D1044184

A CUTTHROAT BUSINESS

Bente Gallagher

PW

PublishingWorks, Inc.
Exeter, NH
2010

First Printing
PublishingWorks, Inc.
151 Epping Road
Exeter, NH 03833
603-778-9883
603-772-7200

Distributed to the trade by
Publishers Group West

Designed by Anna Pearlman

LCCN: 2009907343
ISBN-13: 978-1-935557-07-4

Printed on recycled paper

A CUTTHROAT BUSINESS

1.

Forewarned is forearmed, they say, and in justice to—well, everyone!—I guess I must admit that I was forewarned. It's just that when people told me that real estate is a cutthroat business, I didn't think they meant it *literally*.

My name is Savannah Martin, and I sell houses. Or I should say that I try, because I'm brand new at my job, and truth be told, haven't sold so much as a lean-to yet. I should have realized, when the call came in about 101 Potsdam Street, that it was too good to be true.

It was about quarter of nine in the morning on the first Saturday in August, and I was at work. As usual. For the past six weeks I'd been on call pretty much twenty-four–seven, not exactly what I'd had in mind when I looked forward to setting my own hours, and I haunted the office like the proverbial ghoul.

I guess I should also mention that I didn't actually have anything else to do. I used to work at the makeup counter at the mall, but when I got my real estate license, I quit my job and started living off my savings in the hope that my dwindling bank balance would give me the incentive I needed to succeed. So far it hadn't worked, and if something didn't change soon, I'd have to crawl to Dillard's to beg for my old job back. And that was assuming it was still available, with the way the economy was going these days.

But that was why, when the phone rang, I snatched it up on the very first ring, and had to take a couple of steadying breaths before I put the receiver to my ear. "Good morning. Thank you for calling Walker Lamont Realty. Savannah Martin speaking. How may I help you?"

"Savannah Martin?" a male voice repeated.

I nodded. "Yes, sir."

I waited for him to comment, but instead he just continued chummily, like we were old friends. "See, Savannah, it's like this. I was supposed to be meeting Miz Puckett at eight, to see 101 Potsdam Street, but I've sat here for forty-five minutes, and I ain't seen hide or hair of her."

"I haven't seen her this morning, either," I answered, my heart starting to beat faster. Someone was interested in buying 101 Potsdam? And my colleague and competitor Brenda Puckett had dropped the ball . . . ? "Though it isn't like her to be late." Much more like her to be early, so she could feel superior when you merely showed up on time. "Are you able to wait while I try to call her?"

My caller said he was, and I put him on hold before dialing Brenda's cell phone, and when there was no answer, her home number. There was no answer there, either. I got back on the line. "Sir, I'm sorry, I can't get in touch with her. But if . . . that is . . . I mean . . ."

My tongue tripped over itself in its eagerness to offer help. The caller didn't say anything, but I could sense amusement through the line. I gritted my teeth and tried again. "If you'd still like to see the house, I'd be happy to come out and open the door for you . . ."

I held my breath. The Italianate Victorian and surrounding two acres were listed for almost a half million USD, a fairly high price for Nashville, Tennessee. The commission would pay my rent and keep me in gasoline and Ramen noodles for the rest of the year, at least.

"You sure you can spare the time, darlin'?" The voice was a baritone, husky and low, with a hint of velvety roughness that made him sound like he'd just rolled out of bed.

I assured him, with all the sincerity I could muster, that there was nothing I'd rather do than be of service to him. He chuckled, but didn't comment. Even so, the ripeness of the chuckle brought a blush to my cheeks. I ignored it, promising him I'd be there in fifteen minutes, and then I wasted the first thirty seconds of that time doing a (premature) victory dance before I grabbed my purse and headed out the door. If I was going to get from the office to Potsdam Street in the fourteen and a half minutes left to me, I would have to get my tail in gear and keep my foot glued to the gas pedal the whole way.

This may be a good time to explain about Brenda Puckett, the Wicked Witch of the South, or, as she prefers to think of herself, the Empress of Everything. She's a short, plump woman with big hair and a bigger ego, approximately fifteen years older than I am and at least fifty pounds heavier. And she has disliked me from the moment she first set eyes on me. Could be because I'm younger and thinner—though certainly no reed, it doesn't take *that* much to be thinner than Brenda—or could be because my blonde hair is my own and didn't come out of a bottle, the way Brenda's did. Or maybe I just wasn't deferential enough the first time I met her. Through no fault of my own, I assure you. How was I supposed to guess that the dumpy, middle-aged woman in the ill-fitting blouse, padding around the front office in her stocking-feet, wasn't the cleaning lady, but one of the most successful realtors in Nashville? She sure didn't look it. But she wasted no time in correcting my mistake, in terms that could have curled my hair had it not already had some curl of its own, and she still held it against me six weeks later. The thought of being able to put one over on her made me feel all warm and fuzzy inside as I skidded around the corner of Potsdam Street, narrowly avoiding a head-on collision with a souped-up green Dodge, and gunned the car up the street.

It took me four minutes longer than the fifteen I had promised before I could pull my pale blue Volvo—the safest car on the road—to a stop behind the sleek, black Harley-Davidson waiting in the circular driveway. The man straddling the seat matched the motorcycle: dark, muscular, and more than a little dangerous. The T-shirt might as well have been painted on for all that it left to the imagination, and the tattoo peeking out from under the left sleeve looked like the tail end of a viper curled around his bicep.

I hesitated before I opened the car door. Real estate can be a scary business on occasion. Those of us who are involved in it advertise our faces and phone numbers all over town, then agree to meet total strangers who call, claiming to want to see an empty house somewhere. Often in an area that isn't the best, like the one I found myself in now. Sometimes—rarely, but it happens—one of us gets attacked. And there was something about this man that suggested that I ought to step carefully. So I did, both because it seemed prudent and because the gravel was difficult to navigate on four-inch heels. "Sorry I'm late. I'm Savannah Martin . . ."

And then I stopped—dead, if you'll pardon the pun—when he removed the mirrored sunglasses and I met his eyes.

They were as dark as those on a Jersey cow, and surrounded by long, thick, curving eyelashes. There's nothing wrong with *my* lashes—nothing a liberal application of makeup can't correct, at any rate—but I would have sold my soul to possess his. He could hawk mascara for Maybelline with those lashes. Not that *that* was the reason I was staring.

"Struck speechless by my good looks, darlin'?" His voice was amused.

"Sorry," I managed, fighting back a blush. How mortifying, to be caught staring! "For a second there you looked familiar, but . . ."

"You ain't never forgotten me?" He grinned. White teeth flashed against golden skin, and a ghostly memory stirred, like an alligator in a swamp, but it subsided without breaking the surface.

"Um . . ." I said, distracted. The grin widened wickedly.

When I didn't say anything else, he added, "Been back to Sweetwater lately?"

So he was from back home. Well, it made sense. The drawl, slow as molasses, was pure South, and he wasn't someone I had met recently, or I would have remembered.

"A few weeks ago," I said slowly, running mental mug shots past my inner eye. "You?"

"That'd be telling." Another grin curved his lips and the alligator stirred again. I concentrated, and almost had it, but just as I was about to reach out and grasp it, it slipped through my fingers once more.

"You couldn't give me a hint, could you?"

I smiled hopefully. He contemplated me in silence for a few seconds before he said accommodatingly, "Sure. Columbia High."

I nodded. Of course. He was someone I had gone to high school with. That explained it. Long enough ago that I wouldn't necessarily remember him right off; not so long ago that I had forgotten entirely. But there had been hundreds of students in my high school, from all over Maury County and beyond. How in the world did he expect me to recognize him after all this time?

And then the brick dropped, or the alligator reared, or whatever. I jumped back. "Oh, my God! Rafael Collier. You're . . ."

"Guilty as charged." He made a little mocking half bow. His voice was pleasant, but his eyes were anything but. They had turned as black as the metal of the motorcycle he'd been riding, and approximately twice as hard. I swallowed and opened my mouth. And put my foot in it.

"I thought you went to prison."

He lifted an eyebrow. Just one; the other didn't move so much as a fraction of an inch. "That was twelve years ago, darlin'. I got out."

Obviously. I swallowed again and took another step back.

Rafe Collier had been a senior in high school when I was a freshman, so our paths hadn't crossed much. I knew who he was, of course—everyone did—but we'd never had much to do with each other. I don't think we exchanged more than three words in the year we both attended Columbia High. Or maybe three—"Looking good, sugar!" followed by a wink—but no more. He graduated the next spring, by some miracle of God, or maybe because some of the teachers passed him so they wouldn't have to deal with him for another year.

It wasn't surprising. Rafe was the quintessential small-town bad boy, updated for the new millennium. Gone were the days of tight jeans and leather jackets; Rafe had worn his jeans baggy and enough gold around his neck to post bail for murder one. I knew he'd gotten arrested the summer after he graduated, and seeing as he was the kind of kid whose yearbook entry had identified him as "most likely to spend the rest of his life behind bars," I had assumed he would be shuffled from one correctional facility to the next until he dropped dead and saved society the expense of keeping him. I certainly hadn't expected to come across him now.

"What are you doing here?" I asked, with more curiosity than tact.

"Looking at this house." He nodded toward it. I glanced at it, too.

"You must have done pretty well for yourself if you have a half a million dollars to spend on a ramshackle hundred and fifty-year-old house in a bad . . . um . . . I mean, *transitional* neighborhood."

Narrow escape there. Brenda Puckett would have had my head on a platter if she had heard me refer to the property as being located in a "bad" area. She's the queen of puffing, which is realtor-speak for making something sound better than it is without actually lying about it. Lying outright is called *intentional misrepresentation* and is illegal, but puffing is considered a necessary evil.

Rafe didn't take the bait about his finances. "Nice save," he said instead, mildly. I grimaced. He added, with a look around, "What's so bad about this? Looks better'n where I grew up."

I glanced around, too. "It doesn't look like any part of Sweetwater I've ever seen."

"You prob'ly didn't come down my way a lot," Rafe said dryly. "You grew up in that big mausoleum on the hill, right?"

I wasn't sure I'd classify my ancestral home, the Martin Mansion, as a mausoleum, but it was big and square with white pillars and sat on a little knoll just outside Sweetwater proper, so I assumed we were talking about the same thing. "I guess."

"You prob'ly still had slave quarters out back and brought in darkies to do the housework."

His voice was flat. I shrugged. I wouldn't have put it exactly like that, but yes, my mother sometimes employed some of the young women in the area—black and white both—to clean house or help with the cooking or serving for one of the many parties she held. Rafe's own mother had been among them, if I remembered correctly, though it didn't seem diplomatic to bring it up at the moment.

"Thought so," Rafe said.

There wasn't much either one of us could say after that, so the silence lengthened. A black youth in a shiny green car with chrome wheel wells and a sound system that threatened to shake the fillings from my teeth drove slowly by, staring at us from a half-reclining position in the front seat. It looked like the same car I had seen on my way here. Rafe followed it with his eyes until it was gone before he turned to me. "So when you say the neighborhood's bad, you mean it's full of black folks?"

I hesitated. Every real estate agent learns about testers: people who are hired by the Real Estate Commission to make sure agents aren't violating the fair-housing laws, which preclude discrimination based on race, religion, gender, national or ethnic origin, familial status, and a few other protected classes. I didn't really believe that Rafe Collier was an undercover agent for the commission, but I couldn't afford to be careless. "I'm not actually allowed to comment on the racial makeup of a neighborhood."

"Afraid I might take it personal?" He smirked. I decided not to dignify this comment with an answer, just continued as if I hadn't heard it.

". . . but if you take a drive around the area, you'll see what kind of people live here. And if you're concerned about crime, you can always contact the police department and ask about their statistics."

Rafe snorted. "Yeah, that's gonna happen."

I shrugged. Rafe didn't seem to have anything else to say, so I nodded toward the front door. "You still want to go in?"

"If it ain't too much to ask."

I reverted to realtor-mode, polite and distant. "Of course not. It'll just be a second while I get the door open." I headed up the stairs to the porch with him behind. Far enough behind that I worried that my skirt was too tight and made my derriere look big. When I reached the heavy front door I stopped, frowning. The little black lockbox hanging from the handle was open, and empty. "Where's the key?"

"If I knew that," Rafe said from behind me, "you think I woulda called you?"

"It was more of a rhetorical question." The key wasn't in the lock, but when I reached out and tried the doorknob, it turned in my hand. "You didn't try the door, I suppose?"

"If I had," Rafe repeated, "you think I woulda called you?"

I hesitated. Some people might have been too cautious or too law-abiding to enter an empty house alone, especially when it said *No Trespassing* in letters two inches high on the door, but Rafe Collier . . . ? "Probably not. You would have just walked in."

"Like I'm gonna do now." He reached out and gave the door a push. It opened with a protesting shriek. It must have been decades since anyone had oiled the hinges.

I hesitated for a second on the doorstep. The house was cool and dark, with all the draperies closed against the sun, and there was a certain safety in being outside, in the open. Inside the thick walls, nobody could hear me if I screamed. Not that I had any reason to think I'd be doing any screaming, but I'm a woman, and not stupid, so the possibility is usually at the back of my mind.

"After you," Rafe said. I looked back at him. He quirked an eyebrow. I couldn't very well refuse to go in, considering how I'd practically begged for the chance to come here. I forced a professional smile, took a deep breath, and stepped over the threshold. Rafe came in behind me and pushed the door shut. I moved a little further into the hall, out of his reach, before I looked around.

We were standing in a huge entry, giving way to a long hall running the depth of the house, with doors leading off it to the left and right. It didn't look as if anyone had lifted a finger in here for at least twenty years. There were cobwebs draping the fifteen-foot ceiling like canopies, and mouse droppings scattered across the scuffed wood floor. There was peeling wallpaper, sagging doors, and posts missing from the banister, and everything was overlaid by a thick layer of dust. A faint metallic scent that I knew I'd smelled before, but which I couldn't place, hung in the air, along with the odors of dankness, mold, dirt, and dust.

"Know anything about the owner?" Rafe asked, looking around. His nostrils were quivering too, I noticed.

I shook my head. "Not other than that he or she hasn't been taking care of the place. But when I see Brenda on Monday, I'll ask her." He didn't answer, and I added, "There should be five rooms down here and five more upstairs, plus the third floor and basement. Where would you like to begin?"

"May as well go up." He stepped onto the staircase, just to our left.

The second floor looked much like the first. Rafe wandered down the hall and opened one of the doors.

A room with peeling paint and a sagging ceiling met our eyes. It was empty except for dust and debris and a soiled mattress in the corner. The mattress squeaked and rustled, and I squeaked too, and backed up hastily. Rafe shot me a look over his shoulder.

"I don't like mice," I said defensively. He smirked.

"Those ain't mice, darlin'. Those're rats."

I took another step back, feeling the color draining from my face. Rafe grinned and closed the door.

The rest of the second floor looked pretty much like the first room, with shredded wallpaper and cracking plaster, scuffed and gouged wood floors, and chunks missing from the ceilings where water had gotten in. As Rafe walked from room to room taking it all in, his face impassive, I snuck glances at him, wondering what he was doing here, really.

All right, so I know that just because a guy was a bit of a hellion in high school, doesn't mean that he couldn't have straightened himself out by thirty or so. People do it all the time. He might have a good job and a stock portfolio and be able to qualify for a half-million-dollar loan without any problem. Anything was possible. Unlikely, but possible.

"You know," I said casually, "I didn't ask what you do."

He glanced at me, in the act of opening another door. "Do?"

"For a living."

"Oh." He shrugged. "This'n that."

He turned back to the door. I nodded gravely. This and that? What did *that* mean?

Eventually we ended up in the third floor ballroom, where I stood at the top of the stairs admiring the dust motes dancing in the streaks of sunlight while Rafe prowled and peered into closets and dark corners.

"Are you looking for something in particular?" I asked finally. He shot me a look over his shoulder.

"Why?"

"I thought maybe I could help. If you're checking for dry rot or something."

"Oh. No, I ain't looking for anything special."

He turned away, to contemplate a picture of a black Baby Jesus forgotten on the wall behind the door. I left him to it. If he *was* looking for something in particular, he obviously wasn't going to tell me what it was, and whatever it might have been, he didn't find it, because he was still empty-handed and silent when we went back down the stairs.

"Just the first floor left," I said brightly when we stood in the downstairs hall again. "Parlors, sitting rooms, dining rooms, and other formal-rooms. Ready?"

Rafe nodded, unmoved. I headed off down the hallway with him right behind.

The first room we entered was empty. It was a formal parlor or sitting room, with faded, peeling wallpaper sporting big, red cabbage roses, and a rather nice fireplace on one wall. The moth-eaten draperies were closed, leaving the room in semi-darkness, and while I

14

walked over to the window to pull them aside, Rafe went directly to the adjoining door into the next room. He stopped in the doorway, as quickly and completely as if he had walked into an invisible wall. I took one look at him, at the tense muscles and somehow brittle posture, and moved to join him.

2.

I think I knew before I got there what I would see. (Although if I had known how bad it was going to be, I would have stayed where I was.) Somewhere in the back of my head I must have recognized that metallic scent of blood; plus, it just wasn't like Brenda Puckett not to show up for an appointment.

This time she'd been in the wrong place at the wrong time. She was lying on her back in front of the fireplace, in a pool of blood. Her fat, little hands were outflung and her black skirt was twisted around her ample hips, exposing chubby, dimpled thighs. Her eyes were staring straight up at the ceiling, surprised, and across her throat was a gaping wound. And that was all I saw, because the room started spinning very fast, and everything went dark while small, glowing specks danced in front of my eyes. From very far away I could hear a voice saying,

"Savannah . . . Savannah! Oh, shit!" I felt an arm snaking around my waist, pulling me close to a hard, masculine body, and then I really did faint.

I came back to myself as I was unceremoniously dumped on the front porch. A strong hand pushed my head down between my knees and that same voice said, rather critically, "Keep your head down. I'll be back."

His steps retreated into the house. I concentrated on breathing slowly in and out, and clenching my stomach against the nausea rising in my chest.

It felt like I was sitting there forever, while the world spun and Brenda's dead body floated before my eyes, but I don't think it was more than a couple of minutes before Rafe sat down next to me, with a dripping wad of paper towels and a searching glance. "You all right?"

I nodded shakily, wiping my face with the cool water. "I think so. Thanks. What . . . ?"

"Think maybe you oughta call this in?"

"What? Oh, the police! God, yes!" I fumbled in my bag for my cell phone. Rafe watched my hands shake, but he didn't offer to help. After a long few seconds I managed to pull the phone out and turn it on, but I couldn't keep my fingers steady enough to punch in the numbers. "Here. You do it."

I handed him the phone and listened while he dialed 911 and gave a terse account of what had happened. "They're on their way." He returned the phone to me. I dropped it into my purse without looking. My voice shook.

"You know, when you called and told me she wasn't here, I thought she'd screwed up. I thought she'd forgotten about you, and that I could take advantage of it to pull one over on her. I imagined the look on her face, and I gloated. And all the time she was lying there!"

I buried my face in my hands. I wouldn't have turned my nose up at a comforting pat on the back or a few kind words, or even a polite hug, but Rafe didn't comply. I sniffed a few times and looked over at him. His face was remote, like a bronze statue, and his eyes were fixed in the distance. "You're remarkably cold about the whole thing, I must say," I added spitefully. "From the way you're acting, one might think you saw dead bodies every day."

He glanced at me, but didn't answer.

"Didn't it bother you?" I persisted. "Seeing her like that?"

"Didn't know her," Rafe answered.

"She was a human being!" Granted, I hadn't always remembered that myself, in my dislike of her, but it didn't seem right that he should be so unemotional about her death—her *murder*—as if she had been no more important than a fly. "And nobody deserves to die like that. Alone and scared . . ."

Rafe turned toward me, and I recoiled. His eyes were black as pitch, and about as friendly. I had to work to keep my voice steady. "I'll just . . . um . . . sit here quietly while we wait. Okay?"

I didn't wait, just turned away and contemplated the as-yet empty driveway. After a few seconds, Rafe stood up and walked off in the other direction. A moment later, I heard a creak when he sat down on the porch swing.

We were still in the same positions eight minutes later, when the ambulance came roaring up Potsdam Street with sirens screaming and lights flashing. It entered the circular drive with a spurt of gravel. Hard on its heels was a police car, also flashing lights and sirens. I got up, a little shakily, to greet the incoming horde, while Rafe continued to lounge in the swing.

"Miz Martin?" the first of the cops said. He was around forty-five or fifty, with graying hair and a paunch. "I'm Officer Spicer. This is my partner, Officer Truman."

Truman was younger, no more than twenty-two, and in deference to the occasion, had taken off his uniform cap. "Ma'am," he said politely, as if I were seventy years old instead of twenty-seven.

One of the paramedics, a girl with a nose ring and a wad of pink bubblegum in her mouth, came up to stand next to him. "Where's the diseased?"

I opened my mouth to explain the difference between having a disease and being deceased, but Rafe intercepted me. "I'll show you." He led the way into the house with the girl and her colleague, a boy not much older and still pimply, right behind. Truman joined the influx while I turned back to Officer Spicer.

"They're just kids!"

"It's their job," Officer Spicer said, interpreting my remark, and the feelings behind it, correctly. "They've seen more of it than you." He waited a beat before adding, a little maliciously, "And they may not look as fresh when they come back out. Bad, is it?"

I nodded. "Her throat is cut. There's blood everywhere."

"Tsk, tsk," Officer Spicer said. "I'd better go make sure those eager beavers don't go messing around with anything. Don't go anywhere." He walked into the house.

I stayed where I was. After a few minutes Officer Truman came back out, looking pale and clammy, and took a walk in the garden. He might have been looking for evidence, but I suspect that what he was after was a handy bush to throw up behind.

At about the same time, Rafe came back, and sat down on the porch swing without a word. No queasy feelings there, apparently. Time passed. A few plainclothes police officers showed up, and finally Officer Spicer came back. "I've been told to bring you two downtown," he said. "We're gonna take your fingerprints, and you'll need to make a formal statement. Let's go."

"My car . . ." I began.

"It'll be safe here till we get back. This place'll be crawling with cops before long." He hollered for Truman. Rafe, whose bike was worth at least as much as my five-year-old Volvo, didn't say a word.

The ten-minute trip downtown passed in silence. Rafe and I sat on opposite sides of the squad car without saying a word to each other, and Truman still looked a little green. Spicer was whistling tunelessly between his teeth as he drove, but he didn't talk, either.

Nashville police headquarters are located in a modern four-story building with a fenced, monitored parking lot in the back. Had I been visiting in the regular way, I would have found a parking space somewhere on the street and entered the building by the main entrance. Spicer drove through the chain-link fence into the parking lot and parked in a marked slot.

"I'll walk 'em in," he said to Truman. "You stay out here and get some air."

He herded us through the reinforced steel door in the back and into a utilitarian corridor. Another uniformed officer was sitting behind a desk just on the inside of the door, and we stopped while Spicer told him our names and business. I wondered if Rafe felt as guilty and uncomfortable as I did. If so, I couldn't tell by looking at him.

After the indignity of the fingerprinting, I ended up in an interrogation room like the ones I had seen on TV. The kind with a big mirrored window on one wall and a table with a couple of uncomfortable chairs around it in the middle of the room, and nothing else. And there I sat, with nothing to do but twiddle my ink-stained thumbs and picture Brenda Puckett's dead body in my mind for more than thirty minutes. I don't know what the detectives were doing during that time—grilling Rafe, or just watching me sweat through the two-way mirror—but whatever it was, it had me in a complete twitter by the time the door opened and a woman came in.

She gave me a curt nod. "Good morning. I'm Detective Grimaldi."

"Savannah Martin," I said faintly. Detective Grimaldi sat down on the other side of the table.

"Can I get you anything? Coffee? A soda? Some water?"

"A Diet Coke would be good." Maybe it would help to settle my stomach. She nodded, but didn't leave to get it.

"Tell me what happened earlier," she said instead. I started going over the story again, and had only gotten to the time of Rafe's early morning phone call when the door opened and Officer Truman came in carrying an ice-cold can of Diet Coke. I guess maybe he and/or Spicer were outside the two-way mirror, looking in. I thanked him, opened the can, and took a sip. "I got to Potsdam Street about nine fifteen. Rafe was waiting out front."

Detective Grimaldi consulted a folder she kept in front of her. "Had you been working with him before this morning?" I shook my head. "How did you come to be calling him by his first name?" The look she sent me held a hint of triumph, as if she imagined she had caught me doing something I shouldn't be. My mother would undoubtedly agree.

"I've met him before," I said, telling myself I had no reason to feel defensive, but feeling defensive anyway.

"We grew up together. Or rather, we grew up in the same town. Small place in Maury County, south of Columbia."

"You weren't friends?"

I shook my head. "He's three years older than me and hung out with a whole different crowd."

"When was the last time you saw him?"

"Before today? The day he graduated from high school. Twelve years ago." It was the one and only time I had spoken to Rafe, and although I hadn't thought about it for twelve years, I could still remember every detail. "My girlfriend Charlotte and I had gone to the movies with my brother Dix and his best friend Todd. The movie theatre was in downtown Columbia, fifteen or twenty minutes from Sweetwater. When the movie was over and we were walking back to Todd's car, we saw Rafe."

Detective Grimaldi was quiet. I waited, but when she didn't order me to cease and desist, I continued. "He was sitting on the curb. I think he was drunk, but it looked like someone had beaten him up, too. There was blood on his shirt, and he had a black eye."

I had felt sorry for him, and when Todd had grabbed my arm and tried to hustle me past, I had dug my heels in and insisted we stop. It is the duty of every well-bred Southern Belle to administer to those less fortunate, and Rafe was clearly less fortunate. He was also a schoolmate, although calling him a mate of any of us was surely stretching the point. Still, I felt we owed it to him to make sure he was all right. Dix and Charlotte had been too preoccupied with one another to notice anything less than an earthquake, and Todd had been reluctant, to say the least, to get mixed up in anything. So I had gathered what courage I possessed and had walked over to Rafe to offer him a ride back to Sweetwater.

"Did he accept?" Detective Grimaldi asked. She sounded intrigued in spite of herself.

I nodded. "I doubt he would have, otherwise, but it was very obvious that Todd didn't want him to, so he said yes. He sat next to Todd the whole way home, bleeding on the leather seat of the new car Todd had gotten for his sixteenth birthday, and keeping Todd on the edge of his seat in case Rafe decided to throw up all over the dashboard. If it had been a television sitcom, it would have been funny." It crossed my mind to wonder if he remembered, or if he'd been too drunk or in too much pain to even realize who I was.

"Interesting," Detective Grimaldi said. "But if that was the last time you saw him, I guess you can't tell me anything about his life now? Where he lives? What he does for a living?"

I shook my head. "I don't know anything about him at all anymore. Why don't you ask him? He's around here somewhere, isn't he?" I glanced around the gray concrete walls of the interrogation room.

"He's not being very forthcoming." Detective Grimaldi made another note in her folder. "Let's go back to what happened this morning. Mr. Collier called your office and you drove to 101 Potsdam Street to meet him. Then what happened?"

I recapped the talk with Rafe and our trip through the house, doing my best to remember the details. Yes, the front door had been unlocked. No, only members of the Association of Realtors could open the lockbox; it took a special key card and an individual code. The cards are not available to the general public, and even if a member of the public were to get their hands on one—by bashing the agent over the head and stealing it, for instance—said member of the public wouldn't be able to use it without knowing the agent's personal code. Joe Blow coming in off the street wouldn't have a prayer. No, I hadn't seen anyone else around, except for a lady at the bus stop and a few cars that had gone by down the road. Yes, I'd probably recognize the young man in the green car if I saw him again; I'd gotten a pretty good look at his face. Sure, I'd be happy to look at mug shots. No, I hadn't noticed that the contents of Brenda's purse had been strewn over half the library floor. But I hadn't noticed much of anything; just Brenda's face and the gash across her throat, and then I had fainted. Yes, Rafe had gone back inside after dropping me on the porch. No, I had no idea what he'd been doing; I'd had other things on my mind. Sure, it was possible that he had gone back to look through Brenda's purse; there was no way I could say definitely whether the contents had already been scattered or not. Then again, he didn't know that. But it was more likely he'd just gone back to get me a wet paper towel and to make sure she was really dead. No, I hadn't actually meant that the way it came out . . .

"What was your relationship with Mrs. Puckett?"

"I didn't have one," I said. "We worked for the same company, that's all."

"So you worked together?"

I shook my head. "She had her own team of assistants to do her bidding. I'd see her at the weekly sales meeting, or pass her coming and going, and once she came into my office with a stack of fliers she wanted me to sort and package for her . . ."

It had involved tying every three sheets neatly together with a pretty, color-coordinated ribbon which fought my attempts to finish it in a tidy bow. And it wasn't like I didn't have plenty of my own work to do, after all. Kick-starting a real estate career is hard work even in the best of times, and in the current economic climate, with foreclosures and short-sales running rampant, and people choosing to stay in their houses rather than selling them, it's harder. I resented Brenda for making me do her work for her, and with every knot, I had pictured pulling the string tighter around her plump neck and watching her eyes—small, piggy, *mean* eyes—bug out of her skull. I smiled.

Detective Grimaldi contemplated me for a second. "You didn't like Mrs. Puckett much, did you?"

I opened my mouth to do the proper thing—sugarcoat the truth, i.e., lie—but I thought the better of it. There was probably perjury or something involved here. "Is it that obvious?"

This wasn't good. I was supposed to be better than this at hiding my feelings.

"Can I ask why?"

I shrugged. "She was just difficult to get along with, is all. Self-centered. Bossy. Demanding. I wouldn't have killed her, though. You don't kill somebody just because they're common and loud and make more money than you do."

"Murder has been committed for less," Detective Grimaldi said.

"Maybe, but not by me."

Grimaldi didn't answer. "Did you know she was going to be at 101 Potsdam Street this morning?" she asked after a moment's pause.

I shook my head. "She didn't tell me what she was doing. Except for when she was rubbing something in. Like yesterday, when she had five closings and made sure we all knew it. She might have told Clarice, her assistant."

"Would Clarice have written it down somewhere, if she did?"

I shrugged. "There's an appointment book, I think. You'd have to ask her. *I'm* not on the Brenda Puckett Team, you see."

"I'll do that." Detective Grimaldi made a note in her folder. She didn't say anything else, and after a few moments, I broke the silence.

"So is that it? Can I go?"

"Unless there's something you'd like to add."

I shook my head.

"Take my card, in case you remember something you haven't told us." She handed it across the table to me. I picked it up and glanced at it.

"Thank you. Um . . . when will the funeral be?"

"There'll be an autopsy," Tamara Grimaldi said, as I got to my feet. "The next of kin will be notified when it is completed and the body can be released. Would you happen to know who Mrs. Puckett's next of kin is?"

"She's married," I said, my mind still on the autopsy. "His name is Steven. And there are a couple of kids. Teenagers. I guess I should call and ask if there's anything I can do . . ."

"Give it some time," Detective Grimaldi said firmly. "Go home and take care of yourself first. Officer Truman will drive you back to your car. And don't leave town in the next week or two."

I was almost to the door, walking in a daze, but this last statement made me stop and turn around. "Excuse me?"

She looked up from the folder. "Don't go anywhere. In case we need to talk to you again."

"But it's my mother's birthday on Tuesday. She'll have a fit if I'm not there!"

Detective Grimaldi thought for a second. "Sweetwater?" she asked. I nodded. "All right. You may go to your mother's birthday party. Just don't go anywhere we can't get hold of you."

I promised I wouldn't, and opened the door. Young Officer Truman escorted me to the parking lot and drove me back to Potsdam Street, looking less green and more like himself again. I guess I must have looked about as shaky as I felt, though, because he offered to follow me home, to make sure I didn't get into an accident on the way. He was very sweet and solicitous, as if I were his aged, white-haired grandmother, and I wanted to swat him upside the head and tell him to save it for someone who'd appreciate it, but, of course, I'm far too well brought-up to do something like that.

My car was parked where I left it, and the house and grounds were swarming with cops, both uniformed and plainclothes, just like Officer Spicer had said. None of them paid any attention to me. Rafe's black Harley-Davidson was still there at the foot of the steps when I drove slowly down the graveled drive and turned right onto Potsdam.

3.

I spent what was left of Saturday in my apartment, curled up on the sofa staring miserably at the TV. Usually my cozy one-bedroom rental, with its view of East Main Street through the glass doors of the patio, and the comfortable furniture I had gathered from consignment stores and estate sales over the past two years, made me feel safe and relaxed. Not so today; after what had happened, I jumped every time I heard a noise in the hallway, and the running of water in the pipes made me break into a cold sweat. I went to bed before nine, just because I couldn't stand being awake any longer.

Not surprisingly, I had bad dreams. The corridors and rooms at 101 Potsdam seemed to go on forever, and I ran from room to room calling Brenda's name, ever more hysterically, and all the time I knew that someone else was in the house with me, trying to find me the way

I was trying to find Brenda, but a lot more silently. The dream ended in the library, with Brenda lying on the floor in front of the fireplace. But unlike that morning, she wasn't dead yet. Her eyes were fastened on my face and she was trying to speak, but couldn't because her throat was slit from ear to ear. Blood was bubbling out of the wound and dripping onto the dusty floor. The part of me that was aware I was dreaming wished I would faint again so I wouldn't have to look at it. And then I saw her eyes shift, and felt a presence loom up behind me, and I swung around on my heel, just as the knife came up, and the last thing I saw was Rafe Collier's face—dark eyes narrowed in concentration as he prepared to cut my throat.

I woke up with a scream, so wrapped around with nightgown and sheets that I resembled a mummy. It was five o'clock in the morning, and just beginning to turn light outside. I put away any thoughts of going back to sleep—I'd rather have bags under my eyes than another such nightmare—and swung my feet over the edge of the bed. And watched some more TV. And managed to choke down a piece of toast and a couple of sips of coffee.

By mid-afternoon I was starting to feel a little more human again. I even went outside for a walk, down to the corner market to pick up the Sunday paper. Mostly I wanted to know whether any of the papers had mentioned my name, but I admit that I was a little curious, too.

The murder was front page news, just as it had been the lead story on all the news shows the night before. TOP REALTOR MURDERED IN EMPTY HOUSE! was the headline in the *Nashville Banner*, with a sidebar on the crime statistics in the neighborhood around Potsdam Street. (The *Banner* is a conservative, factual kind of paper.) The stats were staggering: home invasions, muggings, drive-by shootings, gang violence . . . The reporter suggested that Brenda's death could have been the result of a robbery gone wrong, and called for the mayor to do something about the criminal underclass preying on upstanding citizens.

REAL ESTATE QUEEN ASSASSINATED! screamed the headline in the *Tennessean*. (The *Tennessean* is less conservative and more widely read than the *Banner*.) Not to be outdone, the *Tennessean* reporter suggested, none too delicately, that maybe Brenda had been the victim of a sexual crime. Rapes, too, were prevalent in the Potsdam Street area, and the ripe Mrs. Puckett—his word, not mine—might have caught someone's eye. The article was accompanied by an archive photo of Her Highness busting out of a strapless gown, and ripe didn't even begin to cover it.

The last paper was the *City Paper*, which had sent a photographer with a telephoto lens to Potsdam Street to take pictures of the police cars and medical vans. Rafe's black motorcycle had made it into one of the shots, but my Volvo had escaped that honor. Maybe I had left before the photographer got there. It made me wonder how long the police had kept Rafe downtown, and whether the Harley might still be there.

The *City Paper* reporter had had the brilliant idea to interview some of the neighbors, and between them they managed to give a pretty good description of both Rafe and myself. I hadn't noticed anyone hanging out of any windows watching us, but someone must have, because the descriptions were spot-on. "A classy-looking blonde in a tight skirt," was how they described me, while one witness called Rafe "tall and dangerous-looking," and added, "It wouldn't be surprising if *he'd* had something to do with it."

The phone rang just as I was contemplating this last statement, and I steeled myself before picking it up, certain it would be the grieving husband. Steven Puckett hadn't answered the phone when I called yesterday, and I wasn't surprised; if the light of my life had been snuffed out—and Steven might well have considered Brenda the light of his life, difficult as that was for the rest of us to fathom—I wouldn't want to talk to all the well-wishers, mourners, and just plain nosy-parkers, either.

"Hello, Savannah," a smooth voice said in response to my greeting. I managed to bite back a heartfelt "Oh, *God!*" but only just.

"Hi, mother," I said instead, politely. "What can I do for you?"

"How are you, darling?"

"I'm fine," I said, not entirely truthfully.

"You sound tired, darling. You're taking care of yourself, aren't you?"

"Of course I am," I said. "I eat right, I get enough sleep, I give my hair a hundred strokes with a brush every night . . ."

"And you're being careful, aren't you, darling?"

"Of course I am," I said. Mother hesitated.

"It's just that one hears such stories . . ."

I smothered a sigh. I should have known this was coming. Brenda's death would be news all over the state, and quite possibly to the ends of the earth. Wasn't it just too ironic for words? All the notoriety she could possibly desire, and she was dead and couldn't take advantage of it!

"You're talking about what happened to Brenda Puckett, right? She was universally disliked, bless her heart. There must have been at least a dozen people who would have liked to murder her." Including myself, on that day I was tying ribbons. "But there's nobody who wants to murder me, so don't worry." None of the papers had mentioned my name, so mother was unaware that I'd been involved in the discovery, and I wasn't about to tell her.

"A mother always worries, darling," my mother said smoothly. I suppressed an unladylike groan. I knew what was coming, and it didn't help to realize that I had walked right into it. She continued, on cue, "Especially when her daughter is all alone. It's been almost two years since the divorce, darling. Don't you think you should find someone else?"

"I'm not interested in finding anyone else," I said. "One failed marriage was enough, thank you."

Mother thought for a moment. Her next remark might sound like a non sequitur, but only to someone who didn't know her well. "You're still coming down for the birthday party, aren't you?"

"Of course I am."

"I've invited Todd Satterfield to join us. He's back in town, you know, and working for the district attorney's office. You remember Todd, don't you, darling?"

I mentioned Todd in passing earlier, when I was talking to Detective Grimaldi. Todd's daddy has been Sweetwater's sheriff for as long as I can remember—he was the one who arrested Rafe Collier back then—and Todd and I have known each other our whole lives. We'd even dated for a while in high school, more to please our families than because there were any real feelings between us, but we had lost contact when Todd left for college and I went to finishing school and then married Bradley. I knew that Todd had gotten married, too, but if mother was trying to fix me up with him, it was a safe bet that he wasn't married any longer.

"Of course," I said. "How is he? And his wife?"

Mother clicked her tongue. "He's not married anymore, darling. That little gold-digger wife of his—I always suspected that he married her because he couldn't have you. She looked quite a lot like you the one time I saw her, although without your breeding, of course, darling. Anyway, she left him. I thought, now that you're both single again . . ." She let the sentence trail off suggestively. I rolled my eyes.

"It'll be nice to see Todd again. Thanks, mother."

Mother hung up, well contented, and I flopped back

on the sofa with a groan. Great; now I'd have to spend all of Tuesday night swapping war stories with Todd, who had probably been very fond of his wife, despite the fact that my mother didn't like her, and I'd have to commiserate and comfort while the entire rest of my family and Todd's daddy shot us covert glances out of the corners of their eyes to judge how we were getting along. Marvelous.

The phone rang again, and I picked it up with a snarl. If it was my mother calling back with a suggestion for what I should wear to the party, in order to make the best possible impression on Todd, I was going to kill her. "Yes?"

"Ms. Martin?"

Oops. "Yes, Detective," I said smoothly, while my mind started running probabilities. "What can I do for you?" Had they arrested someone? Were they about to arrest *me*?

"I was wondering if you might do me a favor, Ms. Martin."

"Sure," I said blithely.

"The forensic team is finishing up at the house, but we haven't been able to find the key to lock up. It wasn't on the body or anywhere else in the house. I thought you might be able to help."

I hesitated. There was probably a spare key at the office, but the idea of digging through Brenda's belongings was unpalatable. Plus, I didn't want to go back to Potsdam Street. I've always been a little afraid of the dark anyway—I grew up being fed ghost stories by my older brother Dix; *true* ghost stories, the South is rife with them—and discovering a corpse hadn't helped matters any. And in addition to the fear of meeting Brenda's angry ghost, there was the even-less-appealing possibility of meeting her murderer. I've seen enough TV shows to know that the killer often returns to the scene of the crime, and occasionally kills someone else who happens to be hanging about.

On the other hand, I couldn't in good conscience say no.

"Sure." My voice was a lot less happy this time, and Detective Grimaldi noticed.

"If you prefer, I can meet you somewhere and get the key from you. That way you don't have to go back there."

She didn't even bother to try to hide her scorn. "No," I said, stung, "that won't be necessary. I'll take care of it."

She reverted back to her cordial manner. "Thank you, Ms. Martin. I'll be in touch."

She hung up before I had time to say anything else.

So that was how I came to be driving up Potsdam Street around eight o'clock that same evening. I drove slowly, looking around, ignoring the drug deal taking place on the corner, but inspecting the grounds of 101 Potsdam for lingering forensic experts. The drug dealers ignored me and everything else was quiet as I turned the car into the circular drive and crunched up to the front steps. The gravel was a mess from all the cars that had come and gone, and there were cigarette butts and empty gum wrappers littering the front yard. I grimaced. I would have thought cops had better sense than to clutter up their own crime scene with garbage. Or maybe the droppings had come from the reporters or the general public, who had probably stopped by to gawk at the scene of the crime because of all the publicity Brenda's case had received in the media.

I was already a little jumpy from something that had happened earlier: I had stopped by the office to look for Brenda's spare key, and while I was there, someone had walked in, and I had ducked down behind the desk to avoid talking to them. I was planning to come into the office in the morning, to tackle everyone's questions at the weekly sales meeting, but until then I was avoiding people. So when I heard a key in the back door, I switched off the desk lamp and crouched behind Brenda's desk, holding my breath.

The steps, light and quick, went past, and into another office further up the hall. The light came on down there, and spilled out into the hallway. I could hear drawers opening and closing, the rattling of keys or maybe coins, and singing. Then the light was shut off again, and the steps came back. They halted outside Brenda's open door. A hand snaked around the doorjamb and flicked on the overhead light. I held my breath and squeezed my eyes shut.

That brassy tenor voice couldn't belong to anyone but Timothy Briggs, who had spent a couple of years in New York City, trying to get on Broadway, before returning to Tennessee and becoming a realtor. I could even make a pretty good guess as to what was going through his sleek, blonde head as he stood there, and it wasn't that he thought he had heard a noise and wondered if someone was hiding behind the desk. No, he was admiring the office, the second largest in the building, with a solid mahogany desk and a leather chair bearing the permanent imprint of Brenda's broad butt, and imagining the day when it would be his.

I guess I should be grateful that he didn't decide to try it on for size. Attempting to explain why I was hiding behind the desk would have been even more awkward than explaining what I was doing in Brenda's office in the first place. Luckily, after a moment, Tim turned the light off again, leaving me crouched in darkness, before he pranced on down the hall and out the door, whistling merrily. Just before the back door opened again, I heard his voice. "Hey, Larry. It's me, Tim Briggs. Do you have a minute? There's something I'd like to talk to you about."

The door closed with a dull smack, but I waited until I heard the growl of his Jaguar's engine outside before I crawled out from behind the desk. I had already pocketed the key I came for, and I made it down the hall and out of the building without mishap.

And now I was standing outside the door of 101 Potsdam Street, preparing to do my duty and then get out of there ASAP. There was only one problem. There was a light on in the library, spilling out into the front hall. The forensic team must have forgotten to turn it off when they left.

I suppose I could have decided to come back the next day to deal with it, but that would mean another thirty-minute drive. It was easier, if more unpleasant, just to take care of it now. After all, I had a key.

A piece of yellow police tape hung across the front door, and I had to snake my hand under it to find the doorknob. I took a deep breath before I pushed the door open.

It had gotten darker in the thirty or so minutes it had taken me to get here—I hadn't driven hell for leather this time, so the trip had taken a few minutes longer—and the interior of the house was pitch black, except for the glow from the library, casting a yellow square on the dusty hall floor. I took a tentative step into the foyer and stopped. Silence and darkness enveloped me like a shroud. My heart started beating faster. I reached out and tried the ancient light switch on the wall next to the door. It turned over with an audible click, but no light came on. The bulb had probably burned out.

The next second, as if in response, the light in the library went out, too. I stopped breathing, and I had the dizzying feeling that at the end of the hallway someone else was doing the same: peering in my direction just as I was peering in theirs, and blinking at the sudden absence of light.

The way I saw it, there were two things I could do. I could run right down there and investigate, like a good little girl-detective. Maybe one of the forensic experts had discovered that he was missing his petri dish or wedding band or something, and he had come back to look for it. There might not be any danger at all. On the other hand, it could be someone a lot worse. I could end up with my head partially severed from my body, like Brenda.

It wasn't much of a contest. I've never hankered after being the next Nancy Drew, and I wanted even less to be the next Brenda Puckett. I exercised option two: swung around on my heel and ran for safety, down the rickety steps and across the gravel, without bothering to secure the door behind me.

As soon as I was safely locked in the car and on my way down Potsdam Street, I dialed Tamara Grimaldi. "Detective? Sorry to bother you so late, but I was just over at the house on Potsdam to lock up and someone else was there."

"Did you see someone?" Detective Grimaldi wanted to know. I said no. "So how do you know someone was there if you didn't see them? Was there a car parked outside? Or nearby?"

I explained about the light in the library. "When I flicked a light switch in the hall, it went off. I didn't hang around."

"And you don't think it was just a malfunction? That you accidentally tripped a switch?"

I contemplated, then shook my head. "It didn't go off the same instant I flipped the hall switch, like they were on a circuit. It was more like someone heard the click, and then turned off their own light."

Detective Grimaldi didn't sound like she was convinced, but she agreed to dispatch a squad car. "By the way," I added, just as she was about to hang up, "since you mentioned cars, I was wondering about Brenda's—a navy blue Lincoln Navigator, brand new. It wasn't in the driveway yesterday. Have you found it?"

Detective Grimaldi hesitated for a moment. "As a matter of fact we have. In a parking lot a few blocks away."

"I see," I said, although I wasn't sure I did. "Um . . . was it intact?"

"There didn't seem to be anything missing. It was wiped clean of fingerprints, of course, and the only DNA we found is accounted for. Herself, her husband, her children, a co-worker or two . . ."

"It wasn't because someone wanted the car, then?"

"It doesn't appear that way." Detective Grimaldi was remarkably forthcoming tonight. I decided I might as well push my luck and see if it held.

"Why would someone drive her car a few blocks and then leave it?"

"Afraid it might attract attention sitting in the driveway," Grimaldi suggested. "Anyone who saw it— like you or Mr. Collier—would know that Mrs. Puckett was somewhere about."

I nodded. Nashville is not the kind of place where anyone sane would walk, especially in the area surrounding Potsdam Street. "So what did the murderer do with his own car while he was moving Brenda's?"

"We're looking into the possibility that he or she may have arrived in Mrs. Puckett's car." Detective Grimaldi's voice was carefully neutral.

I blinked. "You mean, Brenda picked him up? Or her? But why?"

"For protection," Grimaldi suggested. "If she was concerned about going to meet Mr. Collier on her own."

"And then the person she asked to come along to protect her killed her instead?" Talk about irony . . .

"If she were to ask someone to ride with her, who would she ask?"

My response was automatic. "Not me. I told you we weren't that friendly."

"So who?"

I thought about it. "Her husband, I suppose. It *was* the weekend, and he wasn't home yesterday morning. At least he didn't answer the phone when I called."

"Anyone else?"

"Someone from work. Clarice Webb, her personal assistant. Or Heidi Hoppenfeldt, her protégé. Or Tim, her . . . um . . . partner."

I could hear Detective Grimaldi's ears prick up. "Partner, as in lover?"

I sputtered. "Good God, no. He's as gay as a meadowlark, bless his heart. He's a good realtor, though, and Brenda took 10 percent of everything he made. She was his mentor for a while, and then took him on as a partner when she started working with Heidi."

"And he might have gone with her to Potsdam Street?"

"He probably would have, if she had asked, although I don't know any reason why she should. He would swoon at the first sight of Rafael Collier." And not necessarily in fear. I smothered a giggle, imagining Tim's reaction to Rafe.

"Something funny?" Detective Grimaldi asked courteously.

"Not really. I was just thinking about something."

"I see." Detective Grimaldi's voice was bland, but I got the feeling that she knew exactly what I was thinking. She was a woman, too, after all, so it wasn't impossible that she was thinking about Rafe Collier's broad shoulders and hard muscles and considering swooning herself. Then again, she was a police detective, so it was more likely that she was considering his potential for violence. Unless she wasn't thinking about him at all, of course. It wasn't like she didn't have more important things to worry about.

"I'll send someone out to see if anything's going on at the house," she said finally, "and if you think of anything else that might help, please give me a call."

I said I would, and we both hung up. I amused myself the whole way home by picturing the imaginary meeting between Timothy Briggs and Rafe Collier.

4.

Every Monday morning, Walker Lamont Realty has a sales meeting. Everyone is required to attend. All of us full-time people anyway, although the ones who teach school or wait tables during the week, and who only sell real estate on the weekends, are exempt. On this particular Monday, everyone was there. High school teachers and accountants, supermarket cashiers and guys who cut lawns—one and all had called in sick at their other jobs today. When I walked through the door at a few minutes to ten, every face in the room turned toward me. Timothy Briggs, sitting as close to the head of the table as he could get without actually being there—in Brenda's customary seat, in fact—showed every one of his capped teeth in a blinding smile. "Top of the morning to you, Savannah!"

I smiled back, or more accurately, showed teeth. "Hi, Tim."

"You look smashing today. Have a good weekend?" His bright baby blue eyes were malicious.

"Great," I said dryly, knowing full well that I looked like death warmed over. "Stumbling over a bloody corpse, especially one I know, is definitely my idea of a good time. There's nothing quite like a whole lot of blood to give a girl some color in her cheeks."

Tim tittered. A couple of the others stuck their heads together, whispering, and the rest just stared at me.

"Look," I added—and my mother would have been shocked to hear me tackle the situation so aggressively; we Southern Belles are supposed to be more circumspect— "let's not beat around the bush. I had a lousy weekend, and I'm sure some of you did, too. We may not all have liked Brenda, but she was our co-worker, and I'm sure there are some of us who are feeling the loss." I looked around the table.

"Well, I never!" Clarice Webb puffed herself up, aiming for righteous indignation, but managing only to look like a small, ruffled bantam hen. "I'm sure we were all shocked to hear about what happened to poor Brenda. Shocked!"

She looked around. The others nodded and murmured, but no one actually looked back at her. Even Heidi, Brenda's protégé, kept her eyes on her folded hands. All except Tim, of course. "She was an inspiration to us all," he said primly.

Nothing more was said until Walker glided in and the meeting got underway. I can't really remember much about it, just that there were a few announcements of new listings and sales, and an open house or two were scheduled for the next weekend. I volunteered to sit in on one of them for a couple of hours on Sunday afternoon. It's a good way to pick up clients. Or so they say; like everything else I've tried, it hasn't worked that way for me. But if nothing else, it would make me feel as if I was doing something worthwhile.

After the new listings and open houses were dispensed with and we got an update on how much money the office had generated in the last month—Brenda had sold well over a million dollars worth of real estate in July, while I had, of course, not contributed so much as a dime—the discussion got around to the events of Saturday morning. I had to explain again what had happened, and how I had come to be the one receiving the call from Rafe Collier.

"Since he was Brenda's customer," Clarice said with a sniff, "I don't think *you* should have gone, Savannah. You should have called one of us."

One of the people on Brenda's team, she meant. There were four of them: Brenda herself, Clarice, Tim, and Heidi. The pecking order had Brenda firmly on top and Heidi just as firmly on the bottom, with Clarice and Tim fighting for the top-middle spot. Tim had the other two beat hands down on sales volume, but Clarice had Brenda's ear. Heidi had neither, but she took abuse neither Tim nor Clarice would have permitted. All four of them had stuck together like molasses until now, and now that Brenda was gone, the in-fighting and back-biting would begin. But first they had to put me in my place.

"Savannah was here," Walker pointed out, gently. "It's only fair that she should get to take the calls that come in."

Clarice sniffed again, but didn't say anything else. Walker is outrageously handsome and just as gay as Tim, in an older and a lot more sophisticated way, but he has a spine of steel underneath the stylish designer suits, and he runs a tight ship. Clarice seemed to know it wouldn't do her any good to complain further. When Walker has spoken, the fat lady has sung.

"That's all well and good," Tim said, with another show of caps, for Walker's benefit this time, "but I always got Brenda's leftovers, and he sounds like a particularly tasty one."

He winked at me. A couple of the younger women, and the other gay guys, tittered. Except Walker, of course, who is above that sort of thing. As am I.

"You'd be wasting your time," I said coolly.

"Ooh!" Tim giggled. "That was fast! How do you know that, Savannah?"

The implication was that Rafe and I had engaged in something less than businesslike while Brenda was bleeding to death on the library floor. Or perhaps over the body, while we waited for the police to arrive. I'm sure I looked as disgusted as I felt. "I went to high school with him. He was popular with some of the girls."

The ones who thought his reputation was exciting and who were more susceptible than I to smooth-talking rakes with exotic looks and in-your-face sex appeal.

Tim opened his mouth to reply, something suggestive judging from the gleam in his eyes, but Walker banged his folder on the table. "Enough!"

It didn't make much noise, but had the desired effect. Tim sank back in his seat, not without an amused smile, and Clarice folded her hands piously on the table in front of her.

"Savannah . . ." Walker turned to me, with a tone that brooked no argument, "if he calls back, he's yours."

I nodded, although I wasn't by any means sure I wanted Rafael Collier.

Walker added, over the outraged mutterings, "Clarice, I need you to go over Brenda's workload and divide it between Tim and Heidi. Fairly, if you please."

Tim smirked. Clarice glowered, and I got the impression that she would have favored Heidi outrageously if Walker hadn't said anything.

"For now, at least, I'll handle the listing for 101 Potsdam Street personally. Not to disparage anyone." Walker's gaze flickered to Tim, who closed his mouth again and pouted prettily. "But under the circumstances, I'm sure the owner would feel better if Brenda's superior handled the sale rather than assigning it to a less-experienced agent."

I nodded. It made perfect sense to me. I knew that Walker didn't usually take part in the buying and selling anymore—he contented himself with supervising the rest of us—but with the situation being what it was, I thought he'd done the best he could under the circumstances. Tim looked put out. He had probably hoped the listing would come to him now that Brenda was gone.

"The memorial service is Wednesday at two o'clock," Walker said. "I trust that all of you will attend." It wasn't a question, or a request, it was an order. Clarice nodded vehemently. Tim raised his hand, like an elementary school pupil, and Walker said tiredly, "Yes, Tim, I know you have a closing. But it won't take all day, and I'll expect to see you after you're done. Wear something suitable, please."

Tim, who liked to dress like he was still nineteen and attending drama classes in New York, glanced down at his shiny satin shirt, in a particularly heinous shade of eggplant, and widened his eyes innocently. "Don't I always?"

After the meeting was over, I stepped into Walker's office to tell him I would be going out of town for a couple of days. As I had expected, it was no problem at all. "You're your own boss, Savannah. You know that. You can go away whenever you want."

I nodded. "Especially since I have no listings to service and no buyer clients to show around."

Real estate had turned out to be much harder to break into than I'd realized, back when I'd been on the outside and thought it looked like fun.

"It's a competitive business," Walker agreed sympathetically. "And times are especially tough right now. But if you stick with it, you'll do all right. It takes time. Maybe you'll meet someone in Sweetwater who wants to buy or sell a house. It's always easier to start with your own sphere of acquaintances at first."

Like Rafe Collier. I grimaced. "I'm concerned that, with what's been going on this weekend, and with Tim and Heidi fighting for clients . . ."

Walker smiled thinly. "Don't worry about them. If Mr. Collier calls while you're gone, I will personally ensure that the call goes directly to your voice mail."

I smiled back. "You're all right, Walker. Thanks a lot."

"No thanks necessary. I hired you, Savannah. I'm not going to have Clarice and Tim telling what you can and cannot do. Brenda was a valued member of the company, but she wasn't the managing broker here. This is *my* company, and *I'm* in charge." He nodded decisively. "Have a good time at your mother's. And don't forget Brenda's memorial service."

I promised I wouldn't, and left, wishing I *could* forget, even for a few minutes. But it was going to be a long time before I could close my eyes again without seeing her lying there in front of that damned fireplace.

I got underway a little after three, just in time to catch the beginning of rush hour as the first wave of time-clock lemmings left work and headed south to their homes in the suburbs. It was an awful crush for about thirty miles, until we passed the towns of Franklin and Spring Hill, and after that it was pretty smooth sailing. Just before I reached the Sweetwater city limits, I pulled over to the side of the road and stopped.

What's left of the Martin plantation sits on a few acres of rolling ground just outside Sweetwater proper. It's an authentic antebellum plantation house, completed in 1839, and now that I was looking at it with the eye of someone who no longer lived there, I could see its resemblance to a mausoleum.

It's a good sized building—about five thousand square feet—built of red brick, but with tall, white pillars in the front, and a second-story balcony that runs the entire width of the house. Think Tara, but red. There are eight rooms on either floor; bedrooms upstairs, common rooms downstairs. And yes, we do still have some of the old outbuildings. There's a smokehouse, an old dairy, and one of the slave cabins that Rafe Collier had mentioned. My mother, with her customary elegance, has turned the whole thing into an upscale, very exclusive event venue. Rather than ignoring the Martins' history as plantation and slave owners, my mother is capitalizing on it. People come from near and far to get married on the grounds or the balcony, and occasionally a magazine or film company will pay an outrageous sum of money to snap pictures or shoot a film in and around the mansion. It's chock full of atmosphere, and looks very much like it did a hundred and sixty years ago, in the Old South glory days. Great-

Great Grandmamma Agnes's dressing table is still sitting in what used to be my sister Catherine's bedroom upstairs, and Great-Great-Great Aunt Marie's fainting couch is in one of the downstairs parlors.

My mother was born Margaret Anne Dixon. *Her* mother was Catherine Calvert, of the Georgia Calverts. If you haven't heard of them, don't feel bad; it's only down here in Dixie that it's important to be able to trace our ancestry back to the War Against Northern Aggression, to prove that our families were on the right side in that epic conflict. (I'll give you one guess as to which side is the right one. Down South, folks consider themselves to be American by birth, but Southern by the grace of God.)

My dad was Robert Martin, native of Sweetwater, who met my mother when they both attended Vanderbilt University. He was studying law, she was studying English. Then they got married and produced my siblings and me. I have two: Catherine is the eldest, and was named in honor of our maternal grandmother. Two years after Catherine, my brother was born, and ended up with the name Dixon Calvert Martin. Everyone except mother calls him "Dix." She calls him by his full name and considers herself lucky that the rest of the world doesn't say "Dick." I'm the youngest, and was named for my mother's hometown in Georgia. And I will remain eternally grateful that she wasn't born in Alma or Augusta or Hortense.

My dad died a few years back of a heart attack. It was after that, that mother started marketing the house. Not because she needs the money; she has plenty, both her own and from my dad, but I guess it's something for her to do. Up until the time of dad's death, she stayed busy hosting parties and organizing fund-raisers and being the perfect lawyer's wife, but things are a lot slower and lonelier now than they used to be. I wasn't surprised to see her standing in the open door when I drove up to the front of the house.

I extricated myself from the car and ran up the stairs and threw my arms around her. "Mother!"

She hugged me back, a little less vigorously. "Darling. So good to see you." Her lips were cool against my cheek, and she smelled wonderfully of roses.

"You look great!"

She did. My mother is turning fifty-eight, and looks ten years younger. Her skin glows, and is practically wrinkle-free. Her hair gleams. She has kept her petite figure, and sets it off to full advantage in silk dresses and high heels. It takes a good bit of effort—not to mention money—to maintain the illusion, but it isn't like she can't afford it, after all.

Mother simpered. "Come in, darling. Your room is ready. Dinner is cooking. Would you like a drink while we wait?"

She meant a mint julep or glass of sherry or something equally ladylike. I shook my head. "I'll take my things upstairs first, if you don't mind. But you go ahead."

"No, no, darling. I'll just sit here and wait for you." She smiled. I smiled back and headed up the stairs with my overnight bag.

My room tonight was the same room I grew up in, and it hadn't changed noticeably in the nine years since I left it. It hadn't changed noticeably in the hundred and fifty before that, either. I'd had a few low-brow posters hanging on the wall at one time, and they had disappeared, but otherwise everything was the same. The bed that my great-grandfather Richard Martin was born in still stood against the wall, and Grandmother Eloise's wardrobe was in the corner. I hung my clothes in it and headed back down the stairs for that drink and conversation with my mother.

We spent the cocktail hour catching up, and over dinner we discussed my new career. I had been back home only once since I got my real estate license less than two months ago—for the July 4th family picnic—but at that point everything had been so new that I'd had very little to say about it. I was more forthcoming this time. "It's a nice place to work. I'm glad my friend Lila suggested it, and not only because it's so convenient to my apartment. Walker is very professional and knowledgeable—there are rumors that the governor is considering him for a spot on the Real Estate Commission next year—and most of the others are decent and helpful. I'm not making any money yet, but times are tough for everyone, and I'm sure things will get better soon."

"Any personable young men?" my mother wanted to know. I snorted and pretended it was a sneeze.

"Excuse me. Oh, yes. A number of them, starting with Walker himself. He's not that young—around forty-five, maybe—but he's very well off, absolutely gorgeous . . ."

"Eighteen years isn't so much," mother murmured. I smiled.

". . . and gay. Tim is a turd, but a very successful turd, and also gorgeous and gay. As are more than half the other men. The rest are either married or involved, too young or too old. Except for James."

"And what's wrong with him?" mother asked, resignedly. I grinned.

"Not a thing. He's thirty-two and very handsome. Makes a good living, owns a condo in Green Hills, and drives a Beamer. Dresses well and works out regularly. He's single, straight, has no ex-wives or children, and is looking for the right woman."

"So why aren't you snatching him up?" mother asked.

"He's not interested in me," I answered.

"Well, I never!" Mother sniffed, insulted on my behalf. "Why ever not?"

"He's black," I said. "He wants a black girlfriend."

In fact, I should probably tell Lila Vaughn about him the next time she and I got together for one of our tax-deductible real estate power lunches. Not that she was interested in settling down, having just escaped from a much worse marriage than mine, but she was always interested in making the acquaintance of a good-looking man. If it came to that, I should tell her about Rafe as well.

"By the way, Mom," I said, toying with my cobbler, "you'll never guess who I ran into the other day."

"Who?" mother asked suspiciously. She could tell from my tone that this wasn't likely to be good news.

I told her, and watched her wrinkle her brows. "Who?"

"Rafe Collier. Come on, Mom, you can't have forgotten him. He's three years older than me and you knew his mother slightly. LaDonna Collier."

Mother's immaculately made-up eyes widened a fraction. "The one who got herself pregnant by the colored boy?"

"The same," I said.

"You saw her son? How did that come about?"

"He called," I said. "Not me personally. The office. He wanted to see a house. I'll tell you all about it later. When we're finished eating. I don't want to spoil dessert."

I devoted myself to my cobbler. Mother subsided.

Later, when we were sitting in the formal parlor, on Great Aunt Ida's uncomfortable turn-of-the-(last)-century sofa upholstered in peach velvet, I told her the whole story from beginning to end. Including the part she hadn't heard yet, in which I found the body. And then I watched her turn pale under the meticulously laid makeup.

"How awful for you, Savannah."

"It wasn't pleasant," I admitted.

"That presumptuous, ill-bred young boor. To talk to you like that!"

"Not *that*. Finding Brenda was awful. Rafe Collier is merely annoying." And then some.

"Well, of course, dear. Naturally, finding a butchered body," she shivered delicately, "couldn't possibly compare to having to deal with young Mr. Collier, rude though he may be. Still," she lowered her voice, "you think he might have had something to do with it?"

"The police seemed to think so. Or at least they seemed very interested in him. Kept him for a long time after they finished with me. He was there, after all, and he wouldn't be what I'd consider a particularly law-abiding person, I think."

"No," my mother agreed, with a genteel shudder, "I imagine he wouldn't be."

"He went to prison once, didn't he? Right after he left high school?"

Mother nodded, and lowered her voice. "For assault, dear. Or maybe it was battery."

"Good grief!" I said. I had assumed it had been for stealing a car or forging a check or something relatively—comparatively—innocent; not something as frighteningly violent as assault and battery. "What happened?"

"A bar fight, I believe." Mother clucked. "He was arrested, of course. There was no doubt that he was guilty. It was a particularly brutal beating, from everything I heard at the time. Practically killed the poor man."

We sat in silence for a moment.

"Do you ever see her?" I asked. "LaDonna Collier?"

"Dear me, no," my mother said, smoothing a hand over her impeccably styled, blonde hair. "She was common as dirt, bless her heart. We didn't associate. And now she's passed on, of course."

I blinked at her. "Passed on? Dead, you mean?" Mother nodded. "But she can't have been very old. If she was only fifteen when Rafe was born, and he's three years older than me . . ." I counted rapidly on my fingers, math not being my strong suit, "she'd only be in her mid-forties. What happened?"

"It was quite a to-do, dear. I'm surprised you didn't hear about it on the news up there in Nashville." Mother lowered her voice delicately. "She died of an overdose of some drug or other. At home. By the time someone found her, she had been dead for several days, or maybe as much as a week."

"And nobody went looking for her for all that time? What about the neighbors? And where was Rafe? Didn't she have a job?"

"She worked at the distillery when she was younger," mother said, referring to the Jack Daniels whiskey distillery outside Lynchburg some forty-five minutes away, "but she has been collecting disability for at least ten years. And she lived alone. There's no telling how long she was lying there. She might have called out, but if she did, no one heard her. The Bog is mostly empty these days, and I haven't seen her son since he went off to prison."

"Did it happen recently? LaDonna's passing?"

Mother nodded. "They found her almost two weeks ago now, I'd say. With the heat and all, it can't have been a pleasant task for poor Bob. Here, have some brandy, dear. You're as white as a ghost."

She poured some into a glass and handed it to me. I don't like brandy, but I gulped some anyway. It burned its way down to my stomach and I coughed. "Oh, gosh!"

"What's wrong?" mother asked, concerned.

I took a deep breath. "I chastised him—Rafe—because he didn't seem very upset about Brenda. Like it didn't faze him at all to see her lying there, bathed in blood. I told him that nobody deserves to die that way, alone and scared. And then it turns out that his own mother . . ."

I could still see Rafe's expression when he turned to look at me, his gaze pitch black and threatening; and I remembered recoiling from the icy anger in his eyes.

We sat in silence until I had finished the brandy and was feeling more like myself again. "So tell me about the plans for the party," I said, forcing myself to sound upbeat and normal. "You told me that Todd Satterfield is coming, but who else, except for the family? Who's doing the food?"

We lapsed into small talk about the upcoming birthday party, and nothing more was said about LaDonna or Rafe Collier that night. But the next morning, after I had dropped mother off at the spa, where she was spending a half day being pampered for her party later on, I contemplated the hours stretched out before me, and the catering crew currently taking our house apart, and decided to go for a drive.

Rafe had been correct when he said that I probably hadn't come down his way a lot growing up. I'd never been to the area known as *the Bog*, but I knew where to find it: on the other side of Sweetwater from the Martin plantation. We're on the north, or Columbia side; they're on the southern road to Pulaski. And if the town of Pulaski sounds familiar to anyone, it's probably because it was the birthplace of the Ku Klux Klan. We have so much to be proud of here in middle Tennessee.

I'd driven past the Bog before, looking through the windows of dad's Cadillac, but this was the first time I'd turned off from the highway onto the rutted one-lane track leading down through the trees.

Tennessee is not like Louisiana or Mississippi. We're a rocky state, for the most part. Even in the flatter areas, there isn't much in the way of wetlands. The Bog was not actually a bog, just a rather dank and dismal place. A small creek—or "crick," as we say in these parts—ran through it, a tiny branch of the Duck River. But where it could have been picturesque and pretty, it was just sluggish and muddy brown. It looked unhealthy, like it was carrying disease. A half dozen rusted trailers—mobile homes in my new, professional lingo—were scattered through the spindly trees, and a few shacks squatted here and there among them. Clapboard shacks, low-slung and dilapidated, with leaking roofs and leaning walls. The few cars were American, old and rusted; some had missing parts or sat on cinderblocks, and none looked like they had been driven in the last few years. My immaculate Volvo—the only thing I had gotten in settlement after my short-lived marriage to Bradley Ferguson, aside from the chunk of change that was currently evaporating out of my savings account with every month that went by when I didn't sell a house and make a commission—was as out of place here as a prize brood mare among mules.

I turned off the engine and got out. The slam of the car door sounded very loud in the silence. And it was very silent here. No birds singing, no children playing, no conversations or music. The brook didn't even babble. Very quiet.

Maybe too quiet, as they say in the movies. But I was here, so I looked around anyway. There were no names or numbers anywhere, or for that matter any mailboxes. Nothing to indicate in which of these depressing shacks LaDonna Collier had lived and died. If these people ever got mail, it must all arrive together in the big box up on the main road, and be distributed once someone had carried it all down here. Every place looked deserted, and just as neglected and derelict as the next. There was no sign of life, and no one I could ask for directions. Just for kicks, since I was here anyway, I made my way over to the nearest of the shacks and peered through its dirty window. The interior was empty, save for some debris on the floor. Wire hangers, crumpled papers, roach motels. It didn't look as if anyone had lived there for a while. Stepping carefully around broken bottles, crumpled beer cans, and twigs, I moved to the next home. It was empty, too. Mother was right; people had been deserting the Bog like rats fleeing a sinking ship. There was nothing for me to do here but to go home. I turned on my heel to go back to the car, and stopped with a gasp.

He had moved so quietly through the dry grass that I hadn't heard him, and now he stood between me and the Volvo. For a second, with the sun in my eyes, all I could see was a tall, dark figure, and I recoiled.

He didn't move. Not when I stumbled back, not when the heel of my insensible shoe got caught in a snake hole, and not when I ended up on my derriere on the dusty ground, with my skirt twisted around my hips and my thighs on display. The only thing that moved was his eyes, from my face to my feet and back, with insolent appreciation.

"Didn't your mama teach you better manners?" I inquired coldly, in spite of my burning cheeks. The tiny smile on his lips transformed into a full fledged, dangerous grin.

"Hell, no. My mama always said, 'grab what you can get, 'cause it'll be gone afore you know it.'"

He held out a hand. I hesitated, trying to remember whether anyone had ever said anything about Rafe Collier being in the habit of forcing himself on women.

"Or you can stay there," he added, pointedly. I took the hand and let him haul me to my feet. We stood contemplating one another in silence for a moment.

"Are you following me?" I asked, finally.

"Why'd *I* be following *you*? This is *my* place."

"I thought you were in Nashville," I said.

"I thought *you* were in Nashville."

"It's my mother's birthday. I came down for the party."

He didn't answer. After a second I added, awkwardly, "I heard about what happened to your mother. I'm sorry."

"So you came to offer your condolences?" His voice was dry. I shrugged. It wasn't as if I could tell him that I had come to the Bog out of idle curiosity, because I wondered if there might be a connection between LaDonna's death and Brenda Puckett's murder.

In the silence that followed, the sound of a car engine, backfiring badly, came closer. Turning, I could see an older-model Chevy come bumping down the track. It stopped a few feet away, and the driver's side door opened with a screech. An African-American woman shoehorned herself out from behind the steering wheel and waddled toward us.

She was about my height and age, and approximately three times my weight. Her breasts were the size of volleyballs and she had a behind you could have left a tray of drinks on, with no worries that they'd spill. All of her was poured into a hot pink spandex dress with spaghetti straps, which must have been made for a woman half her size. Her hair was bleached yellow and curled into big, fat sausage curls, and her lips were painted a deep cherry red. She looked like a black drag-queen parody of Shirley Temple. Her eyes were small and half-buried in fat, but she managed to give me a dirty look anyway, before turning to Rafe. "Who she?"

He opened his mouth, but I intercepted him. "I'm Savannah Martin. Who are you?"

She didn't answer, nor give any indication of having heard me. "What you bring her here for?"

"He didn't bring me," I said. "I came on my own."

"What you want with a skinny white chick like that? When you can have Marquita?"

She balanced her weight precariously on one foot and thrust the other ample hip out. I hid a smile. "You know, I'm going to go. I can see you've got your hands full here, Rafe." I gave him a patronizing pat on the arm. The muscles under the golden skin were as hard as granite. He cut his eyes to me, but didn't say a word. Marquita growled deep in her throat, like a Rottweiler. I found myself moving a little faster than usual as I headed for my car.

5.

Mom's birthday party was a big success. Everyone was there: Dix and Sheila and their two kids, Catherine and Jonathan and their three, the rest of the staff from the law office, mom's best friend Audrey, and, of course, the society reporter from the local newspaper, also known as my Aunt Regina. She took my picture and promised to put it in her column, to let everyone know that I was a realtor now and would be happy to sell their houses out from under them.

Sheriff Bob Satterfield had released himself from duty for the evening and was present, and so, of course, was his son. Mom met them at the door, passed Bob deftly into Audrey's capable hands, and snagged Todd's arm, to escort him straight over to me. Her demeanor was that of a devoted pet presenting her lord and master with a fat rat. "Look, Savannah. Here's Todd." She beamed.

"So I see," I said. "Hi, Todd."

"Savannah." He made something halfway between a cordial nod and a gentlemanly half bow. We stood in silence for a few seconds. Mother broke it.

"You look very handsome, Todd."

She smiled. I suppressed an eye roll. This was really a little *too* obvious, even for my mother.

Not that she wasn't correct. Todd did look handsome. At almost thirty he was still lean and had all his hair, and his tall frame was set off to perfection in a gray suit with a blue-gray tie that matched his eyes perfectly. Plus, he's been brought up to be a Southern gentleman, so he knows how to behave. He bowed over my mother's hand and told her how beautiful she looked. Which she did. The spa had tinted her hair a lovely champagne color, and she was relaxed and radiant. I hope I look as good on *my* fifty-eighth birthday.

"And you, Savannah . . ." Todd turned to me, "you don't look a day older than you did in high school."

He leaned in and pecked me on the cheek. I simpered. "Thank you, Todd. That's so sweet." Untrue, but sweet.

Mother beamed. "I'll leave you two to get reacquainted." She patted Todd's arm and shot me a look that said, as clearly as words, *Don't you screw up this time, Savannah!* I grimaced.

"It's good to see you again," Todd said when she was out of range. I turned to him.

"You too. How long has it been? Three years?"

"Four. Your wedding, remember."

"Oh. Yes." How could I have forgotten? Bradley and I had gotten married in Sweetwater, in the same church where I had been christened twenty-three years earlier, and mother had invited everyone I had ever known, including my old boyfriend, to the ceremony. Todd had moved to Atlanta shortly thereafter, and he had gotten married himself just a few months later. I hadn't been invited to his wedding, and had never even seen a picture of his wife.

"I was sorry to hear about your divorce," he added politely. He even sounded sorry, which was nice of him.

"Thank you," I said. "Likewise."

He shrugged. It didn't seem as if he was too heartbroken. Maybe mother was right. Maybe he had married her because he couldn't have me. "Since we're both in Sweetwater again, how about having dinner with me one night? Tomorrow maybe?"

No, if he was still agonizing over his failed marriage, it wasn't apparent.

"I'm really sorry," I said, "but I'm only in Sweetwater for the day. I have to go back to Nashville tomorrow."

"Couldn't you stay one more night?" He looked deeply into my eyes. I hesitated for a moment—I admit it—but in the end duty won out.

"I can't. I have somewhere to be at two o'clock."

"A date?" He smiled, but his eyes stayed sharp. This was getting awfully serious awfully fast.

"A funeral. A colleague of mine was murdered this weekend, and the memorial service is tomorrow."

That did it. He stopped making puppy-dog eyes at me as the professional DA kicked in. "I heard about that. Nasty business." Indeed. "Her throat was cut?"

I nodded. And I must have turned pale, because Todd looked at me more closely. "The news said one of her colleagues found her. That was you?"

I nodded again. Yes, indeed. And the memory of it would probably stay with me until my dying day. Todd swore. "Why would you go and do something like that, Savannah?"

"I didn't do anything!" I protested. "It wasn't like I knew I would find a corpse when I drove out there!" And if I had known, believe me, I wouldn't have gone.

On the other side of the room, Sheriff Satterfield looked up from his conversation with mother and Audrey. I'm not sure if it was the mention of a corpse or our raised voices that had alerted him, but either way we had his attention now. Todd took a deep breath. "I apologize. It was just . . . I hate the idea of you having to face such unpleasantness."

"Thank you, Todd," I said, touched. "That's really sweet of you."

Todd took another breath, but before he could utter whatever it was he wanted to say, his father had turned up next to us. "What're you two young'uns gettin' so het-up about?" He looked from Todd to me and back again. Todd flushed and bit his lip. I smiled sweetly.

"Hi, Sheriff Satterfield. I was just telling Todd that I have to get back to Nashville tomorrow, to go to a funeral."

"Heard about that," Bob Satterfield nodded. He's always been a man of few words. "Sounded bad."

I nodded. "I don't know how you policemen do it, day in and day out. I haven't slept through the night since Friday. Although I hear you had a nasty one yourself a few weeks back."

I crossed my fingers hopefully behind my back. If anyone knew the details of what had happened to Rafe's mother, it was Sheriff Satterfield.

He scratched his bushy, gray head. "LaDonna Collier, you mean? Over in the Bog?"

I nodded. "Mother told me she died. Although she didn't know much about it."

"Ain't much to know," Satterfield grunted. "Bog's mostly empty these days. Bulldozers're due any day. LaDonna was supposed to be gettin' out, too. Guy from the construction company went over there to make sure the place was empty, noticed the stench, and called us. She'd been dead for a week or more. No way to tell what happened."

"No sign of foul play?" I asked, with a smile. Sheriff Satterfield shrugged.

"The way she kept house, who could tell? Looked like a bomb hit the place. Cause of death was an overdose, but there's no way to know if she did it herself, or if someone else was there with her. Nobody's come forward."

"What about her son?"

"Rafe? He don't live here no more."

"But you spoke to him, right?"

Bob Satterfield nodded. "He's next of kin. Had to arrange the funeral. Had her buried up there on Oak Street, next her daddy. Arranged it all by phone from Memphis."

I wrinkled my forehead, then straightened it out quickly, before mother could turn around and disapprove. "Why Memphis?"

"Seems to be where he spends his time these days."

"Oh," I said, surprised. "I assumed he lived around here. Or in Nashville."

"Why'd you assume somethin' like that, darlin'?" The sheriff peered at me from under bushy brows. I grimaced, wishing I'd kept my mouth shut. It was too late now, however.

"Because I saw him in Nashville on Saturday. And down here today."

"Down here?" The two of them exchanged looks. I nodded.

"He was out at the Bog this morning. Cleaning out his mother's house, I assume. It looked like he was working at something, anyway. He was all dirty and sweaty."

Nobody said anything for a moment. "I don't know what worries me more, darlin'," Sheriff Satterfield remarked, "that you went to the Bog by yourself, or that you went to see Rafe Collier." Todd nodded emphatically.

"Oh," I said, shaking my head. "I didn't go to see Rafe. I thought he was in Nashville. He scared the bejeezus out of me when he turned up."

"So what were you doin' there, then, if you don't mind my askin'?"

I blushed. "I wanted to find out about LaDonna. And I didn't want to ask Dix or Jonathan, because I didn't want my mother to find out. She'd probably ground me."

Bob Satterfield smiled. "Helluva woman, your mother."

I shrugged, pouting. Easy for him to say; he wasn't the one who'd get the sharp end of her tongue if she thought I was sniffing around Rafe Collier.

"Why did you want to find out about LaDonna?" Todd wanted to know. I hesitated. On the one hand, I had no real reason to think Rafe had done anything to his mother any more than I had reason to think he had done anything to Brenda Puckett. Not to mention that I suspected that he could make my life plenty difficult if I caused trouble for him. But, on the other hand, it was quite a coincidence that he should be involved, however peripherally, with two possible homicides in the span of a couple of weeks.

In the end I said blandly, "Rafe was with me when I found Brenda Puckett on Saturday morning. If we hadn't turned up, it could have been a week before anyone found her, too."

The Satterfields exchanged a look. "That's right interesting," mused Bob, "innit?"

"Is it?"

"How corpses keep followin' that boy around."

Rafe was hardly a boy anymore, but I refrained from saying so. Something must have shown on my face, though, because Todd glanced at me, then back at his dad.

"Maybe you'd better call for some backup if you're going out there to talk to him. Or better yet, I can come with you."

"Don't mind if you do," Bob said. Todd turned to me. He didn't exactly click his heels together and bow over my hand, but the implication was there.

"Sorry to have to leave so soon, Savannah. It was nice seeing you again."

"Likewise," I answered politely. "Any time you're in Nashville, give me a call, and we'll have that dinner."

"I'll hold you to that." He nodded and followed his father toward the door. Bob paused beside my mother just long enough to say goodbye, then moved on. Todd smiled apologetically and did the same. Mother turned and sent me a look that could have pinned my ears to the wall. *I delivered him right into your hands,* the look said. *What did you do to make him leave?* I tried to telegraph that I hadn't done anything at all, but I couldn't even make myself believe it.

The party wound down around midnight, since the next day was a workday. Mother hires outside help to handle things like clean-up and housework, so we all just left the mess and went to bed. The next morning, after a leisurely bath and breakfast, and a dress-down by mother (the details of which I will spare you), I got in the Volvo and headed back to Nashville.

Brenda's memorial service was scheduled for two o'clock, so all I had time to do was drive home, put my fancy party dress away in the closet, throw the rest of my clothes into the hamper, and change into mourning attire. Walker had made it very clear that he expected us to be on time, dressed appropriately, and I wasn't about to let him down.

Plus, I love black. It makes me look ten pounds thinner and goes great with my pale skin and blonde hair. And it's so easy to accessorize. *Everything* goes well with black. All I had to do was pull my favorite little black dress over my head, hook a pair of pearl earrings through my lobes, step into black sling-backs, and I was ready to go. Not even mother would have found fault with my appearance.

The viewing was going to take place at the Phillips-Robinson Funeral Home in Inglewood, which is only a few minutes from my apartment, and I got there with time to spare. I parked the car in the adjacent lot and headed for the entrance to the big white building, ignoring the humming of the TV cameras a discreet distance away. I should have realized that Brenda's funeral would be attended by the media. Someone tried to get me to talk— maybe they suspected I was the same blonde who had discovered the body—but I kept my head down and kept walking. Timothy Briggs, arriving behind me, was not so restrained. He showed all his teeth in a blinding smile and agreed to speak on camera without batting an eye. "Sure. Always happy to help."

"Yeah," I muttered, "yourself." And the worst thing was, Tim would probably get lots of business because of it. After his boyish face and sappy sentimentality had hit the airwaves, people all over Nashville would remember him when it came time to sell their houses. If I hadn't been so well brought-up, I might have reconsidered and said a few words myself.

". . . a great loss to the profession," Tim was saying, with a straight face, "and my very special friend. I'll miss her." He smiled bravely and wiped away an imaginary tear. The cameras zoomed in. I grimaced.

Misters Phillips and Robinson had opened every room in the place for Brenda's viewing, and every nook and cranny was filled with mourners. Or people who had come to make sure she was really dead, more likely. Nobody seemed too broken up, not even Brenda's own family. Steven was somberly dressed in a brown suit that did nothing for his rather horsey face. Their daughter Alexandra, who was sixteen, wore a slinky black dress that would have been better suited for a cocktail party and someone at least ten years older, while Austin, the son, hadn't even been made to put on a tie, but wore a white shirt, unbuttoned at the neck, hanging over his baggy, black pants all the way to mid-thigh. He kept his hands in his pockets, gazing furtively at the world through shaggy bangs, like a shy woodland creature peering through the brush, while Alexandra's long hair was swept up in a complicated do that also would have looked more at home after dark and on someone considerably more sophisticated. Neither of them looked particularly grief-stricken. Alexandra looked bored, Austin looked fidgety, and Steven looked around. While I stood there in the door and watched, he caught the eye of a plump and pretty fortyish blonde in a blue dress, who walked over and put her hand on his arm. He looked down at her and smiled, and if he was grieving for Brenda, it wasn't evident at that moment.

"For shame," Timothy Briggs's saccharine voice murmured in my ear, maliciously. "Poor Brenda's hardly even cold yet, and just look at her husband."

I did. There was an intimacy in the way Steven and the blonde were looking at each other that hadn't sprung up in the past four days. Alexandra and Austin seemed awfully comfortable with her, too. "Who is she?" I asked.

I was hoping he'd say that the woman was Brenda's sister or something, but, of course, he didn't. "Neighbor-lady. Lost her husband last year. Set her cap for Steven shortly afterwards."

"How long have they . . . um . . ." I flapped my hand.

Tim grinned. "Oh, months!"

I narrowed my eyes. "How do you know? Is it true? And if it is, did Brenda know?"

He giggled. "Sure she did. How do you think I know? She's been going on about it forever. You know what she was like. Hated to lose, hated to share. She threatened to take the kids and sue him for everything he had if he didn't break it off."

"But obviously he didn't," I said, looking across the room at Steven and his ladylove. Tim lifted his slim shoulders in an elegant shrug.

"Who knows? He could have, then. But now it doesn't matter, does it?"

He winked at me and sauntered into the room. A moment later he was swallowed by the well-dressed crowd. I stayed where I was, pondering what he had just revealed.

Brenda had been—not to put too fine a point on it—a shrew. She had busted her butt for years to get to where she was, and although she had succeeded beyond most people's wildest dreams, it didn't surprise me that her family had paid the price. Nor was it surprising that Steven had sought solace elsewhere. Brenda had been approximately as cuddly as a barracuda, and if I'd been married to her, I'd have had an affair, too. However, if she truly had kicked up a huge fuss—which I could totally see her do—Steven had had an excellent reason for wanting to get rid of her. She had probably headed to Potsdam Street straight from home on Saturday morning. What was to have kept him from solicitously offering to drive her there and then, when they arrived, slitting her throat?

"Penny for your thoughts," a voice next to me said. I turned and looked into the angular face of Detective Tamara Grimaldi. She was dressed for the occasion in a severe black business suit whose jacket probably covered the butt of the gun she probably carried.

"I thought it was only on TV that murderers attended their victims' funerals," I answered, obliquely. Her mouth quirked.

"It's not unheard of. Most murders are committed by people close to the victim. But more to the point, I always attend my victims' funerals. You never know who you might see." She looked around the room and added, "Big crowd."

I nodded. "Anyone who's anyone in real estate is here. That black guy over there is the head of the Real Estate Commission. The two women he's talking with are board members. The guy with the beard is the president of the local Real Estate Association. The extremely good-looking man in the gray suit is my boss, Walker Lamont. Brenda's boss, too. And that's Clarice Webb he's talking to. They look upset, don't they? I hope nothing's wrong. Nothing more, I mean."

"I see her husband's found a friend." Detective Grimaldi's voice was carefully neutral.

"A neighbor," I said, "from what I understand."

"Looks friendly."

It did. They were smiling and chatting as if nothing was wrong and his wife wasn't laid out a few feet away.

I had avoided looking at Brenda so far, not being a fan of corpses in general and this one in particular. And Steven had, God knows why, arranged for an open casket. Although I admit it could have been worse. Brenda was dressed in her favorite black, with her plump hands folded across her plump stomach, and a diamond the size of a lima bean on her finger. The undertaker had had the good sense to insist on a high-necked blouse, and nothing below the second chin was visible. I breathed a sigh of relief, although I hadn't really expected anything else. A gaping throat wound isn't something a loving—or even cheating—husband would want to expose to the world.

"Isn't that Mr. Collier?" Detective Grimaldi asked. I came out of my reverie at the sound of her voice.

"Where?"

"Far wall, half-hidden behind the woman in the burgundy dress."

I stretched my neck as far as it would go. "That's Heidi Hoppenfeldt, Brenda's assistant. I guess her mother never told her she shouldn't wear red to a funeral. And yes, I believe that's Rafe Collier she's rubbing herself against."

Heidi is my age and unattached, and what we, in our younger days, used to call *boy-crazy*.

"I think I'll go have a chat with him. Unless you'd like to rescue him yourself?" Detective Grimaldi arched her brows questioningly.

I shook my head. "I doubt he needs rescuing. But if you want to try, be my guest."

"In that case I'll see you later." Detective Grimaldi gave me a cordial nod and wandered off. I watched out of the corner of my eye as she deftly detached Rafe from Heidi's breathless attentions and walked off with him. Heidi pouted.

The service itself got underway shortly thereafter, and the speeches were alternately bearable and agonizing.

Walker was dignified and the real estate commissioner and association president more so, while Steven was composed, at least until he started talking about his and Brenda's children, and then a single tear rolled down his cheek and trembled on his chin for a moment before plunging to its doom on the expanse of his double-breasted suit. And Clarice Webb was a blubbering mess who had to be escorted off the podium by Tim, who patted her hand solicitously while grinning offensively at the rest of us. Heidi was apparently not considered important enough to be allowed to speak.

I left the service as soon as I decently could, without stopping to talk to anyone, and high-tailed it across the parking lot barely ahead of the TV cameras. I was just about to get into my car when someone materialized next to me. I jumped backwards like a flea on a hot griddle, with a little shriek.

"Goddammit!" I added, after I had caught my breath. "Can't you knock or something? You're scaring a year off my life every time you do that."

Rafael Collier smirked. His eyes were covered by mirrored sunglasses, and he didn't say anything. He just stood there looking at me. At least I assumed he was looking at me; it was hard to be sure when all I could see was my own reflection.

"Would you mind taking the glasses off?" I asked peevishly. "I like seeing people's eyes when I speak to them. They're the mirrors of the soul and all that."

"In that case my soul's black as sin," Rafe said wryly. He removed the glasses. I gasped.

He wasn't kidding. The skin around his left eye was puffy and tight, and a lovely purple-black. I use that color (sparingly) for evening eye-shadow sometimes. It didn't look as good on him as I fancy it does on me. I grimaced. "Put them back on, please. It hurts to look at you. What happened?"

"Had a disagreement with someone," Rafe said. When the dark glasses were in place, he looked back at me, but now I could no longer see his expression. I narrowed my own eyes.

"It wasn't Marquita, was it?"

He grinned. "Would that sweet lil' gal do something like this?"

"I wouldn't be surprised," I said. "She could probably take you in arm wrestling, too."

"I doubt it. No, darlin', it wasn't Marquita. I had a run-in with the law."

Oh, God. "Did Sheriff Satterfield do it?" Was this Bob Satterfield's idea of a 'talk'?

"One of his deputies got a little carried away," Rafe said. "Had a score to settle, seemingly. I took care of it." He shifted his weight slightly.

"Sounds painful."

"Was. Can't a'been pleasant for him, neither."

"I can imagine." I looked around. There was a TV camera pointed our way, and I turned my back to it before I added, "I didn't expect to see you here."

"Came to see you," Rafe said, with a glance at the TV crew. He turned away as well.

"Oh." Gosh, he wasn't going to ask me out too, was he? "Um . . . what can I do for you?"

He didn't answer, but his lips curled, and I realized—too late—what kind of response I had let myself in for. To make reference to it would be unladylike, however, so I kept my mouth shut, although I could feel my cheeks heat up. Rafe chuckled. "Got a favor to ask."

"What kind of favor?"

"Not that kind."

"I wasn't thinking that kind."

"Course not," Rafe said blandly.

I bit my lip. He didn't say anything else, though, and finally I asked again, with what dignity I could muster, "What kind of favor?"

"You ever find out anything about the owner of that house on Potsdam?"

Whoops. I flushed. "Sorry. With everything else that's been going on, it totally slipped my mind. I'll do it later today, I promise."

"No problem. You got any free time in the next couple days?"

"For what?"

"I wanna go back there."

I looked up at him, dismayed. "Are you sure?"

Going back to 101 Potsdam Street was at the bottom of a very long list of things I wanted to do. Especially after what had happened last time I was there.

Rafe smirked. "If you're too scared, darlin', I'm sure I can find someone else."

I didn't doubt it. Heidi Hoppenfeldt would jump at the chance to work with him, and Tim would be all over him at the first opportunity. In more ways than one. And whereas that didn't bother me—either of them was welcome to him if Marquita was willing to share—I hated the idea of missing out on the commission in the event that he actually could buy the place.

"I'll do it. But not today. I've still got the reception to go to."

"Tomorrow's fine. Eight?"

I agreed to meet him at the ungodly early hour of eight, then watched him walk away. The TV cameras zoomed in on him as he went past, but nobody pestered him for an interview. I wasn't surprised.

6.

The reception was depressing, mostly because—and this probably won't make much sense—it wasn't. It was more like a party than a funeral; there was happy music playing, and people were eating and laughing and talking shop. Everyone seemed to have a good time. Austin locked himself in the den to play video games, and Alexandra went off to her room with a girlfriend. I barely had time to tell her how sorry I was for her loss before she disappeared.

Steven was smiling when he made the rounds. "Thank you, Savannah." He took my hand and looked deeply into my eyes. "I know you and Brenda didn't always get on well . . ." Brenda must have told him that, because I certainly hadn't. ". . . and I really appreciate your low profile over this whole business. There are a lot of people who would have taken the opportunity to further their own career with all the publicity, but you didn't, and I'm grateful."

"You're welcome," I said. "I've always believed it wrong to take advantage of someone else's misfortune for my own benefit."

Steven smiled. "You're a nice girl, Savannah." He nodded, squeezed my hand, and moved on. I turned, and found myself face to face with the girlfriend. Or neighbor, to put a more charitable spin on it. She was standing a little too close for comfort, and watched me a little too narrowly. "Hello. I'm Maybelle Driscoll." She offered her hand.

"Savannah Martin," I said. She had a surprisingly strong grip for someone so dainty. "I worked with Brenda." I moved back a fraction when she let go of my hand.

"I live across the street." She waved in what I guessed was the direction of her house. "I've known Steven and Brenda for years."

"I'm sorry for your loss," I said, since the situation seemed to call for it. She opened her hands in an apologetic sort of fashion.

"Brenda and I were never close. I used to baby-sit occasionally, when the kids were younger. My husband and I weren't blessed with any of our own, and she was always so *busy*, bless her heart, making those poor, dear children sit in the car while she met her clients. And then, after my husband died, Steven would come over occasionally to give me a hand. With dripping faucets and things like that, you know. Things which are hard for a woman by herself to manage." She smiled. I smiled back.

I'm no whiz with dripping faucets either. Although I'd never stoop to using it as an excuse for seducing someone else's husband.

"I've been thinking about selling," she added pensively—my God, I thought; is she moving in already?—"but I'm not sure."

I nodded sympathetically. "It's a big decision."

She nodded fervently. "Oh, yes! But with Brenda gone, Steven is going to need someone to manage things. Maybe he'll finally be able to make some strides in *his* career, if he doesn't always have to play second fiddle to Brenda!"

Her voice was quite remarkably poisonous when she said Brenda's name, especially considering that our conversation took place at Brenda's funeral. I smiled politely and refrained, with an effort, from showing my reaction.

"If you'd like to talk to someone about selling," I said instead, "I'd be happy to tell you everything I know. Just give me a call."

I handed her my business card. Maybelle smiled sweetly and tucked it into a pocket of her almost—but not quite—too celebratory dress. I excused myself and disappeared toward the buffet, feeling as if I had just escaped with my life. Maybe it was Maybelle who had followed Brenda to Potsdam Street on Saturday morning to slit her throat. At least Steven had shed a tear during his speech, but Maybelle Driscoll gave me the impression been hurt, my ego bruised, and I'd been mad as a hornet, but I wasn't sure I'd really *cared*.

"Did you love him?"

I looked up, surprised. "I beg your pardon?"

Todd repeated it. It sounded exactly the same this time.

"Oh." I finished chewing and swallowing while I thought it over. "I don't think so. I thought I did, I guess. Or maybe not. I married him because it seemed like the right thing to do. *You* know. He was good looking, well off, and from an old Mississippi family. He was studying law, so he fit right in with my relatives. Mother liked him because he was always polite and proper. It was the first proposal I got. I was twenty-three and not getting any younger."

"*I* proposed," Todd reminded me. I smiled.

"Yes, but you were eighteen and going away to college. I was sixteen and still in senior high. I didn't think you meant it."

Todd nodded.

"So what about you?" I added. "I've told you my story. How about yours?"

Todd's story turned out to be quite similar to my own. He'd moved to Atlanta shortly after I married Bradley. If there was a connection, he didn't mention it, and I didn't ask. A few months later he'd met a woman whom he thought would make an acceptable Mrs. Todd Satterfield. He had proposed and been accepted. They'd gotten married. But Jolynn hadn't turned out to be the perfect wife after all. She went through Todd's money

that she could have killed Brenda and square-danced on the remains without feeling a single moment of remorse.

It was just before seven, and I was curled up in a corner of the second-hand faux-suede sofa, dividing my attention between a paperback romance and the TV, when the doorbell rang. While vicariously enjoying the sexual tension between the blonde and beautiful Lady Shannon and the dark and dangerous highway robber, Mac the Black MacTavish, I was keeping an eye on the news for footage from the memorial service. Channel 5 had, for reasons known only unto themselves, decided to include a five-second segment of Rafe Collier and myself in their coverage, and if that doesn't sound like a big deal, I can tell you that five seconds is a lot longer than it seems. We looked very furtive, skulking in the parking lot with our backs to the TV cameras, and he stood a lot closer to me than I had noticed at the time, too. I was flipping between networks, trying to determine whether anyone else was airing a similar segment and crossing my fingers, hoping to God that my mother wasn't watching Channel 5, when the doorbell startled me.

I rent an apartment in a complex on East Main Street. It's gated and for the most part pretty safe, but I made sure I peeked through the spy hole before I answered. What I saw outside made me take an involuntary step back. "Todd?"

Todd Satterfield smiled at the door, over a big bunch of roses. Pink. I guess red would have been too presumptuous. "Good evening, Savannah."

"What are you doing here?" I said.

"Taking you to dinner, I hope. You said any time I was in Nashville, we'd go."

"I didn't expect you *today*!" I protested. Todd shrugged.

"I told you I wasn't busy. Come on, Savannah, let me in."

"I'm not dressed," I hedged. If it had been Rafe outside, he would have made a suggestive remark, but Todd played it straight.

"I'll wait here, then. But don't take too long. I made reservations at Fidelio's at eight."

Fidelio's is one of the nicest restaurants in Nashville; the kind of place where the CEO of Sony Music wines and dines his top artist, and where the director of the Vanderbilt Children's Hospital takes his daughter for her sixteenth birthday. I hadn't been there for several years—couldn't afford it anymore—and the last time had been while Bradley and I were still married. I didn't have great feelings about the place. Then again, the food was good, the stuff in the fridge was depressing, and if Todd wanted to impress me by taking me to Fidelio's, who was I to demur?

It took me a few minutes to get dressed—all right, ten or maybe even fifteen—but as all you girls know, that's actually pretty good. Todd was very complimentary when I finally emerged. "You look beautiful. And you did it so quickly, too!"

I lowered my lashes coyly, and snuck a [...] myself at the same time. The dress was my equi[...] Marquita's hot pink number: not as bright, tight, [...] but with thin straps and enough of a plunge to sh[...] what cleavage I have. I can't hope to match Mar[...] that respect, either, but really, who would want to?[...]

So we went to dinner at Fidelio's and had a nic[...] The food was excellent, the company good, and [...] were only two instances when the conversation was [...] than pleasant. The first came when Todd discovered [...] I had been to Fidelio's before, and what the circumstan[...] had been.

"I think it was our first wedding anniversary." [...] pushed a mushroom around my plate with my fork. "Ou[...] *only* wedding anniversary, because we never made it t[...] our second. Bradley took me here to celebrate. But then [...] this woman showed up, someone he worked with, and he asked her to join us . . ."

"On your anniversary?" Todd was cutting his Veal Marsala into bite-size pieces.

"He talked to her the rest of the night, while I twiddled my thumbs. When I brought it up later, he told me I was being silly, and that it was just business."

"But it wasn't?"

I shook my head. "He married her a week after our divorce was final." I speared the mushroom and ate it.

"I'm sorry," Todd said. I shrugged. It was in the past; it didn't bother me anymore. Much. I wasn't even sure it had bothered me that much at the time. My feelings had

almost as fast as he could earn it, and apparently she wasn't much of an asset to an upcoming young attorney's reputation. She flirted with his boss, drank too much at company gatherings, and didn't keep his house looking the way he wanted.

"She looked like you," Todd said, "so I thought she'd be like you, as well. But she wasn't. She colored her hair, and didn't dress right, and didn't really care about anything but herself." He stabbed his veal with suppressed force, then looked up at me. "Sorry."

"No problem. Bradley wasn't what I thought when I married him, either."

When we dated, he'd been charming, generous, and a perfect gentleman. Once we were married, he turned out to be manipulative, shallow, and lousy in bed.

Of course, he had blamed *me* for his lack of success in that area. I was undersexed. Frigid, even. Impossible to please. Which was why he'd had to go to someone else to get his needs met. It's a bunch of baloney, but I didn't bother to say so; at that point I was just happy to get rid of him. My sister Catherine, who represented me in the divorce, wanted me to broadcast his infamy far and wide. She wasn't happy when I accepted the Volvo and a fair, though hardly extravagant, settlement in lieu of alimony, in an attempt to keep everything on the QT. Very few people knew why my marriage had failed, and that's exactly how I wanted it. I knew that Bradley's infidelity was his fault, not mine; still, the fact that my husband had been dissatisfied with me wasn't something I wanted the world to know. Naturally I didn't tell Todd any of these details; the conversation had been personal enough without that.

The other unpleasant discussion came over dessert, when I informed Todd that I had seen Rafe Collier again. "And he had a black eye. He said he'd had a run-in with the law." Try as I might, I couldn't keep a note of accusation out of my voice.

"It was his own fault," Todd grumbled.

"I don't see *you* sporting a black eye," I retorted.

"You think *I'm* stupid enough to hit him? It was Cletus. Deputy Sheriff Cletus Johnson. Apparently his ex has been hanging around Collier. They used to get into it all the time in high school, too."

"Let me guess," I said. "Cletus's ex-wife is a big black woman named Marquita?"

Todd nodded. "How did you know?"

"I met her out at the Bog yesterday. She seemed to think that Rafe had brought me out there, and she was quite alarmingly possessive of him. Poor man."

"Cletus?"

"Rafe. Have you ever seen her? She's as big as a barn. She'd squash him like a bug."

Todd muttered something. It wasn't complimentary. To Rafe or Marquita.

"So how does Cletus look today?" I added maliciously.

Todd grimaced. "He has a black eye and a split lip, not to mention sore ribs. Collier's not the kind of guy I'd want to tangle with."

I shook my head. Me, neither. In any sense of the word.

It was late by the time I got home. I was alone; Todd didn't suggest coming in, and if he hinted, the hints were too subtle for me to pick up on. He did kiss me, but it was a friendly, non-invasive kiss, and I didn't hold it against him

"I had a good time," he said, clutching my hand and looking deeply into my eyes. I nodded. I'd had a good time, too. Or as good as can be expected, considering that I'd had to dwell on my ex-husband and the failure of my marriage. "I'd like to do it again sometime."

"I'm available," I said brightly. "Anytime you're up this way, just give me a call."

Todd said he'd take me up on that. I smiled and pecked him on the cheek. "Thanks, Todd. Drive carefully."

Todd promised he would. "You be careful, too. Don't go into any empty houses with anyone you don't know. I'd hate to see you end up like Brenda Puckett."

"That makes two of us. I'll be careful." I ducked through the door and into the apartment before my face could give me away. I'm not a good liar, and I was pretty sure Todd wouldn't consider going back to 101 Potsdam Street in the company of Rafe Collier being particularly careful.

Morning came all too soon, and I took a shower and brushed my teeth and did my hair and put on makeup and managed to get to Potsdam Street a little after eight. Rafe was there before me, sitting on the front steps in the bright glare of the sun, looking disgustingly awake for this time of the morning. "Big date last night?" he inquired dryly when I stopped in front of him. I grimaced.

"Do I look that bad?"

"There are bags under your eyes and you forgot to put on glitter."

He tugged one of his ears to show me what he meant. I felt my own earlobes—they were bare—and squinted suspiciously. "Are you a detective or something?"

That suggestion earned me an honest-to-goodness, full-throated laugh. "God forbid. No, darlin', just a man who likes looking at women."

"From what I understand," I said snidely, "that's what got you that black eye, too."

He grinned. "You been asking the sheriff about me?" I shrugged. "Yeah, ole Cletus got a little carried away. Not the first time, neither. Seemed to mind me talking to Marquita."

"That's what I heard."

"As it happens, ain't nothing going on with Marquita and me. And it ain't Cletus's business anyhow. She left him."

"So I understand," I said. Rafe squinted at me.

"Ain't no business of yours, neither, come to think of it."

"I guess not. So are you ready to go inside?" I smiled brightly. He looked at me for a second—debating whether or not to push me further, probably—then got to his feet.

"Sure."

"Let me just open the door for you, and you can look around as much as you want." I got the new key out of the lockbox and into the lock. "There you go. Have fun." I pushed the door open and smiled him in. He didn't move.

"After you, darlin'."

"I think I'll just stay out here, if you don't mind."

He grinned. "Scared?"

I shrugged.

"Don't worry, I'll protect you from the ghostly ghoulies." He lifted his arms and wiggled his fingers suggestively, in the manner of ghostly ghoulies everywhere. Muscles bunched under the tight sleeves of the T-shirt.

"Did it ever occur to you that maybe I'm afraid of *you?*" I asked.

Obviously it hadn't, because he looked stunned. For just a second, before his face and eyes were smooth and under control again. His voice was light. "Can't say it did, darlin'. But now that I know, I'll be sure to keep my distance." He ducked through the door before I had time to answer. I pulled a face. I hadn't meant it *that* way, exactly.

In the end I stayed outside just long enough to— hopefully—give him time to simmer down before I went inside. "Rafe?"

"In here." The voice came from the back of the house. I headed that way.

"What are you doing?"

"What's it look like I'm doing?" He was standing in the middle of the kitchen, looking around. I stepped onto the cracked vinyl and did the same.

Back in the days when the house on Potsdam was built, the kitchen was a separate building at a safe distance from the main house. That way, the house wouldn't catch fire if the kitchen did. As time progressed and cooking over an open flame became a thing of the past, people decided they liked the convenience of having a kitchen that was part of the house, and those houses that weren't originally built with kitchens had one tacked on or inserted somewhere. Back home in Sweetwater, one of the smaller rooms on the first floor was converted to a kitchen. Here, an extra room had been added to the back of the original structure. From the looks of it, it had happened sometime in the thirties, and nothing had changed appreciably since then, except for a new stove and refrigerator. *New* being a relative term; they were avocado green and dated from the seventies.

"This needs a complete overhaul," I remarked, in my cheeriest, most professional tone.

Rafe glanced over at me. "You think?" Both voice and glance were hostile.

"Look," I said, "about what I said earlier . . ."

He shook his head. "No need to apologize. Delicate lady like yourself, ain't surprising you get twitchety round somebody like me."

Twitchety? "You make it sound like I'm a hundred years old," I said. "I'm not twitchety. And even if I were,

I think anyone would agree I have reason to be careful, knowing what I know about you."

"And what do you know about me?" He turned his entire body towards me. It seemed I had made the mistake of getting his undivided attention. Not something I wanted. I took an unobtrusive half step back, and saw his lips quirk. "Scared?" He moved a little closer.

"Should I be?" My voice was steadier than I felt, but with a slight wobble nonetheless.

He grinned. "I don't know. Should you?"

I hesitated. Probably. Here I was, in an empty house—a house where another woman had been murdered less than a week ago—alone, except for an ex-convict who had had the opportunity to kill her, and who was leaning over me, looking like he wouldn't mind taking a bite. He was close enough that I could feel his breath stirring the hair at my temple. It took all my self-control to say coolly, "If I thought I was in any danger, I wouldn't have agreed to meet you. And, of course, I told my office where I was going and with whom."

Rafe nodded sagely. "Course." He straightened up and added, "So if anything happens to you, they'll know I did it. Smart."

I nodded. It would have been, yes. A pity I hadn't thought of it until now.

In the silence as he stepped back, giving me the chance to breathe again, we could hear footsteps in the front part of the house. Slow, dragging steps, coming closer. My heart started beating faster. Rafe took a step forward, between me and the doorway. It must have been one of those automatic guy things, for I certainly hadn't given him any reason to want to protect me.

The footsteps turned into the hall. I held my breath. Any moment now, we'd be able to see someone through the open door. Rafe shifted his weight, distributing it properly for a fight. His muscles tensed and he flexed his hands. I could see what Todd had meant when he said that he wouldn't want to tangle with Rafe. I wouldn't want to tangle with him, either, although there was no denying that the way he moved, smooth and controlled like a predatory animal, was beautiful.

The footsteps stopped. Then a quavering voice called out, "Who's there?"

7.

I started breathing again as a small, shriveled black woman stepped into the doorway. Her face was so wrinkled she resembled a raisin, but she looked like she might have been pretty in her youth. At the moment, her gray hair was sticking out every which way, as if no one had taken the trouble to comb it for several days, and she was wearing a stained and faded housecoat and fuzzy blue slippers. She blinked from one of us to the other. Rafe relaxed, although he didn't move away from me. "Morning, ma'am." His voice was surprisingly polite, with the merest hint of a tremor. Maybe he hadn't been as unaffected as he had appeared.

The old lady squinted at him, then shuffled a couple of steps closer. Finally, a toothless smile spread over her face and she put her hand on his arm. Her quavery voice was delighted. "Tyrell! I ain't seen you in forever. Why didn't you tell me you was comin', you naughty boy?"

"Who's Tyrell?" I murmured. Rafe didn't respond. His attention was focused on the beaming ancient in front of him.

"I didn't know it myself till just now."

"Well, it's great to see you, baby! And lookit here! Who's this you brought home to show your mama?"

She peered around him to me. I smiled politely. She smiled back, widely, before she focused her attention back on Rafe. Or Tyrell, as he clearly was to her. She lowered her voice, and seemed to think I wouldn't be able to hear. "She's a looker, ain't she? But them ain't breedin' hips, boy. You sure she'll be able to get that baby out?"

I sniffed. This remark was offensive on so many levels I wasn't even sure I had caught them all. I could see from the tightening of Rafe's lips that he was suppressing something—a grin, most likely—but his voice was soothing. "She'll be fine."

The woman smiled back. "You're lookin' out for her, ain't you, boy?" She reached up—way up; she was barely five feet tall—and patted him on the cheek.

A car door slammed outside, and just as quickly as that, the atmosphere in the kitchen changed. The old woman stiffened, and her hitherto vague brown eyes became sharper. "They're comin' for me." She glanced over her shoulder towards the front hall. "Filthy cops. You won't let 'em take me away, will you, Tyrell?"

Rafe hesitated, for just long enough to make her take another look at him. Something seemed to switch over in her brain, and her eyes narrowed. "You ain't my Tyrell.

What're you doin' in my house? Help! Intruders! Help! Help!"

Rafe took a step back, straight into me. I grabbed hold of him to steady myself while outside in the hallway someone picked up speed and came barreling through the door, fetching up in the kitchen with a gun in both hands. I did my best to shrink behind Rafe's bigger frame. The old woman shrieked and crumpled in a heap on the floor. Rafe lifted his hands slowly, in the universal gesture of surrender.

"Christ!" a disgusted voice outside the door said. "Put the gun away before you shoot someone."

Officer Truman flushed and lowered the weapon just as Officer Spicer came trotting through the door. He took in the situation at a glance, and didn't seem too surprised. I guess a beat cop gets used to seeing all sorts of things. He nodded cordially to me. "Mornin', Miz Martin. Mr. Collier. Sorry about that. And where's . . . damn, she's fainted. Oh, well. It'll make it easier to get her in the car. Last time she gave us a hell of a time."

He nodded to Truman who, having secured his gun in its holster, bent and lifted the old lady in his arms. He headed for the door with his burden, and I addressed myself to Spicer.

"Where are you taking her?"

Spicer didn't seem to mind sharing the information with me. "Back to the nursing home. She keeps walking off, and they keep calling us to bring her back. Poor old bird." He shook his head.

"Who is she?" I asked, although I was pretty sure I already knew the answer. This had to be the homeowner; who else would worry about intruders?

Spicer's words confirmed my theory. "Name's Jenkins. Lived here up till just a few weeks ago. Can't remember it ain't her home no more."

"Alzheimer's?"

Spicer shrugged. "Or she's just forgetful. Happens to most of us when we hit eighty or so."

I nodded. When I didn't say anything else, Spicer tipped his uniform cap and started to walk off. He stopped after a few steps and turned back. "What happened here, anyway?"

"Oh." I glanced at Rafe, who was standing next to me, sunk in thought. "We came back to see the house one more time. We were interrupted last time, you know." Spicer nodded. "We'd only been here a few minutes when Mrs. Jenkins turned up. She must be an early riser."

Spicer confirmed that she was. "Old folks don't sleep so good no more. Nursing home attendant said she disappeared before breakfast. Ain't but a quarter-mile walk."

I nodded. "At first she was worried about us being here, but then she seemed to think she recognized Rafe. She called him Tyrell." I paused, hoping that Spicer could give me some more information, but if he had any, he chose not to share. "Then we heard the car door slam, and she realized you were coming. I don't think she likes it where she lives now."

"Ain't the nicest place in the world," Spicer agreed.

"She asked us—Rafe, really—to help her, and when he didn't say yes right away, she must have realized he wasn't Tyrell after all. She started screaming for help, and that's when Truman came running in."

"I'll have a talk with the boy," Spicer grunted. "Can't have him pulling his weapon on innocent bystanders. Though I don't mind telling you it'll make it easier with Mrs. J. Last time we did this, we thought we'd have to taser her."

"That poor old lady?"

"Hey, lemme tell you, she can be a handful. She scratched both of us, and bit Truman. I guess I'd better get her back there before she wakes up." He tipped the cap again and headed for the door. This time he didn't stop. I waited until I heard the car door slam and the tires crunch before I turned to Rafe.

"That was interesting."

He shrugged. I added, "Do you want to look around some more? We could go upstairs again. Or downstairs. You didn't see the basement last time."

"I think I'm done. Thanks." The "thanks" was an afterthought. He sent me a distracted glance as we headed out of the kitchen.

"No problem. So do you want the house?" I smiled optimistically.

"Who wouldn't want this?" He looked around at the peeling wallpaper, the dull wood floors, and the sagging ceilings.

I grimaced. "Right."

"I'll let you know."

"You do that. Here, why don't you take one of my cards? That way you can call me if there's anything you need." I dug a couple of business cards out of my purse. "In fact, take several. Spread the joy."

He accepted the cards with a grin. "When you say 'anything' . . ."

"I mean something vaguely related to real estate. Like, you want to buy this house. Or you want to see it again. Or you want to see another house. Or you'd like the name of a good mortgage broker."

"Right." He pocketed the card, although he didn't stop smiling. I locked the front door and put the key back into the lockbox in case someone else wanted to see the place. When I straightened up, Rafe was still standing in the same spot. We looked at each other in silence for a few seconds.

"Well . . ." I said finally, awkwardly, "it's been nice seeing you again." I was surprised to find that I sort of meant it.

"You, too." That grin still wasn't going anywhere.

"I guess I'll . . . um . . . go now." I gestured towards my car. He nodded pleasantly. "Places to go, people to see. I've got to stop by the office to let them know I escaped unscathed. I'll . . . um . . . see you around."

"I'll call you."

"Right."

He didn't say anything else, so I did what I'd said I'd do, and went. Down the stairs and over to the car. Into the driver's seat. Down the drive and through the gate. He was still standing on the porch when I turned the corner, and I was pretty sure he was still grinning, too.

Clarice, Tim, Heidi, and Walker had their heads together when I walked into the office. Walker was stone-faced, and Clarice looked so much like a hen that I slowed down, frowning. "What's wrong?"

Tim straightened up. "Well, hello, Savannah. Late night?" He smirked. I smiled back, but didn't ask for clarification. Tim's choice of words was bound to be a lot more cutting than Rafe's. He added, cheerfully, "Have you seen the *Voice* today?"

The *Nashville Voice* is a weekly paper that comes out on Thursday morning, just in time for the (long) weekend. This was the first issue since Brenda's death, so it wasn't surprising that they had published something about her. What I didn't expect to see was a six-page layout with a headline that screamed BRENDA PUCKETT KICKS THE BUCKET! in letters three inches high. The accompanying photograph showed Brenda at her worst: taken from below, so all three of her chins were prominently displayed and her elephantine calves looked like tree-trunks. Her mouth was open, as if she were yelling at someone, and she was gesturing with a finger. It wasn't the middle finger, but it looked rude nonetheless.

"Ouch," I said, averting my eyes. Tim giggled.

"This is terrible!" Clarice was wringing her hands. Heidi nodded fervently.

"What's the article about?" I inquired.

It was Walker who answered, in a heavy voice. "Apparently someone has remembered that Brenda once was investigated by the Real Estate Commission. It's twelve or thirteen years ago now."

"Fifteen," Clarice said.

"Investigated for what?" I wanted to know.

Walker hesitated. I waited, and eventually he felt compelled to explain. "It had to do with a property she owned in downtown. An office building she wanted to convert to apartments."

"And?"

Walker shrugged. Elegantly. I turned to Clarice. "You've worked for Brenda for a long time. Don't you know anything about it?"

Tim tittered and glanced at Clarice. She pursed her lips, unwillingly. "I hadn't started working for her yet when this was going on."

"So you don't know anything about it?"

Tim giggled. "Nothing more than what's in the paper," Clarice said firmly. I turned back to Walker.

"Why are they bringing it up again? If it was fifteen years ago, it can't have anything to do with what happened to her."

Walker's voice sounded as if the words were being dragged forcibly from him. "I guess they're implying that she might be engaged in something similar again. Some shady deal that could make someone want to kill her."

I hesitated. "Was she?"

"Well, I never!" Clarice sniffed.

Walker raised his voice. "If she was, I hadn't heard about it."

I nodded. I hadn't really expected him to know and not make it stop. Walker Lamont Realty was Walker Lamont's pride and joy. He had built it up from nothing to a very well-respected, profitable company that handles a lot of upscale clients and expensive properties. If someone was doing something that might damage the reputation of the company or of Walker himself, I would expect him to land on them like a ton of bricks. "This isn't going to hurt you or the company, is it?" And by extension, the rest of us. Not that I personally was in a position to be hurt much. If the company went belly-up, I'd have to find another broker who'd take me on, but that was as bad as it could get for me. Walker was another story. He'd have to go back to being a sales agent in someone else's brokerage firm, and something like this wasn't exactly going to improve his chances of getting that coveted spot on the Real Estate Commission, either.

His face was sober. "We'll just have to hope that it doesn't. It probably won't, but you just never know."

I looked around. "Would anyone mind if I read the article? I'm sure someone will ask me about it sooner or later, and I may as well know what they're talking about."

Tim giggled. Clarice sent me a look of loathing. "Knock yourself out," Walker said. "We've got a stack of *Voices*. No one's going to mind if you take one."

Clarice looked like she minded, but she didn't dare speak up. I took a paper and stuck it in my bag before I went to my office, a converted coat closet off the reception area. While the computer booted up, I opened the *Voice* and started reading about Brenda.

The Wicked Witch of the South had started in real estate during a time when interest rates were almost 20 percent and suburbia was the place to be. The urban neighborhoods, so popular now, were blighted areas where no one wanted to live. Brenda had been ahead of her time in seeing the revitalization currently going on in our inner-city neighborhoods. Her foray into the downtown arena had taken place too soon, was all. If she had waited twelve or fifteen years, she could have made a killing. Investors were developing lofts and condos all over downtown these days, and selling them for big bucks. Or had been, until the bottom dropped out of the market last year, and everything slowed down.

At any rate, instead of paying off big time and making everyone involved super rich, Brenda's plan to make the Kress office building into upscale condominiums had backfired. It had left her with a smudge on her record, and had left her business partner facing disgrace, bankruptcy, and a criminal investigation.

He was employed in some branch of banking or finance, the article said, and he had been channeling other people's funds into Brenda's project when he couldn't come up with the capital for the ever-increasing renovations out of his own pocket. Somehow—and the article didn't go into detail, although it hinted darkly at something similar to insider trading—Brenda had managed to bail out just before the whole thing came crashing down. Her partner had not been so lucky. Left holding the bag, he killed himself rather than face the music.

His widow had brought a lawsuit against Brenda, claiming self-dealing and breach of the realtor's code of ethics, but nothing had ever come of it. All the current members of the Real Estate Commission had declined the *Voice*'s invitation to comment—not surprisingly, as they had all come aboard long·after the Kress case had been forgotten—and although Lawrence Derryberry, the reporter for the *Voice*, had tried to contact the widow, he had been unable to find her. I wasn't sure whether that meant that she was dead herself by now, if she had remarried or otherwise changed her name, or if she just plain didn't want to be found.

The article was long on speculation and innuendo, but short on facts. It didn't even mention the name of the widow. Not that something like that ought to be difficult to find. Unless the woman had a good reason for wanting to stay under the radar, of course. Like, for instance, if she had been at 101 Potsdam Street on Saturday morning to cut Brenda's throat . . .

Okay, so I knew that finding Brenda's killer wasn't my job. Tamara Grimaldi got paid to do it, and I should just leave it to her. She seemed capable, and besides, snooping is unladylike. It wasn't as if I had a personal stake in the matter to justify my interest. The detective didn't suspect me—I'd been elsewhere when Brenda was killed—and I didn't care enough about any of the others to worry about them being suspected. Except maybe Walker, but nobody in her right mind would suspect him. On the other hand, Rafe Collier was my client now, by default, and maybe I owed it to him to keep him out of jail. As long as he was innocent, of course. Which I wasn't ready to bet my life on. Still, for my own safety as well as for any other reason, surely it couldn't hurt just to make a few inquiries.

I started on one of the people search engines, by typing in *Rafael Collier* and leaning back in my chair while the computer worked. It ticked and buzzed for a while, then dinged to let me know the search was complete. There were a few people who shared the name Rafael Collier, but none with an address in Memphis, or Nashville, or Sweetwater, or for that matter anywhere in Tennessee. Or in West Memphis, Arkansas. So the sheriff had either misunderstood about Rafe living in Memphis, or Rafe had lied. Imagine that. I stuck my lower lip out and switched to Google.

The thing about Googling somebody is that you get hits on all sorts of things. Every Rafael with a presence on the Internet showed up, as did every Collier. It wasn't very

often that both names converged, but it happened once
or twice. None seemed to apply to the Rafe Collier I knew,
unless he was actually a professor of micro-engineering at
Yale or a pediatric dentist in northern California or in the
habit of winning online poker tournaments. (I wouldn't
put it past him.) The only bona fide mention I could find
was in the *Sweetwater Reporter*—where Aunt Regina writes
the society column—and it was from a couple of weeks
ago, when LaDonna Collier's obituary had run.

The obit was pretty basic, with just the bare bones.
Name: LaDonna Jean Collier, daughter of Wanda and
Jim, both deceased, and sister of Bubba, ditto. Date
of birth: some forty-five years ago, and date of death
as determined by the medical examiner. Cremation had
already taken place, and there was no mention of flowers
or contributions to be sent to a favorite charity. I guess
maybe Rafe, if it was he who had drafted the obit, hadn't
expected anyone to care enough to want to send flowers.
It didn't seem as if he had cared overmuch himself,
because there was nothing about "dearly beloved" or
"missed" or any of that sentimental twaddle. "Survived
by her son, Rafael," was as far as it went.

Since I was on the *Sweetwater Reporter*'s site anyway, I
went to their homepage and typed in "LaDonna Collier"
for an internal search. There I found another oblique
mention, from the time the body had been discovered.
Sheriff Bob Satterfield confirmed that LaDonna Collier
had been found dead in her home in the Bog, but
emphasized that the police had no clues, and were unsure

that a crime had even taken place. They had not yet
notified the next of kin. But once they had a chance to go
through the house, the sheriff said, he was confident that
they would be able to find a way to contact him. There
was stuff there from thirty years back, so it would take
a while, but Sheriff Satterfield was sure the information
they needed was there somewhere. As indeed it must have
been, because I knew they had found Rafe eventually.

The *Reporter*'s online archives didn't date back far
enough for me to discover anything new about Rafe's
arrest twelve years ago, and without knowing more about
it, I didn't know where else to look. So that was pretty
much it for Rafe Collier, at least for now.

Next I decided to visit the Metropolitan Nashville
government website. If I couldn't do any more research
about Rafe, I could at least do some research *for* him, and
maybe figure out why he was so interested in that house
on Potsdam while I was at it.

Property assessments are a matter of public record, at
least in the state of Tennessee, and our powers that be, in
their infinite wisdom, have laid them out on the Internet.
In great detail. Property address and color photograph,
owner's name, square footage, and number of rooms—
it's all there. There's even a schematic drawing of each
house, to make it easier for potential burglars to get
around. It's a great resource, whether your purposes for
checking are nefarious or not.

The official owner of record for 101 Potsdam Street
was Tondalia Jenkins. The previous owner had been

one Douglas Jenkins—a father or husband maybe; now deceased—and before that, the property had belonged to someone named Hausmann. Tyrell Jenkins wasn't mentioned, as owner, co-owner, previous owner, or anything else. There wasn't even an *et ux* he could be hiding under.

Which was just fine as far as it went; Dix, Catherine, and I don't show up as owners on our mother's house, either. It's hers outright, to do with whatever she wants. But if she tried to sell it, you'd better believe we'd be there with bells on to keep an eye on the transaction, and if there had been any question at all about her legal competence, which there certainly seemed to be in the case of Mrs. Jenkins, we'd make sure she had an attorney-in-fact to handle everything for her. We would not be leaving her to handle things on her own the way Tyrell seemed to be doing.

There wasn't anything I could do about it, though. Turning my mind to other things, I finished up my session by Googling the Kress building, but all I could come up with were realtor websites advertising condos for sale, plus the homepage for the Downtown Neighborhood Association. There was no information online about Brenda's botched plan of fifteen years ago, nor any mention of the resulting lawsuit. I guess the Nashville papers weren't any better than the *Sweetwater Reporter* about online archives. But whereas I couldn't very well drive down to Sweetwater and walk into the *Reporter*'s offices and start looking at microfiche without causing all my friends and relatives to have heart attacks over my interest in Rafe Collier, visiting the downtown Nashville library's research room was no big deal. I turned off the computer, gathered up my handbag, and set out.

8.

On my way downtown, I took a detour through the Potsdam area. Not because I had any business there, but just out of idle nosiness. I had left Rafe on the front porch of 101 Potsdam Street four hours ago, and although I doubted he was still there, I wanted to check.

I was in two minds about Rafe. On the one hand, I didn't feel as if I was in any danger from him. He'd startled me, and crowded me, and even—jokingly, I thought—threatened me, but I hadn't gotten that nervous, creeped-out feeling one gets from some people. I wouldn't go as far as to say that I enjoyed his company, but I wouldn't go out of my way to avoid it, either. On the other hand, I knew he was dangerous. I had only his word for it that Brenda never showed up for their appointment. He could have met her and killed her and then called me, pretending to have been waiting for forty-five minutes. I had no idea what his motive might have been, but it needn't even have been anything personal; with his background, someone could have hired him to get rid of her. Brenda had been so universally disliked it was amazing she'd survived as long as she had, and the *Voice*'s insinuation that she might have been mixed up in something illegal and/or unethical again made a lot of sense. Once a crook, always a crook, right? And it seemed to me that one would need a certain personality-type to slit someone's throat. It's not like pulling a trigger from a safe distance, or poisoning someone's food while they're not looking, or cutting the brake cables on someone's car, hoping for a tragic—and fatal—accident. Throat-slitting is up close and personal and seems to require a particularly brutal, yet unemotional personality. A personality a lot like Rafe Collier's.

But if he did kill Brenda, why involve me? He could have just walked away, gotten on his bike, and disappeared. Nobody would have known that he was ever there. Unless someone had seen him, of course. One of the neighbors, maybe. The young man in the green car, maybe. Or unless he was afraid that he'd left evidence behind, and he wanted to be sure that he could explain away anything the forensic team found. His fingerprints and DNA must be in the police database from when he was arrested before, and it'd be impossible to get around hair or fingerprints found in the house if he claimed never to have been inside.

The driveway of 101 Potsdam Street was empty, and I continued on down the street while my thoughts kept churning. I was so preoccupied that I almost ran the stop sign at the corner of Potsdam and Dresden, and came within five inches of hitting a Chrysler with a middle-aged man behind the wheel. He mouthed an insult, to both my race and gender, before he drove off in a cloud of smoke. His car obviously had engine problems, and I supposed that was punishment enough for calling me names.

I was just about to turn the corner and follow him when I caught sight of something in the parking lot across the street. It was a black motorcycle, parked in the shade under a tree, and although I'm certainly no expert, it looked familiar.

I inched forward, peering beyond the rows of glossy-leaved magnolias. The parking lot flanked a long, low building with lots of windows and faded, blue curtains. A motel? I narrowed my eyes. Was it possible that I had discovered—entirely by accident—where Rafe lived?

But no. The sign at the entrance said *Milton House* and below the name, in smaller letters, *Home for the Aging*.

All right, so I know I said earlier that I don't want to be Nancy Drew. I do, however, have a healthy share of what my mother calls unladylike curiosity. At the moment, it was twanging like a steel-guitar string. This must be the nursing home where Tondalia Jenkins lived. It was the right distance from the house for her to have walked, and it was the only nursing home I had seen around here.

And *that* looked an awful lot like Rafe Collier's bike. But if it was, what was he doing here? Did it have something to do with Brenda's murder? Or was he perhaps—my eyes narrowed—talking about the house? Telling Mrs. Jenkins that if she'd take it off the market, he'd buy it directly from her, without using an agent? Thus doing away with Tim and myself, and cheating us both out of our commissions?

I didn't think; I just reacted. I pulled into the parking lot and found a spot close to the entrance. Then I stalked inside, ready to do battle.

The reception area was dingy, with threadbare, green carpet and a utilitarian desk. I dredged up a smile from somewhere and plastered it across my face. "Excuse me?"

The desk nurse, middle-aged and plump, looked up from her issue of *Ebony*. "Yes?"

"Do you have someone named Tondalia Jenkins living here? I'd like to see her, please."

"Miz Jenkins already has a visitor." She didn't close the magazine, and I found my eyes drawn to a photo spread showing five or six dark-skinned men with their shirts off. Muscles bulged and the nurse's eyes did, too. I rather hoped mine didn't, but I wasn't entirely sure.

"That's all right," I said. "He's a tall guy in jeans and a T-shirt, with a tattoo of a snake wrapped around his arm, right? Looks a little like number four down there, but without the braids."

The nurse nodded. "Miz Jenkins said he was her grandson."

Of course she had, poor, confused old woman. And naturally it hadn't occurred to the nurse to ask Rafe to prove it. Not when he looked like one of her photo spreads come to life. I pried my teeth apart. "We're old friends. He won't mind if I drop in."

She tossed her head. "Lucky girl. Room 114, down the hall on the right."

I thanked her and headed in that direction.

Officer Spicer had said that the nursing home where Mrs. Jenkins lived wasn't the nicest place in the world, and now that I was inside it, I had to agree. The interior of the Milton House looked almost as bad as the house on Potsdam, with peeling paint and chipped industrial tile on the floor, and it smelled worse: sour and clinical at the same time, with traces of antiseptic and bodily excretions left too long without being cleaned. It's amazing how some of these places manage to get and keep the Health Department's seal of approval. I would sooner shoot one of my loved ones than allow them to live in a place like this, and I couldn't blame Tondalia Jenkins for trying to escape. I would have done anything to get out, too.

The door to room 114 was shut, but I could hear a murmur of voices inside. They stopped when I knocked on the door. It was silent for a few seconds, and then the door opened a crack. Mrs. Jenkins's wrinkled face peered out. "Yes?"

I smiled. "Hello again, Mrs. Jenkins. Remember me, from this morning?"

It didn't look like she did. "You from the Health Department, baby?"

I shook my head. "Sorry, no. We met this morning at your house on Potsdam Street. Remember? I was there with . . ."

It was all I got out, because now the door was pulled all the way open and Rafe looked down at me, above Mrs. Jenkins's head. And although I won't quote the old adage about looks that can kill, I could tell he wasn't happy to see me. His eyes were black and hard, his lips were set in a tight line, and somehow he managed to look even taller and more imposing than he usually did.

He didn't speak to me, just stepped around Mrs. Jenkins and into the hallway. "Guess it's time to go." He grabbed me by the arm.

"You'll be back, won't you, baby?" Mrs. Jenkins smiled toothlessly up at him. Officer Spicer had said that she had bitten Officer Truman, but I had a hard time figuring out how that could have happened when she had no teeth. Gummed him, more likely. Left him with a drooly, wet spot on his starched uniform shirt. The thought made me smile, and she smiled back.

"You take good care of my boy, ya hear?"

She patted Rafe on the arm. He didn't say anything, just nodded to her before he propelled me down the dusky hallway toward the reception area. His legs were a lot longer than mine, and I was wearing high heels again. I had to take two steps for each of his. The nurse at the duty desk got halfway up from her chair and stared at us with her mouth hanging open, but she didn't say anything. Maybe she didn't realize that I was being more or less kidnapped, or maybe the look on his face warned her off. Either way, she didn't interfere, just let him walk me through the lobby without lifting a finger.

We erupted out of the double doors with enough force to knock them both back against the wall. The next second I was knocked back against the wall, too. Or not exactly knocked; it was the shock more than the impact that drove the breath out of my lungs. Nothing that Rafe had done so far had led me to believe I was in any danger of being manhandled by him. "What the hell are you doing here?" he wanted to know, between clenched teeth.

I could have asked him the same thing, but I refrained. He was too close for comfort and too upset for me to take any chances with. Instead, the truth fell out of my mouth without any additional prompting. "I recognized your motorcycle when I drove by. And I wondered what you were talking to Mrs. Jenkins about."

His eyes narrowed to black slits as he looked down on me. "My private conversations ain't none of your business."

"They are if they concern me," I said, tilting my chin up. He lifted an eyebrow.

"Why'd I be talking about you?"

I shrugged. "I thought maybe you were discussing the house. You might have contacted Mrs. Jenkins to try to get her to sell the house directly to you rather than going through us first. You could probably get a better price that way. And she wouldn't have to pay a commission. Everybody wins. Except for Tim and me, of course."

"Course." There was a glint of . . . was it relief, in his eyes? "Sorry to disappoint you, darlin', but I ain't planning to go behind your back to cut you out of your commission. This ain't nothing to do with you. I had some other business to take care of."

He had eased off just a fraction, and it gave me the courage to confront him. "You're not still letting that poor woman believe that you're her son, are you? That's not only unethical and illegal, but downright mean." He didn't answer, and I added, "If this other business involves taking advantage of her . . ."

"Ain't much you can do about it, if I am."

"I can warn her!"

He shrugged. "Go ahead. Fat lot of good it'll do you. She thinks I'm family, remember? And she don't know you from Adam. She didn't even recognize you when you knocked on the door. She ain't gonna believe anything you say."

"Then I can warn the nurses and tell them to make sure you don't get in to see her."

"Ain't a nurse alive that can say no to me," Rafe said with a smug grin. I sniffed.

"I can call the police and tell them that I think you're planning to rip her off. Revoke your parole, or whatever. Detective Grimaldi is already interested in you because of Brenda's murder, and Sheriff Satterfield isn't positive that your mother's death was entirely accidental . . ."

The sight of his jaw tightening made me subside. For or a second or two he didn't say anything. Then he moved closer to me again; so close that I could feel his body heat and the tension of his muscles through the fabric of my clothes. To anyone watching, we probably looked like a courting couple, but there was nothing romantic about the look in his eyes. His voice was low and deathly calm. "You ain't accusing me of killing my mother, are you, darlin'?"

I hesitated. I was, sort of, but there was something about him—it could have been the warning in his voice, or maybe the flat, black eyes, reminiscent of a cobra preparing to strike—that made it seem like a supremely bad idea. "Um . . . no."

"That's good. I'd hate to think you thought so little of me as that. C'mon."

He removed me from the wall and towed me after him across the parking lot. I gulped. "Where are you taking me?"

"This is your car, ain't it? Gimme your keys." He held out a hand. I scrabbled in my handbag and dug out my key chain. It didn't occur to me to refuse. It did occur to me to slash at him with the keys, on the off-chance that it would make him let me go, but by the time the thought crossed my mind, it was already too late. He snagged the keys out of my hand, disengaged the alarm, and opened the door. "Get in."

I slid behind the wheel and waited for the order to move over into the passenger seat. It didn't come. Instead, he dropped the keys in my lap. "Go home. And don't come back here."

And with that, he slammed the car door and disappeared.

The first thing I did was lock all the doors. Then I had to wait for my hands to stop shaking before I could fumble the key into the ignition and crank the engine over. By the time I got out to the street, the Harley-Davidson was long gone, and to be totally honest, I wasn't sure I minded. Nancy would have followed it, to try to discover anything else she could about him, but personally, I felt that I knew all I needed to know about Rafael Collier, and after this, believe me, I wasn't eager to confront him again.

I thought about postponing the research trip to the library, but in the end I decided to go after all. It beat going home in a tizzy; at least I'd have something to do for a couple of hours until my lacerated nerves healed.

I was just pushing the library doors open when my cell phone rang. The number looked vaguely familiar, but wasn't one I recognized immediately. I punched the accept button and put the phone to my ear, heading back out onto the baking sidewalk. "This is Savannah."

At first I heard nothing but music in the background, and I wondered if maybe it was a crank call from someone whose idea of fun it was to scare people. Under the circumstances, Rafe Collier's name came to mind. Then a voice asked, "Is this Miss Martin?"

The voice was female, sounded young, and was also vaguely familiar. I confirmed that I am, indeed, Savannah Martin. "What can I do for you?"

Another pause, then, "This is Alex. Alexandra Puckett. Brenda's daughter."

No wonder I hadn't recognized the voice. The one and only time I had spoken to Alexandra was at the funeral the day before, and she had said less than a half dozen words to me. "Hi, Alexandra. What can I do for you?"

"I just . . . um . . . wanted to talk to you."

"Sure," I said. "Go ahead."

"Not on the phone." I had a vision of her casting a furtive glance over her shoulder.

"Would you like to get together? We could grab an early dinner somewhere."

"Maybelle's cooking dinner. I have to stay home. Plus, dad's got something he wants to talk to us about."

"Oh," I said. "Well, then . . ."

"I could meet you later. At a bar, or something."

"How old are you again?"

She sighed gustily. "I've been to bars before, okay? Mom used to take me sometimes. To business meetings, like that."

"She held business meetings in bars?"

"Not like in real bars, you know. But, like, cool bars. Hip bars. Like the FinBar and Beckett's." The two names she mentioned belonged to establishments within walking distance of the real estate office. They were clean and well-lit, the sort of places where nobody drank too much or started fights, and the atmosphere was pleasant and not at all rowdy. Very suitable for two young ladies on their own.

"Sure," I said. "I'll go to the FinBar with you. So long as you know I won't buy you anything with alcohol in it. When?"

"Um . . . six thirty?"

"Won't that upset Maybelle's dinner?"

"She eats early," Alexandra said with disgust. "Five o'clock. Six thirty is perfect."

I agreed to meet her there, and put the phone away as I headed back into the library again.

A wasted two and a half hours later, I was on my way to the FinBar. In my possession were the names of three men who had killed themselves between fourteen and sixteen years ago. (Without a specific date, and with only Clarice's word to go by, it was difficult to narrow it down any further.) Joey Shoemaker, an insurance salesman, had driven his car through a guardrail and into the Harpeth River on his way home from work one night. It could have been an accident, but then again, it could have been deliberate. A case of insurance fraud was under investigation at his company at the time, implicating Mr. Shoemaker. The second man was Graham Webster, who had left his job at a small credit union early one day, claiming a headache, and had gone home to his house in Hendersonville, where he had pulled the car into the garage and proceeded to poison himself with carbon monoxide. His wife had found him dead when she came home from her own accounting job at the end of the day. And William Bigelow, the local manager of a national mortgage company, had shot himself through the head at the family's vacation cabin on the Cumberland Plateau, leaving a message for his wife of his intent.

Of the three, my money was on Webster, as it didn't seem likely that the other two would be in a position to be handling a whole lot of cold, hard cash. But I don't know much about such things, so I could quite well be wrong. Plus, I wasn't sure it was even one of these three. I could have missed something, or the death might not have been written up in the paper, or it could have happened at an earlier or later date. Walker had said the event took place twelve or thirteen years ago, and maybe he, and not Clarice, was right. I ran out of time, though, so I had to be satisfied with what I had.

Alexandra was already seated at a table in the corner, sipping a drink, when I came through the door at FinBar.

"That looks like Coca-Cola," I remarked, sliding down on the chair opposite from her. Alexandra sniffed.

"Yeah. So?"

"Just making sure. You want anything else?"

"Like a beer?"

"I was thinking more like a hamburger or a basket of chips and salsa. Unlike you, I haven't had dinner yet."

She rolled her eyes. They were heavily made up with shadow and mascara. I wondered if she was trying to hide that she'd been crying, or if she was just taking advantage of having no mother to tell her that she couldn't leave the house looking like a hooker. "No thanks."

"No problem." I ordered a Diet Coke for myself—no sense in rubbing the girl's nose in something she couldn't have; plus, it was a lot cheaper than a real drink—as well as an order of nachos, and then leaned back in my chair. "So what did Maybelle cook for dinner?"

Alexandra twisted her face into a hideous grimace. "Cabbage rolls. With boiled potatoes and gravy. Yuck."

"Cabbage rolls aren't so bad," I said. She shrugged. I added, "What did your mother usually cook?"

"Takeout," Alexandra said.

"I see."

"She was too busy to cook. So we ate out a lot, and ordered in. My favorite's pizza." She smiled. It was a funny, almost secretive smile, but it lit her face up for a second before it was gone.

"I like pizza, too," I said, although the thought of it doesn't make me smile the way Alexandra did.

We sat in silence for a little longer. My drink and the nachos came. I took a sip. "So how are you holding up?"

She shrugged.

"What did you want to talk to me about?"

She was playing with her glass, using it to make a pattern of wet rings across the table, and she answered without looking up at me. "The other day at the funeral, someone said you're the one who found my mom."

I nodded. "She had an appointment to meet a client at eight, to show him that house on Potsdam Street. When she didn't show up, he called the office. I went out there, and that's when we found her."

"Was that the guy you were with at the funeral?"

I wrinkled my forehead. "I wasn't with anyone at the funeral." Except for the minute or two I'd spoken with Tamara Grimaldi, but surely Alexandra didn't think Detective Grimaldi was a man. And, of course, Tim, but she knew who Tim was.

"In the parking lot, after the service was over. I saw you on the news."

"Oh. Yes, that was him."

She took a nacho and pulled it towards her, trailing cheese. Her eyes were on it instead of on me. "Are you sleeping with him?" she asked.

"Are you crazy?" I answered.

She glanced up. "I just thought he looked hot."

"He's not my type. Not yours, either."

"How do you know what my type is?"

"I don't," I said. "But I know what type he is, and trust me, you wouldn't want to be involved with him. He's also at least ten years too old for you."

"Boys my age are boring."

"Boys your age will be thirty one day, too. Maybe then you'll be ready for them."

I grabbed a nacho from the plate and popped it into my mouth. Alexandra rolled her eyes and sucked on her Coke. We sat in silence for another minute or two.

"So tell me about it," she said, finally. "What was it like?"

I hesitated. "Did your dad let you see your mom afterwards?" She shook her head. "But you saw her at the funeral. So you know that she looked a lot like herself."

"Only deader," Alexandra muttered. I shrugged. No arguing with that.

"To be honest, I didn't look that closely at her on Saturday. I fainted. There was a lot of blood. But I could tell that she looked surprised, rather than scared or angry. I don't think she knew what was happening before it happened."

Alexandra nodded. "One of the papers said she was . . . you know . . . raped . . ."

I shook my head. "If she was, I didn't see any signs of it. She was wearing all her clothes, and like I said, she didn't look angry or afraid."

"That's good." She took another sip of Coke.

"Yes, it is." I thought for a second and then added, "Would you happen to know when she left home on Saturday morning?"

She looked suspicious. "Why?"

"Just curious. I was wondering how much time there was between her getting there and Rafe getting there. But if you don't want to tell me, that's okay."

Alexandra shrugged, looking down at her glass. "I was asleep. I didn't get downstairs until after ten, and by then everyone was gone. Austin spent the night with a friend, and daddy had gone out somewhere. All I know is that she said she had to leave early."

I nodded. So nobody in the Puckett household had an alibi. Not that I seriously suspected any of them. Except maybe Steven. But he had probably just been across the street, in Maybelle's bed, stealing some time for himself while Brenda was working. I grimaced and changed the subject.

"So did you and your mom come here a lot?"

Alexandra shook her head. "Just when—you know— she didn't want to do things in the office. Because . . . um . . ." She faltered. I arched my brows inquiringly, and she added, reluctantly, "Mr. Lamont can be a little strict sometimes, you know. Not very . . . flexible. About special terms and things like that."

It sounded as if she was quoting her mother.

"Of course," I said smoothly. So Brenda had been in the habit of handling things out of the office so Walker couldn't micromanage anything too closely. Interesting. "When was the last time you were here?"

"Oh, I haven't been *here* for a few months." Alexandra looked around at the FinBar's Irish pub decor. "But we went to Beckett's just a couple of weeks ago. Something to do with that house on Potsdam."

"Your mother made poor, old Mrs. Jenkins come to a *bar*?"

"Who's Mrs. Jenkins?" Alexandra asked. I explained, and she shook her head. "This was a man. Black guy. Worked in a hospital or something."

"Tyrell Jenkins?" I suggested optimistically. Maybe Tondalia Jenkins hadn't signed the sale papers for her house herself after all. She certainly shouldn't have been able to do so. Not legally. Not if she thought some guy she had never seen before was her only son. Nothing says *non compos mentis* like that kind of mistake.

Alexandra shrugged. "Could have been. Middle-aged dude, not hot at all." She took a sip of Coke. I nodded. She added, "So on the morning she died . . . did you see anybody? Or anything? You know, suspicious? Or out of the ordinary?" She peered at me through a curtain of long, dark hair, her blue eyes furtive.

"Not really," I said, wondering who she was worried about my having possibly seen. Herself? Her father? Maybelle? "Just neighborhood people, you know. A middle-aged lady waiting at the bus stop, a black kid in a green car who drove by a couple of times . . . So tell me more about this guy your mother was meeting with at Beckett's."

But Alexandra didn't know anything else about him. Just that the meeting had something to do with the house on Potsdam Street, and that the guy had something to do with the healthcare field. When I asked her how she knew that, she shrugged vaguely.

"Well, was he wearing scrubs or something?"

But Alexandra didn't know. The man had been wearing a suit, so that wasn't it, and she couldn't pinpoint exactly how she knew he worked in healthcare, she just did. I gave up and turned the conversation to innocuous subjects. But at least now I knew that there was something fishy about the listing for 101 Potsdam Street. If there hadn't been, Brenda wouldn't have had any reason to work out the details in the dark corner of Beckett's Bar.

9.

Alexandra hung around until about eight, drinking Coke and eating nachos, and then said she had to leave. With what had happened to Brenda, Steven wanted to keep his kids extra close, and he had imposed a nine o'clock curfew. I walked Alexandra to her car, which was an almost-new, candy apple red Mazda Miata. "My mom gave it to me when I turned sixteen," Alexandra explained. She looked at the car for a second, and I swear I saw tears in her eyes, before she turned away and opened the car door. "See you, Savannah."

I nodded. "You take care. Call me if you want to talk more."

I watched her drive away, and then I headed down the street, thinking hard thoughts.

Alexandra must have had some kind of reason for contacting me, but I was darned if I could figure out what it was. It didn't seem as if wanting to talk about her mother with someone sympathetic and not too far removed from her own age had been it. She hadn't asked me any tough questions, none I hadn't been prepared for, anyway. On the other hand, she'd been remarkably forthcoming with answers to the questions I asked her, even going so far as to tell me about Brenda's ways of getting around Walker's professional supervision.

If Brenda had opted to handle the contract for 101 Potsdam Street at Beckett's Bar instead of at the office, surely that must mean that there was something about it she didn't want Walker to know. Brenda was dead and couldn't object to my going through her stuff, but I was pretty sure I knew what Clarice's reaction would be if I walked into the office tomorrow and told her I wanted to see the file for 101 Potsdam. I could go over her head and ask Walker for it, but then I'd have to explain why I wanted it, and I didn't want to do that until I was sure I wasn't making a fuss about nothing. Walker was already reeling from the shock of Brenda's murder, and then the story in the *Voice* had hit him again. His appointment to the Real Estate Commission might already be in jeopardy, and I didn't want to do anything to mess it up.

All this brought my mind back to the office. There was no one there now to object to anything I did. Clarice was compulsively neat, so it shouldn't take much more than a minute to find the file. I'd be in and out in no time, without anyone realizing that I'd ever been there. And then I'd know once and for all whether Tondalia Jenkins had signed the papers herself, or whether she had had an attorney-in-fact—Tyrell, for instance—who had done it for her.

It took just a few seconds to unlock the back door and turn off the alarm, and I made sure that Brenda's office door was latched securely behind me before I turned on the ceiling light. The small strip of light under the door wouldn't be noticeable to anyone outside the building, and the chances that someone else would show up at this time of night were surely pretty slim. I ought to be safe for the short time it would take me to find what I was looking for and get out.

I was helped by Clarice's devotion to Brenda and her compulsive attention to detail. Everything was obsessively neat. The piles of paper on the desk were stacked by size, with the largest piece on the bottom, and the smallest on top. Every corner was aligned perfectly. Every paperclip was in the paperclip holder, every rubber band in its place, and every last blank on every last form in every last file was filled in appropriately.

The files were arranged alphabetically, each file drawer clearly marked: A–E, F–K, L–O, etc. The filing cabinets were locked up tight, but there was a set of keys in the desk where I had found the extra key for the house on Potsdam earlier in the week. In the Active Listings drawer, everything was sorted by number, chronologically. I flipped through the manila folders; 16 Sunflower Lane and 19 Orchard Place gave way to 1023 Landsdowne Court and 1141 Tyne Boulevard. I frowned and went back to the beginning. The folder for 101 Potsdam Street wasn't there.

There were a couple of different explanations for something like this. The first, that Clarice had made a mistake and neglected to make a file, I discarded as extremely unlikely. Clarice would never make a mistake like that.

The second, that the folder had been misfiled in all the hoopla, was easy enough to check. After rifling through all the Active Listings folders, I could say with certainty that the file I was looking for wasn't among them. Nor was it sitting around on someone's desk.

The third possibility, that it had been misfiled somewhere else, was more difficult to determine, due to the sheer volume of folders. There were six six-drawer filing cabinets in the room, and that wasn't even a drop in the ocean of listings that Brenda had handled in her twenty years in the business. She had a rented storage unit somewhere, where she kept everything that wasn't current. The Potsdam Street file was current, and should have been in the office, but there was just the chance that it had been taken to the storage unit by mistake sometime recently. Or on purpose, if Brenda hadn't wanted it sitting around where someone—like me, or Walker—would have access to it. I had no idea where the unit was, but the desk drawer held, in addition to the keys to the file cabinets and the spare key to 101 Potsdam, a key ring with a couple of keys marked *storage unit*.

I stood and looked at them for a moment, biting my lip. There were three of them, all seemingly identical, and chances were that no one would notice if I just borrowed one for a couple of days. I could come back tomorrow night or Saturday morning and put it back. I usually did floor duty on Saturdays anyway, and I was usually alone.

So if there was the slightest chance that the Potsdam folder was at the storage unit, I should check it out. I owed it to Mrs. Jenkins, not to mention to the Realtor's Code of Ethics. (Although someone could argue that borrowing the key—stealing is such an ugly word, don't you think? And I *was* going to bring it back—without telling anyone wasn't too ethical, either. I put that thought out of my mind.) With a key, I wouldn't even really be breaking in, and since I worked in the same office as Brenda, nobody was likely to question my right to be there. Even so, my heart was beating double-time as I painstakingly twisted one of the keys off the chain.

While I was doing it, my thoughts kept going. There was a fourth place that the folder could be, and that was somewhere else in the building. If, for instance, Walker had taken it out of Brenda's filing cabinet and put it in his own now that he was handling the listing, or if Brittany the receptionist had it on her desk, or something like that. But before I could act on this idea and slink into Walker's office to snoop, something happened. I'd been in the office long enough to feel comfortable, and I wasn't keeping an ear peeled for noises anymore. I had no idea that anyone else had arrived until the connecting door into Clarice's and Heidi's shared office swung open. All I had time to do was drop the storage unit key into my skirt pocket and nudge the drawer shut with my hip before I turned to face the door.

Clarice stood in the doorway, looking as if all her dreams had come true at once. "Savannah!"

"Oh," I said dumbly. "Hi, Clarice."

"What are you doing?" She scanned the room suspiciously, but there was nothing to see. Thank God I hadn't found the 101 Potsdam Street file, or it would be sitting in plain view on the desk right now.

I thought quickly. The excuse I came up with wasn't great, but it had the benefit of being unprovable. "I needed a blank Buyer Representation Agreement."

"At nine o'clock at night?" She glanced pointedly at the reproduction filigree clock ticking daintily away on top of one of the filing cabinets.

"I just had a drink at the FinBar. It was easy to stop by on my way home." And if she thought the drink had been with a potential client, whom I wanted to sign to an exclusive representation agreement ASAP, so much the better.

"And you thought you might find one on Brenda's desk?" It wasn't so much a question as a comment on the stupidity of my excuse. It was obvious she didn't believe me. I shrugged, pouting. She added, with unmistakable relish, "I'll have to tell Walker that you were here, you know." She smiled in happy anticipation. "And believe me, he isn't going to be pleased. You may find yourself out on your ear, my fine girl."

It sounded as if nothing would please her more.

"Walker likes me," I said, with more confidence than I felt. "He won't fire me for going into Brenda's office. Even after hours."

"Snooping in other agents' files to give your own client an added advantage is illegal. And Walker isn't the man to let anyone get away with anything illegal." She tittered.

It was an unusual sound, not common to the Clarice I knew. I looked more closely at her. She was dressed the way she always was, in a dowdy skirt and blouse and sensible shoes, with her graying hair in its usual severe bob, but there was something different about her tonight. Her eyes were brighter than usual, and there was an air of suppressed excitement about her. And I didn't think it had anything to do with catching me red-handed in someone else's office. That was just an added bonus, like the cherry on the sundae.

My mother impressed upon me from an early age that one catches more flies with honey than with vinegar. I smiled. "You look nice tonight, Clarice. Are you going on a date? Or coming from one?"

Flattery works (almost) every time. She preened. "Going, actually. Although it isn't really a date. More like a business meeting. A late business meeting."

"Right," I said, hiding a smile.

"I just came to pick something up." She turned on her heel and made for her own desk, in the adjoining room. I sauntered to the door and watched as she unlocked a desk drawer and pulled out a plain manila envelope and a piece of paper.

The key went into her pocket, and then she handed me the piece of paper and smirked. "Are you ready to go, Savannah? Have everything you need?"

I glanced down at the form in my hand. It was a Buyer Representation Agreement.

"Yes, thank you." I snagged my handbag from the corner of Brenda's desk. We walked out together, and Clarice set the alarm and locked the door behind us quite ostentatiously, as if to ensure that I couldn't get back inside. It didn't bother me, since I had no plans to go back. Although the alarm wouldn't have stopped me if I had wanted to.

"Have a nice night, Savannah." She smiled, obviously pleased with having ruined what was left of my evening, and trotted briskly across the street toward the parking lot. The envelope bobbed in her hand, and the one-and-a-half inch heels on her sensible shoes went click-click against the pavement. Her late-model white Cadillac was parked two spaces over from my Volvo, but she didn't suggest that we walk together. I stayed where I was until she had gotten into her car and pulled out into traffic, and then I crossed the street and got into my own car. My thoughts were rattling around in my head like peas in a tin can the whole way home.

It was still reasonably early by the time I got to the apartment, so I kicked my shoes off, picked up the phone, and called Sweetwater. "Hiya, Dix. This is your sister Savannah."

"What's this I hear about you and that Collier guy?" my brother answered, without so much as a how-do first.

"Yes, it's nice to talk to you, too," I said, pulling a half-eaten half gallon of ice cream out of the freezer. Chocolate Mocha Fudge. Yum. "I don't know. What is it you've heard about me and the Collier guy? And from whom?"

"Oh, come on, sis!"

"No, I mean it. How am I supposed to prove or disprove anything if I don't know what you've heard?" I rooted around in the silverware drawer for a spoon, and finally managed to find one. Stainless steel, part of a set I'd bought for $10.99 at Target two years ago, after having left all my wedding silver for Bradley and the new Mrs. Ferguson.

This reasoned argument resonated with my legal eagle brother, who admitted, "I had lunch with Todd Satterfield today, and he told me you've been seeing Collier."

"Todd said that? What's wrong with him?" I curled up on the couch, spooning ice cream straight out of the cardboard container and into my mouth. All my fancy china was back at the Fergusons' townhouse, too. Including my crystal ice cream bowls. "I haven't been seeing Rafe. All right, I've *seen* him, but I haven't been seeing him. Not as in *seeing*, seeing."

"You'll never be a lawyer if you can't express yourself better than that," Dix said.

"I don't want to be a lawyer," I retorted. "I'm the black sheep, remember? The only Martin child who didn't get a law degree."

"You could have had a law degree if you wanted. You dropped out and married that jerk Ferguson instead."

"That's exactly my point," I answered. "I didn't want a law degree. That's why I dropped out to marry that jerk Ferguson."

"At least you admit it," Dix said. "There was a time . . ."

"He didn't seem like a jerk when I first met him. Now I know better. And real estate isn't that different from lawyering. I still deal with privilege and fiduciary responsibility and legal signatures and things like that. My real estate classes were pretty much the same as Property Law 101 back in college. Except now I get to go look at houses every day, and you know how I've always enjoyed that."

Dix agreed that he did. I was one of those little girls who always opened doors when I visited my friends' houses to see where they went. And growing up in an antebellum mansion in the middle of a town full of Victorians and foursquares and craftsman bungalows hadn't hurt, either.

"But to get back to the point," I continued, "the *real* point, which is that I have not been seeing Rafael Collier. I have no idea why Todd would tell you that I have."

"He's probably worried about you," Dix said. "Like the rest of us when we heard. Collier's bad news. Stay away from him."

"Believe me," I answered sincerely, "that's exactly what I plan to do. I just don't understand how anyone who knows me could think that I'd get involved with someone like him." I dug a chunk of fudge out of the ice cream container and popped it in my mouth.

"Well, you *are* the black sheep of the family."

"There's a big difference between dropping out of law school and becoming romantically involved with a criminal," I said, around the fudge. Dix drew a breath.

"So you admit he's a criminal?"

"Enough of the cross-examination, okay? I have no idea what he is or isn't. I've tried to find out, but I can't. And that leads me to the reason why I called you."

"You want me to look into Collier?"

I blew out an exasperated sigh. "No, Dix. I don't. This has nothing to do with Rafael Collier. Or only indirectly. You know a little bit about tracking down people, right? Heirs and such?"

"A little," Dix said cautiously, and went on to expound on what he only knew a little about. I cut him off after a couple of minutes.

"That's great information, but what I really want to know is how to go about finding someone if I've got nothing to go on but a name and a location where they lived at one point."

Dix thought for a moment. "I'm not sure you could without more. Who are we talking about?"

"The son of a woman named Tondalia Jenkins." I told him about the house on Potsdam Street. "It's just not right, Dix. I haven't figured out how yet, but Brenda Puckett must have taken advantage of that poor, old woman somehow, and now she's stuck in a nursing home that would turn your stomach if you could see it, let alone smell it, and she's got Rafe Collier breathing down her neck . . ."

"He probably thinks she's got something worth stealing," Dix said.

"If so, he must be crazy. She's clearly as poor as a church mouse, bless her heart. The only thing of value she owns is the house, and even that isn't worth much in its present condition. Nowhere near as much as Brenda listed it for. Or if it is, it's only because of the land. But that's beside the point. I'd just like to find out if her son is still around and can help her. There's nothing I can do about it personally; I'm not a family member, and it would probably be a conflict of interest or something anyway, but she ought to have someone looking out for her."

"Fine," Dix said, "I'll see if I can get a line on him. I've done this kind of thing before. But just to be safe, I think I'll check out Collier, too. I'll get back to you tomorrow."

I told him I appreciated it, and we both hung up.

The first thing I did the next morning, after the usual morning ritual of makeup and hair, coffee and cereal, was to pull out the Yellow Pages and look up *Storage: Household & Commercial*. As I should have expected, there was page after page of storage companies, from A-1 Self

Storage to U-Stor-It, and without some idea what I was looking for, there was no way I could find out which of them Brenda had used. I toyed with the idea of calling them all, to ask if Brenda Puckett was a customer, but there were too many. It would take forever, and they probably wouldn't tell me anyway. There had to be a simpler solution.

My father always used to say that the easiest way to get something you want is to ask for it. I decided that his advice made sense, and headed for the office. Someone there would be able to tell me where Brenda kept her stuff. But when I walked in, with a cover story all developed and rehearsed, I was brought up short just inside the door by loud wailing and lamentations. Brittany looked up from the reception desk with red eyes and quivering lips. When she saw that I wasn't anyone important, like a potential client, she looked down again without a word.

"Good grief," I said. "What's the matter?"

She didn't answer, just sniffed and pointed down the hall. I headed in that direction. And I'll admit that I was, rather self-centeredly, wondering if this had something to do with my late-night search of Brenda's office and Clarice's threat to report me to Walker. Was I about to get fired? It seemed incredible that Brittany would expend this much effort and this many tears on my own humble person, but I admit it, the thought crossed my mind.

The loud wailing came from Clarice's and Heidi's shared office, and when I arrived at the door, I saw that it issued from Heidi, who was sitting behind her desk, clutching a sodden tissue and having her hand patted by Walker. Tim was perched on the edge of Clarice's desk a few feet away, watching the proceedings. His features were unusually solemn, although he couldn't quite hide the gleam at the bottom of his bright, baby blue eyes.

"What on earth is going on?" I asked. All three of them turned to me, and Walker opened his mouth. Heidi's wailing drowned out anything he attempted to say.

"Oh, Savannah! It's so awful!" She subsided into blubbery hiccups.

"What's awful?" I looked from Tim to Walker. Tim gave a tiny, almost imperceptible, one-shouldered shrug, as if to say he was sure *he* didn't know. Walker gave Heidi's hand a final pat before he gave it back to her, and turned to me.

"I'm afraid I have some bad news, Savannah."

Oh, God. "Before you say anything else," I said, "let me explain. I wasn't really doing anything wrong. I just wanted to look at the file for 101 Potsdam Street, and I wasn't sure Clarice would let me. That's the only reason I was here last night."

I had to raise my voice to get the last sentence out, because Heidi had started howling again. Walker raised his own voice. "You were here last night?"

I nodded. "Clarice said she was going to tell you. Isn't that what this is about?"

Tim giggled, and Walker sent him a quelling look. "I'm afraid not. I have bigger concerns right now than you looking at Brenda's files without permission. Although I wish you hadn't. Why didn't you come to me first?"

"I didn't want to bother you," I said. "With everything else that's going on, I figured you had enough to worry about. And I didn't think anyone would ever know, but then Clarice came in and caught me, and . . ."

An ear-splitting howl from Heidi cut me off in mid-sentence. I turned to her. "Do you mind? Whatever it is, it can't possibly justify this much noise."

"Clarice is dead," Tim said. I turned to stare at him, and then at Walker, speechlessly. Walker nodded.

"But I saw her last night," I protested. "She was fine." More than fine, in fact. Excited and eager, like a kid on Christmas Eve; certain in the knowledge that good things were coming her way. "What happened?" A car accident on her way home, maybe?

"We don't really know," Walker said, with a glance at Heidi. "I don't know if you know this, Savannah, but in all the years she's worked for Brenda, Clarice has never once been absent without prior notice. When she wasn't here by nine this morning, and didn't call to say she'd be late, I had Brittany call her. I was . . ." He hesitated briefly, then seemed to reach a decision. "I have been concerned about her mental state. You two weren't close, so you may not have noticed, but Brenda's death has been hard on Clarice."

To be quite honest, I hadn't noticed. Clarice had been upset, naturally, but I didn't think her behavior had been anything out of the ordinary. A murder in the office is enough to make anybody jittery, and Clarice had been closer to Brenda than anyone else. Still, I hadn't seen any behavior that had led me to worry about her mental state. Then again, as Walker said, we hadn't been close.

"When she didn't answer," he continued, "I drove over to her house to make sure she was all right."

"So you're the one who found her?"

Walker nodded. "I called the police, and they sent a detective out. The same one who is handling Brenda's case."

"So was Clarice murdered, too?" Tamara Grimaldi was a homicide detective, so it seemed like a reasonable question. Heidi squealed like I had stuck a knife in her. Tim sent her a dirty look.

"I don't think we can assume that," Walker said. "It seems to me that the police would do it this way simply because there's a connection between Clarice and Brenda. It doesn't necessarily follow that they think both women were murdered."

"I suppose not," I conceded. "So what happens now? Do we all have to prove where we were last night?"

Heidi stopped wailing for a second. Tim said, "That shouldn't be a problem for you, Savannah. You were here, going through Brenda's drawers. No pun intended; I know you don't swing that way. No, wait . . . you can't prove you were here, because Clarice can't vouch for you." He smirked.

"Obviously," I answered coldly, "she couldn't have vouched for me anyway, since she was very much alive when she left here, and must have died later. I went home alone. What about you? Can you provide an alibi for last night?"

"Most of it." Tim smirked. "Although there were those twenty minutes once in a while, when we slept . . ."

I grimaced. "Oh, gack! Don't take me there. Please."

"You asked," Tim said unrepentantly.

"I think," Walker added, with a stern glance at him, "that it may be too early to talk about alibis. We don't know what happened to Clarice. The detective is stopping by this afternoon to talk to all of us. Will you be available, Savannah?"

"Of course," I said.

"I think she may be especially interested in what you have to say, if indeed you saw Clarice last night. You may be the last person to have seen her alive, and maybe you can shed some light on her state of mind or where she was going, things like that." He looked at me.

"I don't know how much help I'm going to be," I answered. "She didn't tell me where she was going, or with whom, just that she was having a late meeting with someone. How did she . . . ?"

"The police asked me not to discuss any of the details with anyone," Walker said, and included Tim and Heidi in his next statement. "The detective will be here at noon, so if you have anything you need to do today, please rearrange your schedules to allow you to be back here by then. I'm sure we all want to get to the bottom of this as quickly as possible."

"Of course," I said. Walker nodded and walked out, returning to his own office across the hall. I heard the key turn in the lock. Tim drifted away, too, and Heidi and I were left together.

10.

I admit it, I felt awkward. Heidi and I have never gotten along well, and the truth was that I didn't like her. She was common, and catty, and would do anything to get ahead, just like Brenda. I'm well brought-up, however, and she seemed sincerely, if disproportionately, distraught. I took a couple of steps closer to her.

"Is there anything I can do for you?"

She sniffed and shook her head.

"Are you sure? Would you like me to go across the street and get you a Jamocha or a scone or something?" There was a coffee shop down on the corner, and from what I had seen of Heidi, she enjoyed her food. She wasn't as big as Brenda—yet—but it looked as if she was trying to emulate her mentor in that, as well as in everything else. "I'll be happy to do it," I added, secretly thankful for my own self-control. Although after the ice cream last night, maybe I didn't have as much room to talk as I thought I did.

Heidi looked up, eyes swimming with tears. "You don't even like me. Why are you being so nice?"

"I'm always nice," I said. "And I feel bad for you. You've lost both of your mentors in a week. It must be difficult."

That set her off again, howling and wailing. Tim came out of his office, sent her a disgusted look, and closed the door, none too gently. Heidi bawled louder. I sighed. "What's the matter, Heidi? You weren't this upset when Brenda died." She didn't answer. "Is it just because you shared an office with Clarice and you're going to miss her, or is something else wrong? Did something happen?"

She sniffled. And snorted. And blew her nose loudly in the tissue before she looked up. "She screamed at me."

I stepped a little closer. "Clarice?" She nodded. "When?"

It had been yesterday afternoon, just after five o'clock. Everyone else had gone home, even Brittany, and only Clarice and Heidi had been left.

"What did she scream at you for?" I wanted to know.

"I don't know!" Heidi wailed.

"What started it?"

Heidi sniffed deeply and said that it had been a misunderstanding.

"What kind of misunderstanding? Come on, Heidi. Think. Maybe it has something to do with what happened to her!"

Heidi looked stricken. "Do you think?"

"I don't know," I said, "because I don't know what happened. But if you tell me, maybe I can figure it out."

So she told me. With lots of pauses for sniffles and snorts into the tissue.

The story actually boiled down to very little. Clarice had left her desk at one point to use the powder room. While she was gone, Heidi had had need of a manila envelope. There had been none in the supply closet—with all the hoopla surrounding Brenda's death, someone had probably forgotten to buy more; I should have used *that* as an excuse last night!—and Heidi had thought that maybe Clarice had one in her desk. Rather than wait for Clarice to come back, she decided that she would just take a look herself. Nothing wrong with looking for a manila envelope, after all. It was a shared office, and she had looked in Clarice's desk for things before. Always with Clarice's permission, but still. And that was how she had come across this envelope.

"Clarice said she came back here last night to pick up a manila envelope," I said pensively. "I wonder if it was the same."

Heidi said she was sure she didn't know.

"So what was in it?" I asked.

At first Heidi hadn't realized that there was anything at all in the envelope. It had looked and felt empty, and hadn't been sealed or addressed to anyone. She had congratulated herself on having found what she needed without having to go the office supply store, and had taken the booty over to her own desk. And it was then, when she opened it, that she realized there was indeed something inside.

"It was just one piece of paper, or maybe two. I only saw the top sheet, but I think there might have been another underneath." She wiped her eyes on the tissue. I grimaced—she had just blown her nose in it—and fetched another from the box on Clarice's desk. Heidi added, "But I never got a chance to see for sure, because Clarice came in, and when she saw what I was doing, she *screamed* at me!" She sniffed, huffily this time.

"And then what?"

"Then she *snatched* the papers out of my hand and *stuffed* them back down in the envelope, and locked it in her desk. And then she asked me what I thought I was doing and who had put me up to it. I told her I'd just been looking for a manila envelope to send a pre-listing packet to a customer, and that there weren't any in the supply closet. She said, 'Well, then you'd better go buy some, shouldn't you?' and made me leave!"

"So you went to the office supply store?" Heidi nodded, and pointed to an unopened package of manila envelopes on her desk. "And you didn't see her after that?" She shook her head. "Huh!" I said. "So what was in the envelope?"

The paperwork for 101 Potsdam Street, by any chance?

"That's what was so strange," Heidi said. "It wasn't anything special at all. Just a contract or something having to do with Clarice's pay."

I wrinkled my forehead. "What do you mean?"

"It was like the one I signed when I started working with Brenda. Terms and duties and things like that. Like, I don't have to pay for any advertising or anything, and Brenda gets me leads that I work, and when they close, I get 60 percent of the commission, after Walker's share."

I didn't comment. My split is seventy-five–twenty-five, with Walker Lamont Realty taking 25 percent and me keeping the rest of my—as yet—nonexistent compensation, but I don't have to share my 75 percent with anyone. Then again, I have to do all my own advertising, and no one gives me any leads, so maybe I was the one holding the fuzzy end of the lollipop. "So what did Clarice's contract say? And why was it such a big deal that you saw it?"

"I don't know!" Heidi moaned, wringing her hands. "It looked the same. Sixty-forty split after the agency take, except that Clarice's duties were different than mine."

I nodded. "Maybe she just didn't want you to know how much she makes. Payroll records are supposed to be confidential. It may be as simple as that."

"But she screamed at me!" Heidi said. "And now she's gone and she can't ever say she's sorry!"

She subsided into wracking sobs. I stared at her for a second before I found my voice. "That's true. But you can look toward the future knowing that you were right all along. I hope it makes you feel all warm and fuzzy inside." Heidi looked unsure, as if she suspected she was being insulted, but wasn't really positive. Eschewing subtleties, since they didn't seem to be necessary, I added briskly, "By the way, would you happen to know of a good storage place? Brenda used one, didn't she?"

Heidi nodded wetly. "Stor-All on Dickerson Road. She's kept her stuff there for years, so they must be good. Brenda wouldn't pay money for something that wasn't."

"You've been there, right? Can you tell me where it is? I don't know if their offices are open tomorrow, and with the police interviews this afternoon, I should probably take care of this now."

"Sure." Heidi nodded.

It was as simple as that, and I didn't even need the excuse I'd rehearsed in the car. Three minutes later I was on my way, and twenty minutes after that, I was standing outside the Stor-All, wondering what to do now. The units weren't labeled, and there were approximately ten thousand of them. I couldn't walk from one to the other until I found one the key would fit in.

My father's adage ran through my head again, and I figured I'd give it another try. It had worked very well the first time, after all. And if it didn't this time, all I had to do was wait, and try something else later. So I walked confidently into the small office and bestowed a smile on the old lady hanging out behind the counter. "Good morning. My name is Savannah Martin, and I'm looking for Brenda Puckett's storage unit. Can you point me in the right direction?"

She squinted at me through bifocals. "You with the police, hon?"

"Gosh, no," I said. "Have they been here?" I ought to have realized that they would come; Detective Grimaldi wasn't the type to ignore something as obvious as the murdered woman's storage unit.

The receptionist nodded. "Twice. First, a couple of uniforms stopped by on Monday and took away a few boxes. They brought 'em back on Wednesday. And then late yesterday, a single guy showed up. Didn't look much like a cop, but he said he was, and when I asked him if he needed me to let him into the unit, he said no, he had access. He spent an hour or so inside, but he didn't take nothing with him when he left."

Suspicion filled me. "What did he look like?"

"Tall guy. Dark hair, dark eyes, tattoo on his arm. Drove up on a bike. I guess he was undercover." She shrugged.

"That figures," I said.

"You know him?"

"We've met."

She wheezed. I guessed it was supposed to be a laugh. I pried my teeth apart and added, as I put a business card on the counter, "I'm not with the police. I'm from Brenda's office, and I need to get in to look for a file. I have a key." I held it up. She squinted at it, but didn't seem to notice anything amiss. Which indeed there wasn't, since the only thing amiss was me.

"No problem, hon." She slid off the stool and ducked under the counter. "I'll take you over there."

"You don't have to do that . . ." I began, but it was too late; she was already standing next to me.

"This way." She trotted out of the office and down the path between the storage units. It was all I could do to keep up. She was in amazingly good shape for being close to the century mark, but, of course, her Nikes were a lot easier to move in than my three-inch heels. "Don't think I've seen you here before, hon," she said while we were on our way. "Usually it's Brenda's assistant . . . what's her name again? Clara? Clarissa?"

"Clarice."

"You sure it ain't Clarissa?" I said I was. "Oh, well . . ." She continued, without missing a beat, "And sometimes it's that new girl. The one with the brown hair. Crumbs."

"Excuse me?"

"She's always got crumbs on her dress. Like she's always eatin' something."

I hid a smile. "Her name is Heidi Hoppenfeldt. And she does like to eat."

"I even saw that good-looking gay guy earlier this week. Monday morning, I think it was. Just before the cops were here."

"Tim? Yes, he works with Brenda, too." Although as far as I knew he wouldn't have had any business here on Monday morning.

"How 'bout you? You new?"

I explained that I had worked with Brenda for about six weeks when she died. "I didn't have time to get to know her well, or Clarice either. Or Heidi, for that matter. They work together, I just work in the same office."

"So what're you doin' here, then, hon?"

She was sharper than I had given her credit for. "I guess you haven't heard yet. Clarice passed away last night. Heidi is understandably very upset, and I'm filling in." I crossed my fingers behind my back.

"No kiddin'? So Clarice is dead, huh? It's just a couple days since I seen her, and she looked just fine then." She turned a corner and trotted down a side street. I followed.

"I saw her last night, and she was fine then, too. I'm not really sure what happened to her. The police are coming this afternoon to talk to us all, so I guess I'll find out. Some kind of domestic accident, I think."

She nodded. "Can be nasty, them domestic accidents. More people die at home than in car crashes, did ya know that?"

I didn't. "Are you sure those numbers don't include people who just pass away quietly in their own beds? A lot of people die in traffic accidents."

She shrugged. I added, "You didn't mention anything about Clarice coming to Brenda's storage unit recently."

"That's 'cause she didn't, hon. Got her own unit, just on the next aisle there." She pointed over the roofs of the storage units.

"Really?" I followed the direction of her finger. I don't know why; it wasn't as if I could see anything. She nodded and came to a halt outside one of the units.

"Here we are, hon. Got your key?"

She held out a hand, liberally freckled with liver spots. I dropped the key into it. She fitted it into the lock and twisted. The lock opened, and she took a step back. "Go on, hon. Knock yourself out. Just make sure you lock up again when you're done."

I promised I would, and she jogged back toward the office. I pulled the heavy door open, and stepped inside.

Other people's research is pretty boring, so I won't subject you to a detailed account of how I spent the next two hours. Suffice it to say that I sifted through a lot of file boxes, a lot of files, and a lot of pieces of paper, all while my thoughts churned and jumped from place to place. Too much was happening too fast, and I was getting too many pieces of information to be able to keep them all straight.

First things first. The police had been here on Monday, looking through Brenda's storage unit. If they had missed anything, or it had been among the stuff they brought back on Wednesday, Rafe would have found it when he searched the place on Thursday.

And what was up with Rafe, anyway? Surely he wasn't really a cop; that must have been something he said to be allowed access to the place. After all, with two years in jail behind him, it wasn't likely that the Metro Nashville PD would take him on, was it? Nor that he'd want them to, from everything I knew about him. I could see him making the claim, though, knowing that if he sounded confident enough, and if he batted those enviable eyelashes, the impressionable old lady in the front office would let him in without question. More interesting, to me anyway, was how he had opened the storage unit. If he had declined the receptionist's help, he must have had the means of getting in himself. But where had he gotten a key? No one had broken into our office and stolen one, or I would have heard about it. We've got deadbolts and an alarm system and a lot of expensive tech stuff that Walker wants to protect, not to mention confidential client files, and I doubted that anyone could get in and out without setting off the system. Rafe could have broken into Brenda's house, I supposed, but surely it was as well protected as the office, if not more so. Or he could—novel concept—have taken the key off her corpse last Saturday morning, after he killed her. Maybe that was why her purse had been ransacked and her belongings strewn everywhere. He might have wanted information about the owner of 101 Potsdam—maybe Tondalia Jenkins was obscenely wealthy, in spite of looking like a bag-lady—and when Brenda refused to tell him anything, he'd lost his temper and killed her. But in that case, why had he waited almost a week to visit the Stor-All? Why not stop by on Saturday afternoon, when the police were busy with the crime scene?

I had no answers, just more questions, so I went on to pondering the next thing, which was Clarice's death. I was somewhat dismayed to discover that I wasn't really sorry she was dead. I hoped it had been quick and that she hadn't suffered, but we're all going to die sometime, and it must have been Clarice's time, was all. And at least she'd died happy. Maybe she'd eaten something on her date last night that had caused her to have an allergic reaction or something. Or had a little too much wine with dinner, and had fallen and hit her head when she got home. Or just plain had a heart attack from all the excitement. Brenda's death, Heidi's apparent snooping, my snooping, and a hot date, all in one week . . . it'd be enough to make anyone's heart a little dickey. Detective Grimaldi's assignment to the case was surely, as Walker had suggested, just because of the connection to Brenda's murder, and not because there was anything fishy about Clarice's demise at all.

I did my best with the paperwork, opening every cardboard box and file cabinet I came across, but eventually I had to concede defeat. The Potsdam file wasn't here. However, I did find something. At the bottom of the oldest cabinet in the way-back corner of the small room, I discovered files with information about all the properties Brenda had ever owned. Personally owned, I mean. And there I found the file for the Kress building, and opened it.

The eight-story office building had been Brenda's first big purchase. Up until then, she had bought a few small houses and duplexes that she had either fixed up and resold for a modest profit, or that she was holding and renting out. She had taken out second mortgages on all of them in order to buy the Kress building. It left her stretched, and with no money left over to do the work necessary to convert the run-down offices to upscale apartments, she had taken on a partner. As it happened, he was the banker who had agreed to re-mortgage everything, and that was probably unethical and illegal, too. Their contract specified that she owned the building and he was going to come up with the necessary money for renovations, and they'd split the profits fifty-fifty when the condos sold. It wasn't difficult to deduce what had happened. The partner had dumped in everything he owned, and when that wasn't enough—because it always takes more time and money than expected to renovate something—he'd started using other people's money. Eventually, when the whole thing had threatened to come crashing down around their collective ears, Brenda had managed to off-load the building. She hadn't made a dime, but had gotten out with her shirt, while her partner had been left holding the bag. Once he realized what he was in for, he'd taken the coward's way out rather than face the music.

All of this was information I knew already from the *Voice* article. The one thing I didn't know was the man's name. It was with bated breath that I turned over the last sheet of paper and peered at the signature page.

The signature itself was illegible, and faded with time, but someone had kindly typed the names of the signatories underneath the signature lines. As I had suspected, the banker's name had been Graham Webster.

Digging out this tiny bit of information had taken an inordinate amount of time. When I checked my watch, I realized I needed to head back to the office for the meeting with Detective Grimaldi.

On my way to the car, I stopped in the office to tell the ancient receptionist I was finished. She was eating a tuna sandwich and watching a soap opera. "Did ya find what you were lookin' for, hon?" she asked between bites.

"Some of it," I said. "I just wanted to tell you I was leaving. I've got to go talk to the police about what happened to Clarice Webb."

She swallowed a chunk of sandwich. "Think they'll be by to look at her unit?"

"I guess that depends on what happened to her." If she fell in the bathtub and hit her head, I didn't see why they'd investigate further. Then again, who knew?

She nodded. "If you've got some pull with that cop, hon, the one who was here yesterday . . ."

I nodded.

"Tell him it wouldn't hurt none if *he* was to come back here to check out this other unit, too. Them other cops was nothin' to look at, but he was a handsome devil." She winked. I smiled politely and promised I would pass the remark on the next time I saw Lucifer. Although, between you and me, I had something else I wanted to ask him first, and that was whether he was now in possession of a file folder with the paperwork for 101 Potsdam Street.

11.

By the time I got back to the office, Tamara Grimaldi was already there, and closeted with Walker. A couple of the other agents were hanging out in the reception area, whispering, but rather than sit there and commiserate about how awful everything was, I figured I'd use the time constructively. So I excused myself and went into my own small office, and got to work on a list of everything I had thought of earlier. I had hoped that putting what I knew down on paper and seeing it in black and white would spur some kind of epiphany, but it didn't. It still seemed like a whole lot of unrelated circumstances, and the most obvious constant I noticed weaving through it all was Tondalia Jenkins. It was her house that Brenda was murdered in. She visited it frequently, and might have done so on Saturday morning. She lived at the nursing home where the Lincoln Navigator had been found. She was confused, and might have killed in what she would consider self-defense, if she had believed Brenda to be an intruder in her home. And Brenda had taken advantage of her somehow; I just didn't know how yet. But Mrs. Jenkins was also a tiny, frail woman, twice as old and less than half of Brenda's considerable size, and Brenda wasn't the kind of gal to stand still and let someone come at her with a knife. Especially someone she could knock flat with a swat of her hand.

Rafael Collier was another constant. He'd arranged for Brenda to be there, at the house where she was murdered, on Saturday morning. He'd been there himself. He wouldn't have had any problem overpowering her and slitting her throat. He probably owned several knives. He was familiar with the nursing home. And he was inordinately interested in 101 Potsdam and Tondalia Jenkins for no apparent reason.

A stray thought buzzed through my head, and disappeared, too quickly for me to get a good look at it. I banged my fist against my forehead and swore. In a ladylike manner, of course.

"Headache?" a dry voice inquired from the doorway. I jumped. Tamara Grimaldi smirked. "I'm ready for you, Ms. Martin."

"Sure," I said. "Come in."

"Mr. Lamont has kindly allowed us the use of his personal office. If you don't mind . . ."

She gestured. I snagged the piece of paper I had been writing on from the desk and stuffed it in my handbag on my way through the door. Every eye in the front room was on me as I followed Detective Grimaldi past the sofa and down the hall toward Walker's office.

"Have a seat." She sat down behind the desk and gestured me toward one of the chairs in front. I sat and folded one leg over the other, tugging my skirt hem. The bright turquoise color had seemed happy and cheerful this morning, when I hadn't known that I'd be dealing with another death in the firm, but now it seemed horribly inappropriate. Neither of us said anything for a moment. When Detective Grimaldi didn't break the silence, I felt like I had to. (It's a well-known interrogation technique. Sales technique, too. Remain silent and force your opponent—suspect, potential customer, ex-husband— to speak first.)

"I didn't expect you to get to me this quickly."

"Oh, you're a very important witness." She smiled, but it didn't reach her eyes, and didn't make me feel at all at ease. "Why don't you tell me what happened last night."

"Oh," I said, "so you've heard about that?"

She nodded. "Mr. Lamont mentioned that you had seen Clarissa."

"Clarice. Yes, I did. It was right here—or rather, in Brenda's office across the hall—at about nine o'clock."

She scribbled something on a legal pad in front of her. "What were you doing here that late?"

"You mean Walker didn't say?" She didn't answer, just looked at me, and I continued, "All right, all right. I came to snoop. I wanted to find out what I could about that house on Potsdam Street, where Brenda died. See, when I was there yesterday . . ."

"What were you doing there?" Detective Grimaldi interrupted. I squinted at her.

"Conducting business. Showing the house to a potential buyer. You did say you were finished with it."

She didn't answer the implied criticism. "What's the name of this potential buyer?" she asked instead.

"The same as last time. Rafael Collier."

"He wanted to go back there?" She made a note on the legal pad. I nodded.

"He approached me after the memorial service on Wednesday and asked if I would show it to him again. You had said the forensic team was done, so I didn't think there would be any harm in it."

"And what happened when you got there? Something to make you take an interest in the provenance of the house?"

I nodded. "This old woman showed up, and then a police car with Officers Spicer and Truman, and Spicer told me she used to live at the house and had gotten confused and still thought she did. Apparently she escapes from the nursing home regularly, and Spicer and Truman are called in to find her. It made me wonder, because she shouldn't have been able to sign legal papers in her condition."

I decided not to mention anything about going to the FinBar with Alexandra Puckett. There were a couple of different reasons why Detective Grimaldi might find fault with that, and it was just as easy to keep Alexandra out of it by implying that it was Tondalia Jenkins's behavior that had caused my snooping. It had contributed, anyway, so it wasn't even really a lie.

Detective Grimaldi made another scribble on her pad. "So you thought Brenda Puckett might have taken advantage of Mrs. Jenkins's illness?"

"The thought crossed my mind," I said.

"Is that something Mrs. Puckett would do?"

Hell, yes! "I don't want to speak ill of the dead . . ." I began. Detective Grimaldi looked surprised, and I grimaced as I realized that I had been doing very little else since the murder, especially in my conversations with the detective. "I wouldn't put it past her. Did you happen to catch the article in the *Nashville Voice* yesterday?"

Something like a shutter came down over Tamara Grimaldi's face, leaving it smooth and expressionless. "I did, yes."

"Then you know that she didn't always do things entirely by the book. She kept houses on the market when they already had contracts, and accepted higher prices than the list price so she could kick the difference back to the buyer in cash. It's mortgage fraud, at the very least."

Grimaldi made another note. "So you came here last night to snoop. Then what happened?"

"Clarice showed up."

"What was she doing here?"

I explained about the envelope. "She took it out of a locked drawer in her desk. I don't know what was in it." I hesitated for a second before I added, "Although it might have been the same envelope that Heidi told me she'd seen earlier in the day. If so, it just contained Clarice's contract with Brenda, and maybe another piece of paper."

"I haven't gotten around to speaking with Ms. Hoppenfeldt yet," Grimaldi said, in a tone that indicated that she wasn't looking forward to it. "She seems to be having a difficult time, and is lying down in her office. I'll ask her about it when I see her. Let's get back to what happened to you. Clarissa came in?"

I nodded, running through the conversation I had had with the dead woman while Detective Grimaldi made notes on her legal pad. "Can I ask you a question now?" I added when it looked like she had penned her last period. She nodded, although the look in her eyes was wary. "What happened to her?"

Grimaldi hesitated. "Didn't Mr. Lamont tell you?"

I shook my head. "He said he wasn't allowed to talk about it. But maybe he couldn't tell."

"Oh, it wasn't hard to tell," Detective Grimaldi said. I looked politely inquiring, and she added, "Her wrists were slashed. She bled out."

"Oh, my God!" The room spun for a second, and I could feel my own blood leaving my head and pooling in my stomach. At least that was what it felt like. "Did she do it herself?"

"That's the most likely explanation," Grimaldi said cordially. She waited for me to start breathing again, and then asked, "She didn't tell you whom she was meeting last night?"

I shook my head. "I probably wouldn't have known who it was even if she had mentioned his name. We didn't associate outside work."

"But you know it was a man?"

I thought for a second. "Not really. She was married once—her husband died just before she came to work for Brenda, I think—and her demeanor . . . I guess I just assumed she was meeting a man."

"But she didn't specifically say so? Did she mention where the meeting was to take place?"

I shook my head again. "All I know is I saw her drive east from here. Towards downtown and the university area." And the restaurant and nightclub district, as well as 101 Potsdam Street, the Milton House Nursing Home, and Brenda's house on Winding Way.

"And you didn't see her again?"

"No, of course I didn't. I'd tell you if I had."

She didn't say anything for a moment, and I was about to ask if the interview was over when she posed another question. "What did *you* do?"

I blinked. "After I left here, you mean?" She nodded. "I waited for Clarice to leave, then I drove home, called my brother, spoke to him for a few minutes, and went to bed. Why?"

"Alone?"

"Did I go to bed alone, you mean? Yes, I did." I'd been going to bed alone for almost two years, not that that was any of the detective's business.

"So no one can verify your whereabouts after you got there?"

My stomach did a weird backflip. "Not after I hung up the phone with Dix. Why? I thought she committed suicide. Why do I have to have an alibi?"

She didn't answer. "What would have happened if Clarissa had told Mr. Lamont that she had caught you going through Mrs. Puckett's office?"

I drew a shaky breath. "Not a lot. I told him myself this morning. Before I realized that Clarice wouldn't ever get a chance to. He took it better than I expected. But then I guess he had other things on his mind."

Poor, sensitive Walker, going to check up on an employee and finding her dead in a pool of blood. He must have been absolutely sickened. No wonder he had locked himself in his office after telling the rest of us the news.

"But if he hadn't had other things on his mind, how would he have reacted? What did you expect would happen, when Clarissa told you that she'd have to tell him?"

"I wish you'd stop calling her Clarissa," I said irritably. "Her name was Clarice. And I guess I expected a reprimand if I was lucky, and if I wasn't, that he'd tell the Real Estate Commission and they'd give me an official warning and flag my record."

"But that didn't worry you?"

"Not enough that I'd kill Clarice to shut her up, if that's what you're implying. My God, what is wrong with everyone? I'm a nice person! I don't do things like that!"

Detective Grimaldi looked at me unemotionally for a moment, before she said calmly, "I think that's it for now. But stick around, will you? I may have something else I want to ask you."

I promised—grudgingly—that I would stay in the office until she gave me leave to go, and headed for the door. "By the way, Ms. Martin," Detective Grimaldi said as I reached for the door knob, "her name was Clarissa. Not Clarice. Clarissa Webster. Just thought you ought to know." She smiled sweetly. I made a face.

I was almost to my office door when Detective Grimaldi's words penetrated. By then she had asked Heidi Hoppenfeldt into Walker's office and was busy interrogating her. I wondered if I ought to knock on the door and tell her what I knew, or thought I knew, but I decided that it could wait a few minutes. It might just be a coincidence anyway. There are a lot of people named Webster in the world, and just because Brenda had had a brush with a man named Webster fifteen years ago—just about the time Clarice went to work for her, a tiny voice in my head reminded me—there wasn't necessarily a connection there. It was a suggestive idea, certainly, but by no means a sure thing.

And then I realized that if I told Detective Grimaldi about Graham Webster, she'd ask where I'd gotten the information. She had read the *Voice* article, so she'd know it wasn't mentioned there. I could say I'd checked the newspaper archives, of course, and actually come up with Graham Webster's name, but what if she wanted to know how I knew that Graham Webster was the person in question, instead of Joe Shumaker or Mr. Bigelow? Or I could say that I'd asked Dix's help and he'd told me, but then she might call and verify it with him. I'd be forcing my brother to lie, and although he might, if I begged and pleaded and promised to baby-sit every Saturday from now until his youngest daughter was in college, it wasn't right to put him in the middle of a police investigation. No, it didn't appear as if I could tell Detective Grimaldi after all.

The thought of Dix made me wonder if he had discovered anything about Tyrell Jenkins. He hadn't contacted me, so he was either busy with work or didn't have anything to report, but it gave me the illusion that I was doing something. I had no clients (except Rafe, and he didn't really count), no leads to follow, and no business to conduct, but maybe I could do my good deed for the day by tracking down Tyrell and trying to right the wrong that Brenda had done his mother. And it was better than sitting in my office with nothing on my mind except the realization that the police seemed to believe me capable of slitting Clarice's—Clarissa's—wrists and leaving her to die.

The phone rang a couple of times on the other end, and then my brother picked up. "This is Dixon C. Martin, and I can't come to the phone right now. Please leave a message at the sound of . . ."

"Come off it, Dix," I said, tilting my office chair back, "don't you think I can tell the difference between the real you and a machine? What's the matter? Don't you want to talk to your baby sister?"

"Not particularly," my only brother answered candidly. "I found what you want, and you're not going to like it."

"You found Tyrell Jenkins?" My heart started beating faster.

"I found out what happened to Tyrell Jenkins," Dix corrected.

I frowned. This didn't sound good. "He's dead? Or in prison?"

"Dead. More than thirty years ago."

"Damn. I mean, darn. How did it happen?"

"He was shot," Dix said. "A couple of times in the chest, outside his house late one night. The police had no suspects, and no one was ever arrested. The only witness was his mother, who claimed he was shot by a white man in a pickup truck, but you can imagine how much credence was given to that piece of evidence. So I guess that takes care of Tyrell."

"I guess it does. There's no help to get from him. Poor Mrs. Jenkins."

We sat in silence for a moment. Then Dix said, "I've also got some information about your new boyfriend."

"Oh, God! Dix," I said. "He's not my boyfriend, and you didn't have to check him out. There's nothing going on between us. Why did you bother?"

"I didn't, actually." I could hear the shuffling of papers. "It turned out Todd had already started a background check of his own. So he gave me what he had and said he'd add to it as he got more."

I didn't respond for a moment. "You know," I said finally, "I'm not sure how I feel about that."

"What? That your family and friends care enough about you to want to be sure you're not getting involved with someone dangerous?"

"That my family and friends don't believe me when I say I'm not involved with him! Dix, please, listen to me. There is *nothing* going on between me and Rafe Collier. Zip. Zilch. Nada. I'm not seeing him, dating him, interested in him. He's not my type. You know Todd. You remember Bradley. *That's* the type I get involved with. Conventional, settled, respectable. Those dashing rogues are all well and good in fiction, but I wouldn't know what to do with someone like Rafe Collier even if I could get him!" I stopped, panting.

"I think you're protesting too much," Dix said coolly.

"Argh!" I answered.

Dix added, "So does this mean you don't want to hear what Todd discovered?"

"No!"

"You *do* want to hear what Todd discovered?"

"No, I don't. I don't care what Todd discovered. Rafael Collier is a client, nothing more. All I'm interested in is whether he can afford to buy the property he's looking at."

"He can't."

"He can't?"

"Not with what he's got in the bank." Dix shuffled more papers. "And Todd wasn't able to find anything about a job. Looks like he's unemployed. Sorry, sis."

"So why is he interested in the house?" I demanded.

"Maybe he's planning to burglarize it," Dix suggested.

"He must be going for the brass door knobs and the fireplace tile, then. Those are the only nice things in the house. Oh, and the avocado stove and fridge. I suppose he could get twenty bucks for those at a yard sale."

Dix didn't answer. "All right," I said, "since Todd's taken the trouble to gather the information . . ."

"Yes?"

"What happened twelve years ago?"

"What do you mean?"

"Rafe left high school, and left town, and a couple of months later he came back and was arrested. Mother said it was for assault. Does Todd's research say anything about that?"

Dix shuffled papers. "Todd must have asked his dad. I've got a copy of the arrest record here. I'm sure that's not supposed to be floating around . . ."

"It helps to have friends in high places," I commented. "What does it say?"

Dix's voice took on the cadences of someone reading. "The incident took place at Dusty's Bar in Columbia. The injured party was one Billy Scruggs. And I do mean injured. There's a hospital report attached, and Scruggs had a broken nose, broken ribs, a punctured lung, two black eyes, and numerous contusions and abrasions."

"Bruises and scratches," I translated.

"Apparently Billy Scruggs was LaDonna Collier's boyfriend. She must have been pretty upset about the whole thing, because she didn't even come to the sentencing two days later."

"Yikes."

"It says here that Collier didn't get off unscathed, either. He had cuts and bruises, a split lip, a black eye, and a sprained wrist. No wonder his wrist got sprained, the way he was using it. Scruggs was a big guy, in good shape for his age—he was forty-five—and this wasn't his first fight. He'd been arrested a couple of times before, for the same type of thing. Drunk and disorderly conduct, DUI, brawling, domestic assault on his ex-wife . . ."

"Did he have to serve time, too?"

"Not on this occasion," Dix said. "All the witnesses agreed that Collier started the fight. He pleaded guilty to the lesser charge of assault and battery, in order to avoid being tried for attempted manslaughter, is my guess. There was certainly a case for it. He was sentenced to five years and got out in two."

"Thanks," I said. "So what happened doesn't seem to have had anything to do with Brenda Puckett."

"Not really. I'll let you know if I find out anything else."

"About Tyrell Jenkins, right? I don't need to know anything else about Rafe."

"I'll talk to you later, sis," Dix said and hung up. I did the same, shaking my head. It shouldn't be this difficult to convince my family that there was nothing going on between me and Rafe.

My cell phone rang again before I had the opportunity to put it down. "Savannah? This is Alex." Alexandra Puckett. I recognized the voice this time.

"Hi, Alexandra," I responded. "What can I do for you?"

"What are you doing?"

"Just sitting in my office waiting to talk to the police again." I closed my eyes in disgust when I realized I had, once again, spoken out of turn. (Open mouth, insert foot.) Mother had frequently admonished me not to move my mouth so fast that my brain couldn't keep up, but apparently I hadn't learned my lesson yet. Alexandra turned frantic.

"Is it about my mom? Has something happened?"

"No, no," I said soothingly. "It's Clarice. Clarissa."

"Clarice Webb is dead? Oh, my God! Was she murdered too?"

"I don't think so," I said. "It sounds like she committed suicide." Alexandra didn't answer. "I'm sorry," I added. "She and your mom worked together for a long time. You must have known her pretty well."

"Um . . . not really." It sounded like Alexandra was regretting her outburst and was trying to seem calm, so

I wouldn't think anything was wrong. "She and mom weren't friends, you know."

"Really?" I'd always gotten the impression that they were inseparable. Brenda was high-handed and demanding, and Clarice was a sourpuss; still, Brenda had relied totally on Clarice, and Clarice seemed to have adored and admired Brenda.

"Nuh uh. Clarice made my mom give her a job like a thousand years ago, when I was a baby, and she worked really hard, but mom said she had to pay her way too much. And they didn't hang out or anything, except when they were working."

"Oh," I said. That probably shouldn't surprise me. Brenda must have hired Clarice—Clarissa—after Graham Webster died, either to make Clarice drop the lawsuit or because Brenda actually felt guilty and wanted to be helpful. Or both. But I could understand why there was no love lost between them. If I'd been Clarice, and I was holding Brenda responsible for the death of my husband, I wouldn't have wanted to hang out with her either.

"You know," I said, in an effort to change the subject, "you never told me what the big announcement was that your dad was going to make yesterday."

"Oh, that." Alexandra sounded disgusted. "It wasn't anything exciting. Just that he and Maybelle are engaged."

I managed, narrowly, to convert a shocked expletive to a ladylike cough. "Already?" His wife had only been in the ground for a couple of days. Wasn't this rather precipitous?

"He says he's waited long enough and he doesn't want to wait any longer," Alexandra said. After a second she added, reluctantly, "My mom and dad didn't always get along that great."

"I'm sorry," I said, for lack of something better. She gave an audible shrug.

"They argued about stuff, you know. Money, and Austin's grades, and my boyfriend. Stuff like that."

"Parents do that," I agreed, although I couldn't actually remember mine ever doing so. That was probably because I never did anything they wouldn't have approved of. Until I divorced Bradley, and declined to move back to Sweetwater and into the bosom of the family, of course. And until they somehow got the impression that I knew Rafe Collier better than I did. "Especially the boyfriend. If you get involved with someone they don't like—or even if they just think you are—they'll never let you hear the end of it."

Alexandra agreed wholeheartedly. "My mom was usually too busy to notice what I was doing, but then Clarice saw me with Maurice one day, and told my mom, and she just freaked!"

"What's wrong with Maurice?"

"Nothing," Alexandra said promptly.

"Oh, come on!" I answered. "If there wasn't something wrong with him, why would your mother freak out?"

She blew out another of those gusty sighs. "Maurice is black, okay? My mom tried to tell me that it was because

I'm too young, and that she hadn't given me permission to date, but the real reason is that he's black."

"I see," I said. "Um . . . are you sure she wasn't telling the truth? I mean, I know . . . knew Brenda, and I never noticed that she had any prejudices to speak of. As far as I could see, she treated everyone the same." Not necessarily very nicely, but the same. It didn't matter if we were black or white, gay or straight, men or women; we were all subjected to Brenda's magnificent condescension.

Alexandra didn't answer. I wasn't sure whether she believed me or not, but it didn't seem as if she wanted to argue about it, at any rate. I added, "So tell me about Maurice. Where did you meet him? How long have you dated?"

It turned out that Alexandra had met Maurice about four months ago, when he had brought the family a pizza. After that, Alexandra had gotten in the habit of ordering a lot of pizza so she could keep seeing him. They had started dating exclusively at the beginning of the summer. She was obviously head over heels in love with him, and couldn't stop talking about how handsome he was, and how smart, and how sexy.

"So what happened when your mother found out that you were dating?" I asked. Alexandra's voice turned poisonous.

"That witch Clarice saw us in Maurice's car last week. She told mom, and mom totally lost it. I thought she was going to have a heart attack. She threatened to ground me until I'm eighteen unless I agreed to stop seeing him. So I told her I would, just to get her off my back, but I didn't, really. I just had to be more careful, and see him when they thought I was doing other things."

"Like sleeping?"

"Huh?"

"Is that what you were doing the morning your mother died? Seeing Maurice? You said you were home alone, sleeping. But I called your house when I couldn't get hold of your mom on her cell phone, and no one answered."

"Maybe I just slept through it," Alexandra said defensively. "Maybe I don't have a phone in my room . . ."

"Yes, that's likely."

She sighed. "All right. I went over to Maurice's. I had to wait until mom was gone, so it was after seven when I left the house. But when I got to Reinhardt Street he wasn't there, so I drove home again."

I felt a frisson down my back, as if someone had dropped a millipede with cold feet under my blouse. "Maurice lives on Reinhardt?" Reinhardt Street is in the same area as Potsdam and Dresden, a stone's throw away from the Milton House Nursing Home. "What kind of car does he drive?"

"A green Dodge with lots of chrome and zebra seat covers," Alexandra answered promptly. "Why?"

"No reason. Just curious. Listen, I've got to go. The detective is ready for me again."

"Oh." She sounded disappointed. "Give me a call later, okay? Let me know what happened to Clarice? Nobody ever tells me anything."

I promised I would, and hung up the line. And leaned back on my chair contemplating what I had just learned. (No, Detective Grimaldi wasn't ready for me again. I had fibbed in order to get off the phone before I said something else that my brain hadn't vetted.) But this was interesting information. Alexandra was dating a black youth in a green car, of whom her mother disapproved. Surely it had to be more than a coincidence that a black youth in a green car had driven by 101 Potsdam Street when Rafe and I were standing in the drive on Saturday morning. Twice.

Was it possible that Alexandra's boyfriend, tired of Alexandra's mother telling her daughter that she couldn't date him, had taken matters into his own hands and gotten rid of Brenda? And then, because Clarice had been the one to tip Brenda off about the relationship, he had revenged himself on her, too? Was Alexandra Puckett dating a double murderer?

12.

It was almost four o'clock by the time Tamara Grimaldi had finished all her interviews and got back to me. By then, almost everyone else had been dismissed, except for the small crew of detectives scouring Clarice's office for clues. I had spent a couple of boring hours preparing a three hundred-piece mailing to my "sphere of influence"—everyone I had ever known, with the exception of my ex-husband and his new wife—to tell them I was a real estate agent and to ask if they would please keep me in mind if they were thinking of buying or selling. That done, I had descended into reading the tawdry romance novel I keep in my bag for just such occasions, and was just getting to the part where the muscled highwayman was riding off across the moors clutching the swooning form of the heroine to his manly chest when Detective Grimaldi appeared at my door.

"Ready to go?"

I had been ready to go for two hours, but I thought it best not to say anything about that. Instead I rose with alacrity. "Sure. Where?"

She waited until we were outside on the sidewalk before she answered. "Since Mrs. Jenkins already knows you, I thought you might want to come with me when I talk to her."

I stumbled slightly, but told myself it was because of the heels on my shoes and nothing else. "We're going to the Milton House?"

She glanced at me. "Is there a problem?"

I had to hustle to keep up with her long-legged and short-heeled gait. "Um . . . no."

"You don't sound sure."

"No, it's just that . . . well . . . Rafe Collier told me not to go back there."

She sent me another look. "What does Collier have to do with it?"

"Nothing that I know of," I admitted, "but he gave me the distinct impression that he would prefer not finding me there again."

Detective Grimaldi sniffed. "As long as you're with me, I don't see what he can do about it."

I wanted to ask her what would happen later, when I was no longer with her, but I decided against it. She thought I was wimpy enough already, and a complaint like that would only reinforce the impression.

"Haven't you spoken to her already?" I asked instead. "With her being the owner of the house where the murder happened, I mean?"

Detective Grimaldi shook her head. "I spoke to Officer Spicer, and he told me all about Mrs. Jenkins. I didn't see the need to waste my time or hers with an interrogation. I doubt she would have been able to produce anything coherent."

I nodded. Most likely she was right.

"I have to talk to her now, though." She didn't sound pleased about it.

"Sorry," I said. She smiled.

"That's okay. At least I'll have you there, if things get difficult."

Great. Not.

The detective must have shared my low opinion of the nursing home, because I could see her aquiline nose twitch with disgust when we walked into the lobby. "Tamara Grimaldi, Metro PD." She flashed her shield.

The nurse at the desk—the same one who had allowed Rafe to walk off with me the day before— jumped to her feet with a guilty look. "What can I do for you, Detective?" She threw a panicked glance over her shoulder, probably hoping that someone with more authority would appear.

"I'd like to see Mrs. Jenkins."

The receptionist looked like she was thinking of pretending she didn't know who Mrs. Jenkins was.

"Tondalia Jenkins," I said. She looked at me. And recognized me. And looked unhappy to see me. Tamara Grimaldi didn't say anything, just raised her brows. The receptionist, lacking the courage to object, waved her hand in the direction of the hallway. "Your girl there knows the way."

Grimaldi smiled, or more accurately showed teeth. "Much obliged. Come along, Ms. Martin." Once I indicated which room was Mrs. Jenkins, Grimaldi marched down the hall with me trotting behind. By the time I'd caught up, Detective Grimaldi had already knocked on the door.

"Who is it?" Mrs. Jenkins's quavering voice answered. Grimaldi nodded to me. I took a step closer to the door.

"Mrs. Jenkins? This is Savannah Martin. We met yesterday, and the day before. Can I come in?"

I heard a sound inside, and then the door was opened a crack. Mrs. Jenkins's black bird eyes looked out at us. "Oh, it's you," she said, after a moment. "C'mon in, baby." She shuffled out of the way. I pushed the door open and walked in, cautiously. Tamara Grimaldi followed.

The room was not much bigger than my office, and as devoid of charm. There was a hospital bed in the middle of the floor, one metal folding chair—it looked hard and uninviting—and nothing else. No shelf with books, no TV, no table for writing letters or playing cards; not even any family photos or other personal effects. The threadbare blanket was institutional, and Mrs. Jenkins had on the same faded and dirty housecoat and the same filthy, fuzzy slippers as the other two times I had seen her.

The only nice thing about the room was a bouquet of flowers on the windowsill, and even they looked droopy and wilted.

"It looks like your flowers could use some water," I said brightly, attempting to hide my horror at the small, dingy, depressing room. After a long and probably none-too-easy life, she deserved better than this. "Would you like me to take care of it?"

She waved a vague hand. "Sure, baby." I grabbed the vase, which didn't feel like it had any water in it at all, and carried it into the tiny adjoining—doorless—bathroom. Mrs. Jenkins turned to Detective Grimaldi. "Who're you?"

"That's my friend Tamara," I said brightly.

"You look like a cop." Mrs. Jenkins's voice was suspicious. Grimaldi's was calm.

"That's right. I wanted to talk to you about your house. And about the lady who died there."

"Don't know nothin' about it," Mrs. Jenkins said.

"But you listed your house for sale recently," I prompted. "Didn't you?"

Tondalia Jenkins must be in a fairly lucid frame of mind today, because she seemed to know that she no longer lived in the house on Potsdam. "I ain't as young as I used to be, baby. When the lady knocked on the door and asked if I wanted to move someplace diff'rent, I figured I'd better do it."

"And that was Mrs. Puckett?"

Mrs. Jenkins looked vague. "Can't rightly remember her name, baby. Guess it musta been. Big lady. Big hair, big butt, big attitude."

"That sounds like Brenda," I remarked. Grimaldi sent me a quelling look and turned back to Mrs. Jenkins.

"Did you ever see the lady again?"

"She came back once, to tell me she'd found me a place and I had to leave. Next thing I know, I'm here." She looked around. I pursed my lips disapprovingly.

"Do you remember the kind of car the lady was driving?" Detective Grimaldi asked. Mrs. Jenkins was unsure.

"Big? Dark, maybe? One o' them big ones they're allus talkin' about on the news. UFO?"

"SUV?" I suggested. She nodded.

"Big, kinda square car. Saw it when she came the first time."

Detective Grimaldi took over the questioning. It occurred to me that in a way, we were doing the old "good cop, bad cop" routine, with only one real cop and no bad cop at all. Nevertheless, I was clearly cast in the role of good cop, jollying Mrs. Jenkins along and making her feel comfortable, while Grimaldi posed all the difficult questions. "Did you ever see a car like that here? Recently, maybe? In the parking lot on Saturday morning, for instance?"

Mrs. Jenkins shook her head. "Can't say as I did, baby. Nor another time, neither. She just left me here, and that's the last I seen of her."

"Marvelous," I said, wishing that Brenda wasn't dead so I could have the pleasure of killing her myself. Or at least dragging her in front of the Real Estate Commission by her bleach blonde hair and having her license revoked and her professional reputation ruined. It was no more than she deserved.

"You wanna be careful 'bout gettin' upset, baby," Mrs. Jenkins told me kindly. "It ain't good for the baby."

Detective Grimaldi didn't appear to have any more questions, so we made our excuses and headed for the door. We were almost there when Grimaldi did a Columbo and turned back. "By the way, Mrs. Jenkins. Ms. Martin tells me that you like to go for walks. Did you happen to take a walk last Saturday morning?"

Mrs. Jenkins looked blank.

"Not sure? Well, don't worry about it. I'll ask the nurses and see if they remember. How about last night?"

Mrs. Jenkins looked more confident this time. "I didn't go nowhere last night. My grandson was visitin' me." She smiled toothlessly. I opened my mouth to set her straight, looked at her beaming face, and closed it again.

"Surely you don't think she's strong enough to have killed Brenda?" I asked when we were outside in the parking lot again. The receptionist had followed us with her eyes the entire way through the lobby, speaking softly on the phone the whole time, and I had decided to wait until we got outside before I said anything. "She's tiny. And old. And frail. She would have needed a ladder to reach Brenda's throat. Unless you think she used a sword."

"Actually," Grimaldi said, "we've found the murder weapon."

I gaped. "You're kidding! Where?"

She hesitated. "That's privileged information, I'm afraid."

"Oh," I said, disappointed.

"I shouldn't have mentioned it, and I would appreciate it if you wouldn't pass it on, as it pertains to a—two, now—open investigations."

"Of course." I couldn't stop myself from speculating, though, and after a few minutes of driving—and cogitating—I gasped. "Oh, my God! Clarice killed Brenda!"

"It's too early to say that," Detective Grimaldi answered, without looking at me. In justice to her, she was navigating through the busy intersection at Potsdam and Dresden, and probably couldn't.

"But that's where you found the knife? The knife Clarice used to cut her wrists was the same knife that was used to cut Brenda's throat?"

Detective Grimaldi didn't deny it, which was as close to a tacit confirmation as I could hope to receive. I sat in stupefied silence the rest of the way back to the office, trying to make sense of it all. The only thing I could come up with was that Clarice must have snapped and decided to avenge her husband's suicide fifteen years after the fact. Maybe the realization that Brenda was up to her old tricks, taking advantage of Mrs. Jenkins, had tipped the scales. Clarice's appointment last night could have been with someone who knew or had guessed what she had done, and who threatened to report her to the police. Maybe that person had given her an ultimatum—"If you don't contact the police yourself tomorrow, I will!"—and

Clarice had decided to follow her late husband's example before she could get caught and punished.

Or maybe there hadn't been any appointment at all. Maybe her meeting had been with her Maker, and she had geared herself up for it with some liquid courage. Maybe that was why her cheeks had been flushed and her eyes bright. And that special envelope . . .

"Did she leave a note?"

"I beg your pardon?" Detective Grimaldi must have been deep in thought, too. I repeated my question. She shook her head. "Not everyone does, you know."

"I'll take your word for it. So I guess Brenda and Clarice went to 101 Potsdam together last Saturday. Then Clarice killed Brenda and drove the Lincoln Navigator down to the Milton House and parked it there. Was her DNA among the evidence you collected from Brenda's car? You mentioned coworkers . . ."

Grimaldi nodded. "Not that that's in any way conclusive. They worked together, and I'm sure Mrs. Webster was in Mrs. Puckett's car on many occasions. We also found Mrs. Puckett's husband's DNA, Mr. Lamont's, Mr. Briggs's, and Ms. Hoppenfeldt's, along with the children's."

"It's hard to believe that Clarice had it in her. But I guess there's no other explanation, is there? Even without a written confession, the murder weapon is pretty conclusive evidence."

Detective Grimaldi shrugged. We rode in silence the rest of the way to the realty office, where Grimaldi dropped me off with a terse good afternoon and an admonition to stay out of trouble this weekend. I said I'd try, and she prepared to drive off. At the last moment, she called after me. "By the way, Ms. Martin, I wasn't aware that you were expecting. Who's the lucky man?"

"Rafael Collier," I said, without thinking. "I mean . . . I'm not actually pregnant. Mrs. Jenkins misunderstood. That is . . ."

"I see," Detective Grimaldi said.

"No . . ." But it was too late; she had already put the car into gear and driven off. I groaned. That was all I needed; for *that* misunderstanding to get around.

I was still on the road when my cell phone rang. "Savannah?" It was Todd's voice, and it sounded far away and muffled, like he was calling from the car. "Are you by any chance free for dinner again tonight? I've got something I'd like to talk to you about."

I hesitated. I had something I wanted to talk to him about, too. His comment to Dix that I was seeing Rafe Collier seemed to have the whole family in a twitter of apprehension; plus, I really didn't appreciate his taking it upon himself to do a background check on Rafe. It wasn't any of Todd's business who I dated, or—in this case—didn't date, and I wanted to tell him so. But impulse was warring with indoctrination in my mind. Mother had always admonished Catherine and me that we should never appear too available to potential beaus.

Poor Jonathan had gotten a hell of a runaround when he first attempted to date Catherine, I remembered.

Todd's voice continued, temptingly, "We can go back to Fidelio's."

It was a hard offer to resist. Although the cupboard in my apartment wasn't quite bare, the microwavable macaroni & cheese I had to look forward to tonight couldn't compare to the cuisine at Nashville's premier Italian restaurant.

"I suppose I could spare a little time."

"I'll pick you up at seven." He hung up before I had time to say anything else.

I decided to wear black, to show respect for poor Clarice and her untimely demise, and also because (if I may say so myself) it looks great on me. The cocktail dress was short and clingy, and I piled my hair loosely on top of my head and strapped high-heeled sandals to my feet. I was putting the finishing touches on my makeup when the doorbell rang. I glanced into the kitchen at the clock on the stove, as I made my way to the door. It was a quarter to seven. Todd must have made good time on the road.

I guess maybe I should have looked through the peephole before I opened the door, but I was so sure it was Todd outside that I just swung the door back. "You're early . . ." I began, and then fell silent when I realized that the man outside didn't have Todd's sandy hair and gray-blue eyes. I tried to slam the door shut again, but I was too slow. Rafe simply caught the moving door with the flat of his hand, pushed it back, and shouldered me out of his way.

"You can't . . ." I began before I could help myself. He already had, so there was no sense in telling him he couldn't come in. He arched a brow, but didn't point out the obvious.

"Tell me, darlin'," he said instead, stepping so close to me I could feel his breath on my face, "didn't I tell you to stay away from the old folks' home?"

I tried to retreat, but there was nowhere to go. For the third time in two days, I had my back against the wall—literally—and Rafe Collier leaning over me. I kept my eyes straight ahead, not meeting his eyes, when I admitted, "Um . . . now that you mention it, I think you did."

"Wanna explain to me what you were doing there this afternoon, then? With the cops?" His voice hardened on the last word.

"It didn't have anything to do with you," I said.

"No?" His voice was mild, and quite amazingly scary, considering. I looked up, into a pair of hard, black eyes, and shook my head. I really didn't want any misunderstandings on this point. I value my life too highly to take any chances with it.

"No. It had to do with Brenda Puckett and the house on Potsdam. Detective Grimaldi wanted to find out about it, in case it had anything to do with why Brenda was killed."

"That old lady ain't strong enough to cut the throat of a cat." His voice was flat.

"I agree," I said soothingly. "Actually, it seems the police are pretty sure who killed Brenda."

"Yeah? Who?"

He stepped back enough to allow me to draw a deep breath again. I told him about Clarice Webb, a.k.a. Clarissa Webster; her death and the knife she had used to—seemingly—kill herself and her employer. "I don't suppose you saw a dumpy, middle-aged woman who looked like a hen nearby on Saturday morning?"

"Can't say as I did, darlin'. Or I didn't notice nobody like that, anyway. So this was fifteen years in the making? That's a long time to wait."

"I guess some people are patient."

"Some ain't."

That was true. "It looks like the case is closed and the murderer punished, anyway. Poor Clarice. I wouldn't have thought she had it in her."

Rafe shrugged. For the first time he looked at me, comprehensively, from top to toe and back. "Going out?" he inquired, with a quirk of an eyebrow.

I resisted the impulse to cross my arms over my chest. I hadn't considered the dress to be too revealing when I put it on, but now I felt practically half-naked. "As a matter of fact."

"Who's the lucky guy?"

"Todd Satterfield," I said. "He'll be here in the next ten minutes, and I don't think he'd be best pleased to see you, so . . ."

It was a not so subtle suggestion that he make himself scarce. Rafe smiled. "I imagine he won't. Where's he taking you?"

"Fidelio's," I said. He whistled.

"Swanky. Course, he can afford it."

"I suppose *you'd* be taking me to McDonald's?"

He grinned, and I gave myself a hard mental slap. Where had that come from? Now it sounded like I *wanted* him to ask me out, which was *so* not true!

"If you were wearing that"—he looked at my dress—"I don't think I'd bother taking you anyplace except to bed."

It took a second, or two or three, of me gaping like a goldfish with my cheeks on fire before I managed to say coolly, "Typical man. You see a woman in a nice dress, and all you can think about is taking it off her."

"You telling me Satterfield ain't thinking the same thing, darlin'?"

"If he is, he's too polite to say so."

"That what you're looking for in a man? That he's polite?" He smirked.

"It doesn't hurt," I said primly.

"Guess that knocks me right out of the running." He didn't sound too upset about it.

"I guess it does." When he didn't answer, I added, sweetly, "By the way, I stopped by Brenda's storage unit this morning. You didn't tell me you're a police officer. When did that happen?"

He laughed. "It didn't, darlin'. I've got a record, remember."

"So you're not a cop, just a liar?"

He shrugged, setting off a chain reaction of muscles under the black T-shirt.

"Hmpf!" I sniffed. He grinned, but didn't answer. "So are you going to tell me what you found? Was there anything important?"

"Depends . . ." Rafe said, but before he could say anything else, there was a knock on the door. I made a face. I had hoped to have Rafe out of my apartment before Todd showed up.

For a wild second I contemplated asking him to go out on the balcony and climb down the downspout so Todd wouldn't see him—it was only ten or twelve feet down to the flowerbeds below, and he looked like he could handle the trip—but I got a grip on myself. I had nothing to hide, and Rafe probably wouldn't have done it anyway. So I did the next best thing, and put a cheerful, innocent smile on my face when I opened the door. "Hi, Todd."

"Savannah." Todd leaned in to peck me on the cheek while simultaneously handing me another bouquet of roses.

I smiled my thanks and turned to the kitchen to put them in water, and came face to face with Rafe, who had moved closer, in his usual soundless fashion. He winked. I sidestepped.

"Oh, Todd," I said casually, over my shoulder, "you remember Rafael Collier, don't you? From high school? He was just leaving." I sent Rafe a look. He responded with an ironic half bow.

"Of course," Todd said stiffly. "Collier." He nodded.

"Satterfield." Rafe nodded back. "How's the arm?" He smirked.

"Arm?" I repeated, looking up from the flower arranging. "Is something wrong with your arm, Todd?"

"I pulled a muscle a few days ago," Todd said repressively. "It's nothing."

Rafe grinned. I looked from one of them to the other. Todd hadn't mentioned getting hurt in the fight between Rafe and Cletus Johnson on Tuesday night, but that must have been when it happened. "Did you have it looked at?"

"I don't need a doctor to tell me when I have pulled a muscle," Todd said. The two of them eyed each other like a pair of dogs in an alley. I sighed.

"Are you ready to go, Todd?"

"Whenever you are, Savannah," Todd answered politely, but without looking at me. It appeared they were engaged in a juvenile staring contest. I turned to Rafe.

"We're leaving now. Thanks for stopping by." It was as close as I had ever come to out-and-out asking someone to leave my house. Even Bradley had stayed while I left. It felt strange, but liberating.

Rafe didn't seem to have any hang-ups about looking away first, because he broke eye-contact with Todd without hesitation, and grinned at me. "No problem, darlin'. Anytime."

He sauntered towards the door. I called after him, "I still want to hear what you found in the Stor-All."

Todd's look sharpened. Rafe sent me a grin over his shoulder. "It'll cost you."

Todd growled. "Cost me what?" I asked. Rafe didn't answer, just sent me a long look and a wink. It left no doubt whatsoever what he thought a fitting price might be. I was as red as a tomato by the time he disappeared down the hallway toward the stairs. "I'll be in touch," floated back to me.

13.

"What was *he* doing here?" Todd demanded, without bothering to lower his voice or wait for Rafe to get out of earshot. I reminded myself that I didn't have anything to hide. It would also sound silly if I dropped my own voice to a whisper, so I answered normally.

"He . . . um . . . dropped by to tell me something."

"Really?" Todd sounded suspicious. "What?"

"I'm afraid I can't tell you that."

His eyes narrowed. "Why not?"

"It's . . . um . . . privileged."

Todd snorted. "Excuse me?"

I didn't like the snort, or his tone of voice—what business did he have, acting like his privilege was more important than mine?—so I said, "You know how you have attorney-client privilege? Well, I have broker-client privilege."

"You're kidding!" Todd said. I shook my head.

"I'm afraid not. I owe my clients certain fiduciary duties, and confidentiality is one of them. Rafael Collier is a client, so I can't repeat our private conversations."

Todd grumbled, but he was too good a lawyer to object. I permitted myself a tiny, self-congratulatory smile as I walked ahead of him out the door and down the stairs.

Fidelio's was even busier tonight than the last time we'd been there—not surprisingly, as it was Friday instead of midweek—but Todd had called ahead, so there was a table waiting for us. He had sense enough to wait until the—excellent—meal was over, and we were lingering over coffee and dessert, before he returned to the same irksome subject.

"Has he been to your apartment before?" He wasn't looking at me, but gazing around the room as he waited for my answer.

"Who?" I said, looking around, too. "Oh, Rafe? No, he hasn't."

"Did you tell him where you live?"

I shook my head. "I have no idea where he got my address. I have no idea where *you* got my address, either, if it comes to that."

"I asked your mother," Todd said.

Naturally. "Well, I'm sure Rafe didn't. Mother wouldn't have given it to him, and I think he's smart enough to know that."

Todd nodded approvingly. "I'm glad you don't give your personal information to just anyone, Savannah. One can never be too careful, you know. After all, look at what happened to Mrs. Puckett!"

"Actually," I said, "it seems Brenda Puckett was killed for personal reasons, by her assistant."

"Oh, dear," Todd said. "So someone else you work with."

I nodded. "I'm still not sure I understand it. Clarice did everything for Brenda. She picked up her dry-cleaning, and booked her hair appointments, and kept track of her children's birthdays, not to mention all the demands of the business. If Brenda had a closing, Clarice made sure the paperwork got to the attorney. If Brenda needed a termite letter, Clarice called the exterminator, and if Brenda had a new listing, Clarice made the fliers. Brenda would have been totally lost without Clarice, and the way Clarice was blubbering at the memorial service, it certainly seemed like she felt totally lost without Brenda."

"So why are you so sure Clarice killed her?" Todd asked, stabbing his cheesecake with his fork. I tried not to look envious as I sipped my black coffee. I love cheesecake, but mother has me firmly trained not to eat too much in front of a gentleman. It's a holdover from the days when a Southern Belle should have a sixteen-inch waist and eat like a bird. I don't have a sixteen-inch waist—far from it—but I never order dessert when I'm on a date.

I explained about the knife, and Todd protested, "But that doesn't prove anything. Just because the same knife was used in both cases, doesn't mean that Clarice was the one who used it. Any halfway-decent defense attorney could make mincemeat of that argument in court."

"Where it won't ever go, since they're both dead. But what you're saying is that someone else may have killed Brenda, and Clarice held onto the knife so she could kill herself with it later? Or Clarice killed Brenda and someone else killed Clarice? Who would do such a thing?"

"Someone who wanted to avenge Mrs. Puckett's death, obviously," Todd said. I shook my head.

"There's nobody who's sorry that Brenda is dead, believe me. Not even her family. Her husband has a new fiancée already, and her daughter is probably snuggling up to her unsuitable boyfriend as we speak."

"Fine," Todd said impatiently, obviously irritated that I didn't applaud his suggestions, "so maybe someone else killed both of them."

I sat back in my seat. "That would explain why Detective Grimaldi asked me whether I had an alibi for last night."

"The police think *you* may have killed Ms. Webster? Savannah . . ."

"It's just because she caught me snooping in Brenda's office last night."

Todd looked shocked, and I added, defensively, "I was just looking for the folder for 101 Potsdam Street. For Rafe."

"I actually asked you out tonight to talk to you about Collier," Todd said, recognizing a smooth segue when he heard one.

I sniffed. "How flattering."

"I didn't mean it like that. I enjoy your company, Savannah. You know that. I'm just concerned that you're getting involved with someone dangerous."

"In that case," I answered, "let me put your mind at ease. I am not getting involved with him. Quite the opposite. Our relationship is purely professional."

"That's not how I'd describe it," Todd said.

I arched my brows. "What do you mean by that?"

"He showed up at your apartment, uninvited, after business hours, and without you even having told him the address. And the way he looked at you . . . there was nothing professional about that!"

"He's a man," I said. "Men look at women in tight dresses."

"Not that way," Todd said darkly.

"You're being silly," I answered.

"Well, I don't think you should wear anything like that around him again." He glowered at my—really quite conservative, considering—little black dress.

Now, I know he was just being chivalrous, but personally, I hadn't found Rafe's regard all that offensive. Most men ogle women, that's just the way of the world, and although Rafe hadn't bothered to be polite and well-bred about it—probably because he wasn't well-bred or polite—he hadn't made me feel like I had anything to worry about, either. If he truly had plans to tie me up and have his way with me, I doubted he'd be so cheerfully and lecherously up front about it.

"I wore this dress to go to dinner with *you*, Todd," I said soothingly. "Rafe Collier showing up was incidental. Any other time I've seen him, I've been more professionally dressed, believe me."

Todd didn't answer. I added, "So was that all you wanted to talk about, or was there more?"

"There's more." Todd put his fork down and stuck his hand into the breast pocket of his dark suit. He extracted a couple of folded sheets of paper. "After you told me Collier had shown up, I decided to look into him."

"Dix told me." My voice was cool, but Todd either didn't notice, or chose not to let me see that he had. "And I don't think you should have, not without a better reason. You can't arbitrarily do background checks on people just because you don't like their faces."

He unfolded the ominous-looking papers. "I didn't go deep. All of this was available through official channels. There's nothing personal here. He doesn't own property anywhere, at least not in his own name. He doesn't owe money. He doesn't have a credit card. He has two bank accounts—a checking account with a few hundred dollars in it, and a savings account with a few thousand. He's never been married and has no known dependents. Or none he's acknowledged, anyway. He's never been sued. He hasn't been arrested in the past ten years, although he's come to the police's attention on several occasions."

"For what?" I wanted to know, interested despite myself.

"Involvement in criminal activities," Todd answered.

I wrinkled my forehead. "Is he involved in something criminal now?"

"His most recent brush with the law was over Brenda Puckett's murder," Todd said.

"But he wasn't involved in that."

"He was interviewed in connection with it."

"So was I," I said.

"That's different," Todd answered. "You didn't have anything to do with it."

"Neither did he. I had more to do with it than him. At least I knew Brenda and wanted to murder her occasionally myself."

Todd shrugged, as if my objection was a minor point of no consequence and not worthy of remark. Referring to his papers again, he added, "He files income tax, but doesn't appear to have a steady job. He filed as an independent contractor last year, and didn't have enough income to owe much." Todd shook his head in amazement and came down off his high horse for a moment. "He made less than twenty-five grand after deductions, can you imagine?"

I smiled politely, and refrained from mentioning what my annual salary had been for the past two years. "I guess he's used to living cheaply." Although that didn't explain the wickedly expensive Harley-Davidson he'd been riding. But maybe it wasn't his. Or maybe Rafe, like so many other Americans, cheated on his taxes. Maybe he had an undeclared source of income, one that the IRS knew nothing about. Like drug dealing or gun running or murder for hire.

"Listen, Todd, I'm not sure this is any of our business." If Rafe hadn't done anything wrong, it didn't seem right to snoop in his private affairs. And if he had, all the more reason to ask as few questions as possible.

"I just want you to understand what you're dealing with, Savannah." Todd folded the papers again, preparatory to putting them back in his pocket. "Collier is different from the people you're used to. And it isn't just the cultural difference, although . . ."

"What cultural difference?" I interrupted. "He grew up less than three miles from both of us. What kind of cultural difference is that?"

The Satterfields owned a big turn-of-the-(last)-century foursquare in the middle of Sweetwater, where Todd had been raised in almost as much musty splendor as Catherine, Dix, and I. It was a far cry from the squalor of the Bog, but hardly a different world for all that.

Todd didn't answer directly. Instead he said, "The Colliers were no better than they ought to be, Savannah. LaDonna got herself in the family way at fourteen, and Bubba was in jail by seventeen. Old Jim was in trouble with the law his entire life, and you remember what Rafe was like. Dad always used to say it was a matter of time before he ended up either in prison or six feet under. It didn't come as a surprise to anyone when he was arrested."

Of course it hadn't. Everyone in town had been waiting and hoping, and some of us probably hadn't cared particularly whether he ended up in one place or the other, just so long as we didn't have to deal with him anymore. No wonder he hadn't come back to Sweetwater when he was released from prison. No wonder he had chosen to handle the arrangements for LaDonna's funeral by phone. I was surprised he'd come back in person to clean out her belongings instead of hiring a crew to pack them up. Although if he truly was as hard-up as Todd said, maybe he couldn't afford it.

The conversation had put something of a damper on the evening, and we called it a night shortly thereafter. Todd drove me back home in his cushy SUV. He didn't ask to come in for a nightcap, although he did give me a proper kiss this time. There was even an embrace and some tentative probing of tongues involved. It didn't leave me feeling faint or dizzy, or even weak in the knees, but as kisses go, it wasn't bad. I'd certainly had worse. Bradley . . .

But I won't bore you with the details. Enough simply to say that I've come to the conclusion that the weak-kneed, fainting heroine is a convention that romance publishing has come up with to perpetuate the sale of their tawdry novels. They know that none of us are likely to ever meet a real man who sweeps us off our feet, so they keep publishing books with macho, masterful males, thus encouraging us to keep reading, thus perpetuating the myth of the weak-kneed, dizzy heroine. That's my story, and I'm sticking to it.

I waited until Todd was safely on his way before I called his father. "Sheriff? This is Savannah Martin."

There was a beat, and some noise, before the sheriff answered. "Well, hello there, darlin'. What can I do for you?"

"I just wanted to ask you a question," I said. It sounded like the sheriff was entertaining while his son was out, but it could just have been the TV, I suppose.

"And what might that be, darlin'?"

"Well," I said, "I just came home from having dinner with Todd . . ."

"Oh, he's on his way back?" The rustling immediately became more agitated, and I thought I could hear a female voice murmur something.

"I'm sorry," I said, "is this a bad time? It sounds like you've got company."

"No, no, darlin'. Nothin' to worry about." I heard the sound of bedsprings, and imagined the sheriff sitting down on the edge of the bed with the phone to his ear. Good thing technology hasn't provided us with visuals yet, or I might have seen a scantily clad woman hurriedly gathering herself in the background.

"Are you sure? Because I can call back later. Or tomorrow. It isn't urgent."

"Now is fine. If Todd's on his way back . . . That is, anytime's a good time to talk to you, darlin'."

I smiled. "That's awfully sweet of you, sheriff. This won't take long, I promise. I just wanted to check something. Todd happened to mention that Jim Collier, LaDonna's daddy, was a bit of a troublemaker . . ."

"Sure was, darlin'," Sheriff Satterfield agreed readily. The rustling in the background had stopped while I spoke, so I had either imagined it, or the person who had been there had left. "In and out of jail his whole life. Beat his wife, beat his kids, beat the dog, fought, drank, and fornicated. And he was quite the bigot! Whoa! I remember once—long time ago now, before you young'uns were born—some black kids came into the Bog. Old Jim pulled out his shotgun and blasted 'em off his property."

"You're kidding!"

I heard bedsprings squeak as the sheriff settled himself more comfortably. "'Fraid not, darlin'. Filled their behinds full of buckshot, he did. Told me a man has the right to protect his property 'gainst vermin. Had me shakin' in my boots, I don't mind tellin' you."

"He must have been upset when he discovered that LaDonna's boyfriend was black." I kept my voice carefully neutral. The sheriff snorted.

"Upset? Hell! Fit to be tied, more like. Beat that poor girl to a jelly. Was a miracle she didn't lose the baby."

"Oh, my goodness!" I said. "He tried to make her miscarry?"

"Well, no." The sheriff sounded grudging. "I wouldn't go that far. Don't think he knew then she was in the

213

family way. Guess he was just tryin' to knock some sense into her, the only way he knew how."

"Did he ever meet the boyfriend, do you know? Either before or after Rafe was born?"

Sheriff Satterfield answered promptly, "Can't imagine he did, darlin'. Can't imagine the boy woulda survived the meetin'."

I nodded. "That's what I thought. You know, I don't remember Jim Collier. Whatever happened to him?"

"Lived another twelve years, then got hisself drunk one night and fell into the Duck."

The Duck River, the sheriff meant. Probably the little branch of it that ran through the Bog. I blinked. "He drowned?" It seemed a surprisingly gentle end for someone so vile. Not that drowning is a nice way to go, but I had expected something more violent, like a shooting or knifing or bludgeoning. "Accidentally?"

Sheriff Satterfield's voice was as carefully neutral as mine had been a few moments ago. "As far as we could prove. Though there were some said the boy helped."

I gulped. "Rafe? You're joking! He was only twelve!"

"Ain't no way to be sure, darlin'. Both he and LaDonna swore they'd been together all night and hadn't heard a sound, and there wasn't no way to prove different."

"Good Lord!"

"So we kept it quiet. Seemed better just to let sleeping dogs lie. Though I kept an extra-close eye on the boy after that."

I nodded. "I can see why you would. Well, thanks, sheriff. It's been . . . um . . . interesting."

"Any time, darlin'. Was that all you wanted to know?"

I said it was. "I mostly wanted to find out about LaDonna's boyfriend. If anyone had ever seen him, or knew anything about him, or about what happened to him."

"Sorry I can't be much help, darlin'. I never saw him nor heard speak of him much. Old Jim used ta get drunk sometimes and brag of how he'd shot the boy, but that was prob'ly just Jack Daniels talkin'."

"Unless one of those kids he blasted off his property was LaDonna's boyfriend?"

The sheriff thought for a moment before he said, "Prob'ly not. That happened before. When LaDonna was just a wee'un. Long before any of the rest of it."

"All right, then." I thanked him again and hung up. And thought to myself as I got ready for bed that if I had known who had been with the sheriff when I called, whoever had scurried out of there so rapidly when she heard that Todd was on his way back, I would have thanked her for her assistance. Her presence must have rattled the sheriff's brain sufficiently that he hadn't even had the wherewithal to tell me to stay away from Rafe, let alone to question why I was so interested in the events of so long ago.

114.

Every Saturday morning since I got my real estate license, I had gone down to the office to hang out for a few hours, answering phones and keeping my fingers crossed in the hope that someone would call who wanted to buy or sell something. Finding clients had so far proven to be a challenge, made worse by the fact that the entire real estate market was in a slump. After last week's fiasco, I had considered staying in bed this week—the last thing I wanted was for someone else to call me with another dead body—but when the rubber met the road, I ended up going to the office after all. Call it greed, or desperation, or whatever you want, but with both Brenda and Clarice gone, the chances of my finding a client were better than ever, and I wasn't about to let the opportunity pass me by. And before you judge me too severely, keep in mind that I was only about two months away from having my lights and water cut off for non-payment. Bradley's settlement had kept me afloat since the divorce, during the lean times when no one had bought much makeup, but with the start-up costs of becoming a realtor, I had exhausted most of my resources. I had to make a sale soon, or ask mother or Dix for help, and I wasn't looking forward to it.

Unfortunately, the office phones didn't ring that much on Saturday mornings. Home buyers are just as fond of sleeping in as the rest of us, and I'm sure they had better things to do between the sheets on a lazy weekend than worry about finding a realtor.

My own sheets have been empty—of anyone but me—since I left Bradley, and now I sat for a second and processed the thought that I could have asked Todd in last night. He hadn't hinted—was too much of a gentleman to hint—but he probably wouldn't have said no if I'd suggested it. He found me attractive—at least he said he did—and he was only human, after all.

I had never slept with Todd. When we'd dated back in high school, we had both had enough sense to know that it was a bad idea. Plus, like I mentioned before, we dated more because it made our parents happy than because Todd and I were all that much in love with one another. At least I hadn't been in love with him, although if he had truly married his ex-wife because he couldn't have me, I must have made more of an impression on him than I realized.

The idea of going to bed with him still didn't hold much appeal for me, though. He was good-looking enough, certainly, and had all the other attributes a girl should be looking for in a mate: good manners, a nice car, enough money to provide for one in the manner to which one was accustomed, antecedents that dated back to the War Between the States. There just wasn't any spark there. Plus, he'd probably expect me to want to marry him—a gentle-born Southern Belle doesn't sleep with a man she wouldn't want to marry—and I didn't. At least not right now. It was much safer just to continue to live vicariously through the last in a long line of panting heroines in genre fiction.

I sighed and turned my mind to business, which in this case was making sure that the phones were turned on and operational, and then sitting back and waiting for them to ring. For something to do, I pulled out *Tartan Tryst* again, and dove in. But for once, the perils of the heroine at the hands of the dark and dangerous highwayman failed to hold my attention. After a few minutes, I put the book down and decided to finish my search from the other night while I had the office to myself.

I wish I could tell you that I found a really spectacular clue, something that the police had overlooked, but I didn't find a blessed thing. I put Brenda's Stor-All key back in the drawer, after making sure I wiped any fingerprints off on the hem of my skirt, and that was pretty much the long and short of it. The 101 Potsdam Street file was nowhere in Brenda's office, or Clarice's and Heidi's shared office, or Tim's office, or on Brittany's desk, and if Clarice's special drawer had ever contained anything of interest, the police must have taken it. All that was there now was a half-empty package of Italian biscotti and a few magazines, an open box of tissues, and some other odds and ends. The only interesting thing was a romance novel of the bodice ripper variety, which gave me a guilty feeling—Clarice and I had had something in common after all, even if it was just a shared passion for Barbara Botticelli's rogue heroes!—but there was nothing anywhere that explained why she had done what she did.

If she had done it, that is, and hadn't been murdered, too. That explanation was looking a lot more likely, now that I was standing here. Everything about the office was a mute testament to Clarice's devotion to Brenda. A photograph of the two of them, lovingly framed, stood on the desk. All of Brenda's files were conscientiously labeled and filed in the numerous filing cabinets. Clarice's desk calendar kept meticulous track of all of Brenda's appointments. *Alexandra dentist 4:00 PM. Closing 1457 Carteret 11:00 AM. Conference Montgomery Bell Academy 2:30 re Austin. GNAR luncheon 11:30. P/u red suit from cleaners first!*

Clarice herself didn't appear to have had a life outside the office, for none of the notations applied to her. There was nothing written down for Thursday night, so either the appointment had been personal rather than business, or she just hadn't wanted a record of it. On a whim, I flipped back to the previous weekend, to see if Clarice had made a note of Brenda's appointment with Rafe, and maybe even of whom Brenda was taking with her. There was a notation that read, "7:30 101 Potsdam, R. Collier," plus a phone number. Rafe had said that their appointment was for eight, so either Brenda wanted to be early, to open the draperies and make sure things looked as good as they could, or he had lied. Or she had arranged to meet someone else there at seven thirty, killing two birds with one stone, as it were. I took hold of the desk phone and dialed the number.

A couple of rings went by, then a gruff male voice answered. "Car lot."

"Oh," I said. "Um . . . Rafe?"

The voice grunted a negative.

"Rafael Collier?"

"Sorry." He didn't sound sorry. He also didn't sound like Rafe, so I apologized and hung up, feeling stupid

The phone rang again before I had even gotten up from the desk. I picked it up, putting the perkiness back into my voice. "Good morning. Thank you for calling Walker Lamont Realty. Savannah Martin speaking. How may I help you?"

"Savannah Martin?" a male voice said. I rolled my eyes.

"Speak of the devil."

"That sounds promising." I could hear the grin in his voice, and ignored it.

"I want to talk to you."

"I figured."

"What do you mean, you figured? How did you . . . ? Oh, God." I resisted the impulse to knock my forehead against the desktop. It would rearrange my hair, and probably give me a bruise, too. "That *was* your number I called."

"As near as makes no difference. So what can I do for you, darlin'?"

"I want to talk to you," I repeated.

"Yeah, I got that. You wanna know what I found in Brenda Puckett's storage unit, right?"

"Among other things. And I don't want to do it over the phone. Especially not the office phone." I glanced over my shoulder. Nobody was there, but it didn't hurt to be careful.

"I hear McDonald's is having a sale on cheeseburgers."

I shuddered. "I think I'll pass, thank you."

"Fine. We can go someplace else. Be ready at six."

He hung up before I had a chance to tell him I didn't want to go to dinner with him. I also didn't want to wait until tonight to get answers to my questions. So, of course, I tried to call back, but this time there was no answer at all. Gritting my teeth, I added another item to the list of questions and gripes I had, and put it on the back burner until later.

There was one more thing I could do to track down the elusive paperwork for 101 Potsdam Street, and that was calling Detective Grimaldi. It had occurred to me that maybe the reason why the file wasn't here in the office was that the police had confiscated it. Since 101 Potsdam Street was where Brenda's murder had taken place, it made sense that the police would have wanted a look at the file. I dialed.

"Detective? This is Savannah Martin."

"Good morning, Ms. Martin," Tamara Grimaldi said. "What can I do for you?"

"I just wanted to ask a question. Do you by any chance have the paperwork that Brenda Puckett filled out for the sale of the house on Potsdam Street? I need to have a look at it, and I can't find it here in the office, so I thought maybe you had taken it."

I crossed my fingers, hoping that the intricacies of real estate were such that she wouldn't realize I had no business wanting to see the paperwork for someone else's listing.

Apparently she didn't, because she answered readily enough. "We did, yes. But as it wasn't pertinent to the murder—the papers themselves, I mean—we just made a copy and gave the originals back to Mr. Lamont."

"Oh," I said, looking around as if I was hoping to see the file waving at me from somewhere. "I can't find them." Walker might have the file in his office, but I wasn't about to look there. There are limits to my snoopiness, and digging through my boss's files is firmly on the other side of that line. Plus, he usually locked his door when he wasn't around, anyway.

The detective hesitated for a moment. "I can fax you a copy if you'd like."

"You can?"

"Sure. It was yours to begin with. No reason why you can't see it again. Maybe you'll notice something we didn't."

"Great," I said. "I'm at the office." I gave her the fax number. We hung up, and I went over to the fax machine to wait. It rang less than two minutes later, and the first page of a Walker Lamont Realty Exclusive Right to Sell Listing Contract approved by the Tennessee Association of Realtors started making its slow progress through the machine. I gathered all three pages and took them back to my desk, where I proceeded to look them over.

Five minutes later I was breathing hard and having a problem controlling my emotions. I had hoped that maybe Mrs. Jenkins had had an attorney-in-fact, someone who had been looking out for her interests and advising her on what to do, or even signing for her. If such was the case, there was no mention of it in the contract. Tondalia Jenkins had put her own shaky John Hancock to the fact that she was competent to make decisions and not under coercion when she agreed to let Brenda Puckett market and sell her house under an illegal net deal, which gave Mrs. Jenkins the first $100,000 from the sale, and Brenda everything else.

I should probably explain. In a regular right-to-sell or exclusive-agency sale, the listing broker receives a percentage of the sales price as compensation. It can be anywhere from 4 percent up to 12 percent, with the average around 6 or 8 percent. The broker then turns around and shares his or her proceeds with the selling broker, who is the broker representing the buyer. (Confusing, I know.) In a net listing, however, the owner receives a specified—net—amount from the sale, with the excess going to the broker. This is done instead of giving the broker a certain percentage of the sales price. The broker can offer the property for sale at any price he or she wants, and pocket the difference. In this case, Brenda had listed the property for five times what she owed Mrs. Jenkins. She stood to pocket four hundred grand, or would have, if she hadn't been dead.

Net listings are illegal in most states, Tennessee among them. The Real Estate Commission might have looked through their fingers with the dementia thing—all Brenda would have had to do was say that Mrs. Jenkins had acted perfectly lucid and sane at the time of their meeting, and she had had no idea that the woman suffered from Alzheimer's—but they wouldn't have let her get away with the net listing. Lucky for her that she was already dead, and beyond the reach of the long arm of the law.

At noon I gave up the vigil and went home. And not because I wanted to have five hours to primp for my date with Rafe. Every time I thought about it, I couldn't believe I had let him con me into going out with him. I'd never live it down. And with my recent run of luck, we were sure to meet someone I knew, who would tell everyone else where I'd been and with whom, and my family would have a collective heart attack before they had me committed and disowned.

All the same, I did get dressed up for dinner. Not in a sexy little black number, like I had for Todd, but in my most crisply sedate blouse, with French cuffs and a prim collar, and an equally sedate, mid-calf-length skirt. I pulled my hair back in a tight chignon, and even wore glasses instead of contacts. When I stepped back from the mirror, I looked like an old-fashioned school marm. Todd would have approved, but personally, I wasn't so pleased. It wasn't that I wanted Rafe to find me attractive—goodness, no!—but no woman likes to go out on the town looking less than her best. So with four minutes to go, I replaced the glasses with contacts and swiped some more color across my mouth. It was a poor effort, but better than nothing, and it took up all the time I had.

The downstairs buzzer sounded at six o'clock on the dot. I didn't bother answering it—he hadn't shown me the courtesy of allowing me to cancel, so I didn't feel I owed him any consideration in return—I just locked the door behind me and headed down the stairs to the first floor, where I was met, not by Rafe, but by a middle-aged African-American man with a military haircut. "You Miss Martin?" he asked. I nodded. "I'm your driver. Get in." He opened the door of a Lincoln Town Car double-parked at the curb.

I hesitated, and not only because his manners were atrocious. In mystery novels, the heroine always gets abducted when she gets into a cab she hasn't ordered herself. Then again, if Rafe had wanted to abduct me, he could have done it himself yesterday, or the day before, or the day before that. Plus—and the thought only now occurred to me—he might not have any vehicle other than that monstrous Harley-Davidson, and if so, it was really quite considerate of him to send a car instead of expecting me to ride pillion.

So I climbed into the Town Car and sat back against the leather upholstery, enjoying the feeling of being chauffeured and wondering where I'd end up for dinner.

"Where are we going?" I inquired when the car circumvented the downtown restaurant district and headed for the snobbier west side instead. A pair of flat, brown eyes, as expressive as pebbles, met mine in the mirror.

"Can't say."

"You mean you don't know?"

He shook his head. "I mean I can't say."

"You know, but you won't tell me? Why not?" I kept my eyes on him in the rearview mirror.

"Rafe told me, 'get the lady in the car and drive. No talkin', no detours, no answerin' questions. Just drive.'"

I arched my brows. "So you can't talk to me?"

"Nope. Sure don't wanna upset the man." He turned his attention back to driving. I leaned back, looking out of the window at the cars moving past and thinking dark thoughts.

When we turned into Murphy Avenue and I saw a familiar red, green, and white canopy up ahead, I knew where we were heading, and I admit it: I would almost have preferred McDonald's. Almost. Still, I made an effort to smile graciously when I approached the maitre d'. "Good evening. I'm meeting someone for dinner."

That distinguished gent inclined his gray head and murmured, "But, of course, signorina. I'm afraid the gentleman signorina was with yesterday has not arrived yet, but . . ."

"Never mind." I had spotted Rafe over in the corner, carrying on what looked like a flirtation with all three women at an adjoining table. "I see him."

I left the maitre d' in the dust and headed in that direction.

I got a few glances from male patrons as I walked through the restaurant tonight too, but none from Rafe, who was much too busy to notice my approach. The three women were keeping him occupied, and he didn't seem to mind one bit. Not very flattering, I must say. It wasn't until I was standing across from him that he looked up and saw me. I could see his eyes light with amusement when he took in my primly buttoned blouse and tight chignon, but he didn't comment, just grinned as he got up to pull out the chair for me.

He had made an effort to clean up for the occasion himself, which was considerate of him. (Of course, the maitre d' would have refused him admittance had he been dressed the way he usually was.) Tonight's dark slacks and plain, button-down shirt wouldn't win any awards for sartorial elegance, but the women at the next table didn't seem to find any fault with him. The blue shirt made the most of his dusky complexion and dark eyes, and when he walked back around the table, I couldn't help but notice that the slacks set off his posterior very nicely.

Naturally I didn't comment. Instead, I folded my hands demurely in my lap and waited until he was seated again before I smiled sweetly. "It was nice of you to send a car for me. I wasn't looking forward to riding on the back of the bike."

"I figured."

"Although, if you had told me where we were going, I could have met you here."

"Stood me up, you mean."

"No, just . . ." He didn't say anything, but a grin was tugging at his mouth. "Oh, all right," I admitted. "I wouldn't have stood you up—I have better manners than that—but if you had given me the opportunity to cancel, I would have."

"Why d'you think I didn't answer the phone all afternoon? Drink?"

"I beg your pardon?" He nodded toward the waiter, hovering next to the table. "Oh. Yes. White wine, please."

"And you, sir?" The waiter turned to Rafe. The "sir" seemed to be an afterthought, but if Rafe noticed, he didn't let on.

"Just a beer."

The waiter sniffed. "We carry a large selection of imported beer, sir."

"I ain't all that fancy. How about a Bud?"

Fidelio's could oblige with a selection of domestic beers as well, and in no time at all, Rafe was drinking a Budweiser while I was nursing a glass of chilled white wine. The waiter had brought another glass, so cold frost was forming on it, but Rafe had indicated that he preferred the bottle. The waiter had removed the glass with an eloquent sniff. Now Rafe leaned across the table and knocked his bottle against my glass. "Cheers." He poured about half the contents down his throat.

"If you keep drinking like that," I commented, "I'll know all your secrets before the evening is over."

He grinned. "Don't count your chickens, darlin'."

I shrugged and changed the subject. There's more than one way to skin a cat. "That friend of yours you sent to pick me up seems nice. How long have you known him?"

He looked at me for a moment, his dark eyes watchful. Eventually, he seemed to decide that it wouldn't do any harm to answer. "Going on ten years."

"Were you in prison together?" I asked. Maybe the man's loyalty dated back to some occasion when Rafe had stood up against the prison bullies for him or something. Not that he had looked like he would need help taking care of himself. There had been absolutely nothing servile about him, hired hand, or no. In fact, he was the least-polite chauffeur I'd ever encountered. Rafe shook his head in response to my question. "So you met him after you got out? Do you work together?"

"In a manner of speaking."

"At the . . . um . . . car lot?"

He smiled. "The car lot's what you might call a sideline."

"So you're not a used car salesman?"

"God forbid. No, darlin'. I don't sell cars. Drive 'em sometimes, but I don't sell 'em."

"So you're a . . . chauffeur, too?"

My questioning seemed to amuse him, because he laughed. "Not the way you mean."

"Truck driver?"

"Not really."

"Mover? Pilot? Maybe you freelance as a NASCAR driver?"

"Haven't tackled that one yet. No. Might be fun, though." He took another swallow of beer before leaning back and folding his arms across his chest. I conceded defeat with a sigh. He wasn't going to tell me what he did for a living, so I might as well ask him something there was a chance he'd answer.

"Tell me about Brenda's storage unit."

"Ain't much to tell. I was looking for something specific, so I didn't take no notice of nothing else. What were you wanting to know?"

"What you were looking for, for a start. And whether you found it."

He didn't answer for a few moments, just watched me in silence. I was getting ready to squirm when he finally spoke. "I was looking for the paperwork for that house on Potsdam."

"And did you find it?"

He looked away, over to the next table where the three women were sitting. One of them caught his eye and smiled. He lifted one corner of his mouth in return and turned back to me. "Yeah."

"So you know that Brenda Puckett offered Mrs. Jenkins a measly fifth of what she hoped to sell the property for." He nodded. "Did you know that that kind of contract stipulation is illegal in Tennessee?"

He shook his head. "But I didn't have to know that to know it's wrong."

"Good point."

"Did *you* know that the hundred grand is already on deposit with the Milton House?"

It was my turn to shake my head. "How did you find that out? It wasn't in the contract. Not the part I saw, anyway."

"I asked," Rafe said.

"And they told you? Oh, wait. That's right. There's not a nurse alive who can say no to you."

He grinned and toasted me with the beer bottle.

While we had been bantering, the waiter had come back to take our dinner order. I ordered without consulting the menu—Chicken Marsala, the same thing I had had the night before—and waited for Rafe.

"I don't suppose you got cheeseburgers?" The waiter just stared at him, stonily, down the length of his nose. "Guess not. I'll have what she's having." He handed the waiter his menu.

"It won't go well with the beer," I warned. The waiter sniffed. Rafe shrugged. The waiter took the menus and disappeared, his back radiating disapproval. I turned back to Rafe. "They do steaks, I think. You can call him back and . . ."

"Chicken's fine."

"Oh." I bit my lip. "Okay, then. If you're sure."

He grinned. "I ate courtesy of Riverbend Penitentiary for two years, darlin'. Chicken Marsala and beer ain't the worst meal I've ever had."

"Maybe not," I admitted, "but if you're paying these kinds of prices for dinner, you may as well get something you enjoy."

"You afraid you're cleaning out my food budget for the week? Don't worry. I can afford to pay for dinner and still eat tomorrow."

"Good for you," I said, trying not to think about the state of my own checking account and the refrigerator at home. "So you went to Brenda's storage unit to look at the contract for 101 Potsdam Street?" He shrugged. "Or to steal it?" He smirked. "Why would you do something like that?"

He didn't answer, just kept his eyes on the now-empty beer bottle he was turning over in his hands. I looked at him, at the downturned eyes and sweep of lashes across his cheeks, and decided to take a chance on expressing an idea I'd been toying with for a couple of days. The worst thing that would happen was that he'd laugh at me, and even if he did, I'd survive. After all, it wasn't like I cared what Rafe Collier thought of me.

"Tondalia Jenkins really is your grandmother, isn't she?"

He looked up abruptly, and for just a second I saw a genuine emotion in his eyes. Surprise, and something deeper. Then it was replaced with amusement. "Quite the girl-detective, ain't you? How'd you figure that out?"

"Process of elimination," I said modestly. "You're interested in the house, but there's nothing in it worth stealing, and you can't afford to buy it. You don't have the resources in hand, and without a steady job, you won't be able to get a loan."

His eyes narrowed. "How d'you know anything about my resources?"

I did a mental eye roll. He didn't object to the suggestion that he would have stolen things had there been any to steal, but he didn't like the idea that I knew about his financial status. "Todd did a background check on you."

He sat up straight so fast that the beer bottle wobbled. "You had Satterfield look into me? Why?"

"I didn't ask him to," I said. "He did it all on his own. He was worried about me being involved with you."

Rafe leaned back in the chair again, relaxing once more. "I should be so lucky. So what did Satterfield come up with? Other than that I'm broke and unemployed?"

"Not much," I admitted. Rafe smirked, but the smirk faded as I went on to enumerate the things Todd's non-invasive search had found. (So much for Todd's assertion that the search hadn't gone deep.) "You've never been married. You have no children, or at least none you've acknowledged. You don't own a house. You don't borrow money. You file taxes, but you don't have the kind of income Todd thinks is necessary."

"But what does he know?" Rafe murmured. I ignored him.

"And although you haven't been arrested again since you got out of prison, you've been suspected of a fair number of crimes and interviewed in connection with several of them."

"Like Brenda Puckett's murder."

I nodded. "Which brings me back to your interest in the house on Potsdam. And the Jenkinses. Tyrell was your father and Tondalia is your grandmother."

He arched a brow. "What if she is? Ain't no crime for a man to look for his family."

"Of course not. And I'm glad you found her. Especially now that your mother has passed on."

I planned to add something else, but before I could, the waiter arrived. He placed a steaming plate of Chicken Marsala in front of each of us. I waited while Rafe cut a piece of chicken and put it in his mouth. Silence reigned while he chewed.

"So what do you think?" I asked.

He shrugged. "It ain't a cheeseburger, but I guess it'll do."

"It will help you sustain life, anyway." I added, lifting my own utensils, "Just out of curiosity, how did you find Mrs. Jenkins? After all this time? Or did you always know who she was?"

Rafe shook his head. "My ma never talked about my daddy, and if I asked questions, old Jim would hit me, and her, too, if she answered. I learned real fast to keep my mouth shut."

I nodded. I could imagine.

Rafe continued, "After he died, I tried asking my ma again, but all she said was that my daddy was dead, too. Wasn't till last week, when I was clearing out all her stuff, that I found a newspaper notice about some kid named Tyrell Jenkins. She'd written a date on it, a couple months before I was born."

"What made you think it had anything to do with you?" I nibbled delicately on another piece of chicken. Rafe answered readily enough.

"The date. And that she kept it for thirty years. And . . . here, I'll show you."

He put down knife and fork and fished in the pocket of the black leather jacket hanging over the back of his chair. Out came a wallet, and out of that a creased, yellowed piece of newsprint which he handed across the table to me. It was brittle, and felt fragile in my hands. I unfolded it carefully, and caught my breath when I saw what it contained. "My goodness. No wonder Mrs. Jenkins thought you were Tyrell."

According to LaDonna Collier's childlike script, the clipping had come from the *Tennessean*, three years before I was born. A brief paragraph stated bluntly that Tyrell Jenkins, eighteen, had been shot to death by an unknown assailant outside his home on Potsdam Street. Beside the text was a grainy, black and white photograph of a smiling teenager. A yearbook photo, maybe; Tyrell was wearing shirt and tie, and had the fixed look of someone posing. The resemblance to Rafe was uncanny. Tyrell was darker skinned and blunter featured, with an afro that would have made the Supremes envious, but the eyes were the same, fringed by the same long, thick lashes, and he had the same hairline and the same bright grin. Rafe's face was harder and more sculpted these days, but I could remember when he looked a lot like this. I looked from father to son a couple of times before I handed the clipping back. "That's pretty conclusive. Almost as good as a note saying, 'this was your father.'"

Rafe folded the clipping and tucked it back in his wallet, next to—I couldn't help noticing—a thick stack of bills. "That's what I thought. It even talks about the street. All I had to do was check the tax assessor's website for the right address. When I drove up to it, I saw it was empty and for sale, so I called Miz Puckett and asked to look at it. I hoped maybe she'd tell me where the rest of the family was."

"And did she?" I asked innocently. He squinted at me.

"On the phone, you mean? No, darlin', she didn't." And then his voice changed. "Oh, I get it. Nice try."

I shrugged. "I thought it couldn't hurt to ask. Just in case."

"Can't blame a girl for trying." He cut another piece of chicken and chewed on it before he added, "I thought you said Clarice killed Brenda. Why're you trying to pin it on me?"

"I'm not. Not really. It just makes for a nice, neat solution. If you knew beforehand that Brenda had cheated your grandmother out of her house—and you out of your inheritance—and you made an appointment to talk to her about it, and she refused to listen and told you that hell would freeze over before she released Mrs. Jenkins from the contract . . ."

"I might have got so angry I killed the old broad?" He shrugged. "I guess I might."

I squinted. "Really?"

"No, darlin'. Not really. Not when I coulda just broken into her office and taken all the copies of the contract. No contract, no deal."

"It's not as easy to break into our office as into the storage unit."

He didn't answer, but I could tell from his expression that he didn't think he'd have much of a problem. I added, "So what are you going to do now?"

"Don't know that there's much I can do. I ain't got no legal standing, remember. I can't prove who I am. Tyrell's name ain't on my birth certificate, and my ma ain't alive to say it oughta be. And Mrs. Jenkins—my grandma—ain't in any kind of condition to know who I am one way or the other."

"They can do paternity testing for babies these days. Maybe they can test your DNA against Mrs. Jenkins's, and tell whether you're related. Heck, if they could prove that Thomas Jefferson slept with Sally Hemings two hundred years ago, they ought to be able to do something like that!"

Rafe didn't answer, just shrugged. I hesitated for a moment before I added, "My brother Dix—do you remember Dix? He was a year behind you in high school—Dix is an attorney. He and his partners—my sister Catherine and her husband—specialize in family law. He might have some ideas. I could ask him, if you'd like."

He shrugged. "Knock yourself out. Though maybe you'd better not tell him who you're asking for. I don't think he'd want you doing me any favors."

Knowing Dix, he had a point, but before I had time to say anything, I was interrupted.

"Why, Savannah!" a delighted voice behind me said, "I thought that was you!"

15.

Rafe looked past me and smiled. I fixed a bright expression to my own face before I turned around. This was a guy who took no prisoners, and I didn't want to appear to have any chinks in my armor. He'd stick it to me right through each and every one. "Hi, Tim. Fancy meeting you here."

Tim smiled. He must be going somewhere else later, because he was dressed for the evening in a white poet shirt, dripping with ruffles and open halfway down his smooth chest, tucked into a pair of black leather pants that fit his narrow hips like plastic wrap. Rafe's T-shirts had nothing on Tim's pants (although Rafe's shirts were a lot more entertaining to watch, at least for a straight female).

Tim glanced from me to Rafe and back with a bright, speculative look in his eyes. "Out for a romantic tête-à-tête, kids?"

Rafe grinned and leaned back on his chair, causing the thin fabric of his shirt to pull tight across shoulders and chest. I could see the outline of the snake through the left sleeve. Tim's eyes lingered. "Who's your friend, darling?" The question was addressed to me, though his eyes were still on Rafe. I opened my mouth to perform the introductions, although what I really wanted to do was tell Tim to mind his own business. Rafe beat me to it. (The introduction, I mean; not telling Tim to leave.)

"Rafael Collier. Good to meet you." He extended a hand across the table. Tim's manicured digits disappeared into it.

"Timothy Briggs. My, what nice, strong hands you have!"

I rolled my eyes. "Don't you have somewhere to be, Tim? Someone to meet, maybe?"

Tim smiled at me. "Now, now. Don't be catty, darling. I'm just looking." He proceeded to do just that, since Rafe obviously wasn't going to do anything to stop him.

"Horrible what happened to Clarice," I said.

Tim nodded distractedly.

"Coming right on the heels of Brenda's murder like that, it kind of makes you wonder who will be next."

Tim shuddered theatrically, still without looking at me.

"By the way, I hear you stopped by Brenda's storage unit the Monday after the murder. Do you mind if I ask you what you were doing there?"

That did it. Tim tore his eyes away from Rafe. (There's no other word for it.) "I don't know what you're talking about, darling."

"The receptionist said you'd been there," I said. Tim shrugged elegantly.

"Sorry, darling. What would I be doing in Brenda's storage unit?"

"Picking up the contract for 101 Potsdam Street? Because you assumed Walker would give the listing to you?"

I saw something flash in Tim's eyes—anger, maybe, at being passed over, or something more sinister, if my questions were getting to him—but it was gone a second later. "The receptionist must have been mistaken. I haven't been to Brenda's storage unit in months."

"How about Clarice's storage unit?"

"I didn't even know she had one," Tim said easily. "In case it escaped your attention, Clarice and I weren't on the best of terms."

"You must be glad that she's gone, then."

Tim smiled tightly. "I won't tell you I'm not, darling. Although I certainly didn't plan for it to happen like this."

I opened my eyes wide. "You mean you had something to do with it?"

He shook his head, causing the pale blond hair to flop over his forehead. "Oh, no. No, no. I didn't have anything to do with her death. Nothing at all. I just wanted her to leave the company now that Brenda was gone. That's all."

"I see," I said. "The receptionist probably just made a mistake, then."

Tim nodded. "If I remember correctly from the last time I was there, she's quite old. She probably saw someone else blonde and terribly good-looking and thought it was me." He winked at Rafe, who grinned back. I smiled sweetly.

"Thanks, Tim. Say goodnight."

Tim made a moue. "If you're going to be that way." He offered Rafe a limp hand and another melting smile. "So very nice to meet you, Rafael." From the position of the hand, one might almost assume he wanted Rafe to kiss it.

Rafe gave it a squeeze. "Same here, Tim. Enjoy your dinner."

Tim swung around on his heel and, facing me, mimed feeling dizzy and fanning himself vigorously with his hand to show me just how stupendously hot he thought Rafe was. I smiled politely and managed to hold my tongue until he had swayed off to a table on the other side of the restaurant, romantically situated between a palm tree and a tinkling fountain. Somebody was waiting for him there, but with the tree blocking my view, I couldn't see anything beyond a charcoal gray sleeve. I turned back to Rafe.

"Sorry about that."

Rafe shrugged. "Can't fault a man for looking."

"I can," I said. He grinned.

"Is that why you're wearing those clothes? So I wouldn't look?"

I opened my mouth, but before I could deny that such a thought had ever crossed my mind, the waiter appeared. He whisked Rafe's plate away. I gave him mine, too. I'd eaten as much as I decently could without looking like a glutton.

"Would sir and madam like some dessert?"

He looked from one to the other of us. Rafe turned to me, questioningly. I shook my head. "None for me, thanks. Though you may want to try the chocolate raspberry cheesecake. Todd had it yesterday, and it looked good."

He nodded. "One of them, then."

I added, "And some coffee, please. Black."

The waiter took himself and our used plates away, and Rafe returned his attention to me. An arched brow invited me to pick up where I'd left off. I said, reluctantly, "As a matter of fact, Todd asked me not to wear anything revealing."

"You told him about tonight? Afraid you wouldn't make it back home again?"

I shook my head. "It was yesterday. Last night, after you left. He said he didn't like the way you looked at me, and would I please not wear anything provocative in front of you again."

"You think he'd approve of that getup?" His eyes wandered over me, what he could see above the table.

"It's not provocative," I said. He grinned.

"That depends, darlin'."

"On what?" What was provocative about a long-sleeved, primly buttoned blouse and a chignon so severe my eyebrows were elevated, for goodness' sake?

"I s'pose on what's underneath. And what it'd take for someone to get to it."

He smiled, but the eyes that met mine were intent. I opened my mouth, but found I had nothing to say. Rafe didn't speak, either. Leisurely, his gaze snagged on my lips for a moment before moving south. As the seconds ticked by, the curve of his mouth softened and his eyes turned hot. I had a hard time catching my breath. I felt the way you do when you jump into cool lake water and all the air gets slammed out of your lungs. I couldn't breathe, I couldn't think, and for the life of me, I couldn't look away. The sounds around me receded, until all I could hear was a faint buzzing, as if from a bumblebee trapped in a jam jar. The drumming of my own heartbeat sounded uncomfortably loud in my ears.

The return of the waiter broke the spell, and I accepted my cup of coffee with hands that weren't entirely steady. My voice wasn't, either. "I don't know why I ordered this. Could I have a glass of water, please? With ice?"

The waiter didn't react, but, of course, Rafe did. "Have the cheesecake, too, darlin'. You look hungry."

A choking noise came from the table next to us, and one of the women buried her face in her napkin. I opened my mouth to protest, but the waiter was already lowering the plate, and I didn't want to argue in front of him. I waited until he was out of earshot before I hissed, "I told you I didn't want any dessert."

"That was before," Rafe said.

"Before what?"

"Before I got you so hot and bothered you ordered ice water to cool down."

"I am not hot and bothered!" I denied. "And I don't want any cheesecake." I pushed the plate away. For what might have been the first time in my life, cheesecake held absolutely no appeal for me. As a matter of fact, I felt sick. I got to my feet, a little unsteadily. "I . . . um . . . need to powder my nose. Excuse me."

He nodded cordially.

I walked through the restaurant with my head held high, concentrating on putting one foot in front of the other, and without actually seeing where I was going. It was a miracle I didn't knock one of the waiters over or walk right into some happy couple celebrating their anniversary. When I got to the ladies' room, I wasted no time in splashing my face and neck with cold water, devoutly thankful for waterproof makeup.

I was still standing there, dripping, looking at my pale face in the mirror and trying to make sense of what had just happened when someone knocked on the door. It's not common practice to knock on ladies' room doors, so I went to see who it was. I guess I expected Rafe, although I should have known better; he wouldn't have bothered knocking. When I opened the door, I saw none other than my boss, Walker Lamont.

"Oh, God!" I blurted. "What are you doing here?"

He didn't respond to my tone, which was nice of him. Instead he took the question at face value, and gave me a few seconds to pull myself together. "The same as you. Having dinner with a friend. Are you all right, Savannah?" He looked me over, concern in his eyes. I nodded.

"I'm fine, thank you. I was just feeling woozy for a moment. Too much wine, I guess."

The single glass of Sauvignon Blanc wouldn't have affected a child, but Walker didn't know that. He didn't look as if he believed me, though, although he was too polite to say so. Tim would have commented. My mouth made the connection before my brain had caught up. "Are you and Tim . . . um . . . ?"

"We're having dinner. And discussing some business matters." His tone was bland.

"Oh," I said. Walker nodded.

"Tim tells me that you're here with Mr. Collier."

It was my turn to nod, a little nervously. "That's not a problem, is it? I mean, is there a reason why I shouldn't have dinner with him? Other than that my mother would ground me for life and all my friends would think I had completely lost my mind, that is? It's not like I'm actually involved with him, you know. It's just dinner . . ."

"You don't have to explain your personal life to me, Savannah," Walker said.

"I don't want you to misunderstand, though, and think there's something going on between us when there isn't. I'm sure there's some kind of rule about getting involved with clients. See, there's been a . . . um . . . development in the case."

Walker's eyes narrowed. "What sort of development?"

"Well . . ." I hesitated, "it's complicated. And kind of personal, too. Although you *are* my boss, and the listing for 101 Potsdam is technically yours, so I guess it's all right to tell you."

Walker was looking politely inquiring and just a little wary. I did my best to pull myself together and condense the story into a few salient sentences. "See, Rafe Collier is actually the grandson of the woman who owns . . . um . . . *owned* the house on Potsdam Street. His mother died recently, and he never knew his father . . . anyway, it's a long story. Did you know that the listing agreement is for a net deal?"

"I discovered that fact when I took over the listing after Brenda's death," Walker said tightly. "How did you find out?"

"I asked Detective Grimaldi if she had a copy, and she faxed it to me. This morning." Walker's demeanor was making me nervous, and I started babbling, explaining my reasoning. "See, Alexandra Puckett told me that Brenda had met with someone at Beckett's Bar to handle the details of the listing." The guy that Alexandra thought had something to do with the medical field was probably from the Milton House, there to accept his cash.

"Alexandra said that her mother had a habit of doing that when something wasn't right about a listing. So I went to the office to look for it, but then Clarice showed up before I could find it. And I went to Brenda's storage unit, but it wasn't there either. I knew that the police had been there, though, so I called and asked if they had a copy I could see."

"Very industrious of you," Walker said. I shrugged modestly. "So the detective faxed you a copy of the listing?"

I nodded. "Rafe told me that Mrs. Jenkins's share, the hundred grand, is already on deposit with the nursing home where she lives. He's obviously not happy about the fact that Brenda took advantage of his grandmother."

Walker nodded. He looked pale, but that might have been just the glaring light in the bathroom. "What is he planning to do?"

"He isn't sure. He doesn't have the cash to buy the house back, and I doubt the board of directors at the Milton House would be willing to part with the money they were given. If there's no other way to get the house back, I suppose he might sue."

Which would open up a huge can of worms, and involve every single one of us. Every transaction Brenda had ever taken part in would be dug up and scrutinized. Walker would lose his spot on the Real Estate Commission. The agency would go belly-up. I'd have to go back to the makeup counter, and the whole story about Tyrell and LaDonna would come out. Brenda's reputation would take a further hit, and Alexandra and Austin would grow up with a cloud hanging over them.

"Would you do me a favor, Savannah?" Walker's question brought me back to earth, and I nodded. "I have reasons for wanting this kept as quiet as possible. If I can get the situation resolved without any money changing hands, do you suppose your friend might be amenable to that?"

I blinked. Rafe didn't strike me as the type who'd accept charity, but it might depend on the situation. "It couldn't hurt to ask, I suppose."

"Would you mind checking with him, then? Seeing as the two of you are so close?" His voice and face were bland, and it was probably just my imagination that supplied the sarcasm.

"I don't know about that, but I'll float the idea by him. And now I guess I'd better get back out there, before he comes looking for me." Something I definitely didn't want. Especially in the semi-seclusion of the ladies' room.

Walker drew his perfectly groomed brows together in a frown. "He isn't giving you a hard time, is he?"

"No more than usual," I said. "Don't worry, I can handle him."

Walker smiled approvingly. I tried to look confident, although in my heart of hearts I knew that my last statement was—pardon the language—crap, and that the only hope I had of *handling* Rafe Collier was if he allowed himself to be handled.

When I got back, he was making idle conversation with the three women at the next table. The cheesecake he had insisted on giving me was neatly packaged in a Styrofoam to-go box, and my coffee and water were shimmering in the candlelight. The sight of it all—especially Rafe—made my stomach twist unpleasantly, and rather than sit down, I placed a steadying hand on the back of my chair. "I'd like to leave now, if that's okay with you."

"Sure." He rose with alacrity and tossed a couple of bills on the table. They were more than adequate to cover the tab and the tip.

"I didn't mean that *you* had to leave. Just that *I* wanted to."

"What am I gonna do here by myself?"

"You could join them." I looked pointedly at the next table, where all three women were watching us—him—expectantly. He grinned.

"You ain't jealous, are you, darlin'?"

"You wish," I said. The grin widened.

"You bet. So I think I'll just take you home. Just in case you feel like giving me a kiss when I drop you off."

As I turned to leave, one of the women at the next table snagged my sleeve. "If you don't want him, sister, I'll be happy to take him off your hands." She winked at Rafe.

"Be my guest," I said. "If you want him, you can have him, with my blessing."

Rafe grinned, but refrained from pointing out that he wasn't actually mine to give. "She don't mean it," he said instead, putting a friendly arm around my shoulders and squeezing.

"Sure I do," I said—rather, tried to say—but the words wouldn't come. Rafe nodded politely to the threesome.

"Nice to meet you lovely ladies. Y'all have a good evening."

"You, too," all three women chorused. As for the one who had spoken earlier with an envious look, little did she suspect that I intended to ditch him just as soon as I decently could.

That proved to be a more difficult task than I had expected. My first attempt, on the sidewalk outside the restaurant, didn't come off at all. "I'm not really dressed for a ride on the back of the motorcycle, so why don't I just get the valet to order me a cab?"

He smirked. "Nice try, but I ain't sending you home by yourself."

"But there's no sense in you coming all the way back with me when you could just go home yourself."

"Sorry, darlin', but you ain't getting rid of me that easy. I got you here, and I'm taking you home."

"But I can't ride on the back of the motorcycle. Not in this skirt."

Rafe glanced down at it, and back up to my face. There was a wicked glint in his eyes. I took a step back, shaking my head. "Oh, no. I'm not taking it off. Nor hiking it up to my hips, either."

He grinned. "Relax, darlin'. You can keep your clothes on. For now. I had Wendell leave the Town Car in the lot down the street. Come on." He put a hand against my back to steer me down the sidewalk. I let him do it, even if it took everything I had not to flinch from the touch.

Neither of us said much on the ride back to my apartment. I don't know what Rafe was thinking, but personally, I was planning what to say when we got there, and how I would handle the various scenarios that might present themselves. My first choice would be to simply say goodnight in the car outside the gate. Failing that, I'd say goodnight outside the door, without unlocking it. If he absolutely insisted on coming in—and I knew I couldn't stop him if he did—I'd let him go in first and make sure he didn't get between me and the door. If he did . . . But I'd deal with that situation if I got to it. Which I wouldn't. Because I'd simply say goodnight in the car outside the gate; it was that simple.

"I'll walk you up." He had the engine shut off and his door open before I even realized we'd pulled up to the curb.

"You don't have to . . ." I began, but it was too late; he was already out and coming around to open my door. "Really, I don't mind going up by myself."

"That's all right. I don't mind, either." He extended a hand and hauled me out of the car.

Scratch Plan A. I let him walk me up the stairs to the second floor and tried again. I had barely managed to turn to him and open my mouth when he was already talking. "Keys?"

"Wha . . . what?" I stammered. He grinned.

"What if you can't get in? Let me see your keys."

I dug the keychain out of my handbag and held it up. He arched an eyebrow and nodded to the lock. Scratch Plan B, too. I sighed and unlocked the door. "Happy now? You've walked me to the door and I can get in."

His eyes crinkled. "Ain't you gonna ask me in for a nightcap?"

"I don't think that would be a good idea," I said primly.

"Afraid you won't be able to keep your hands off me?"

"In your dreams," I said.

He smiled, but didn't speak. It wasn't necessary. I didn't speak, either, because I wasn't sure what to say. The idea that I was starring in Rafael Collier's pornographic daydreams was more than a little disturbing.

As I stood there, dumbly, his eyes dropped from my eyes to my mouth, and I felt a stab of abject panic. God, he wasn't going to kiss me, was he?

It looked like he was. His eyes flicked back to mine— deep and dark; the kind of eyes a girl could drown in if she wasn't careful—and he leaned closer. I could feel my own eyes go out of focus, and I thought I was going to pass out from the sheer terror of it.

He grinned and dropped a kiss, not on my mouth, but on my forehead. His voice was amused. "You'd think I was Jack the Ripper. You can let go now, darlin'."

I blinked and started breathing again. "Huh?"

"My jacket. You can let go."

"Oh." I realized I was clutching the soft leather with both hands and moved back as if I had burned myself. He laughed.

"Makes you wonder what'd happen if I got you into bed."

"Don't worry about it," I managed, "because that will never happen."

"You sure about that, darlin'?"

I nodded. I was positive. If the thought of him kissing me scared me so much I almost passed out, there was no way I'd even entertain the idea of him taking me to bed. In fact, from here on out, I was more determined than ever to have absolutely nothing at all to do with him.

16.

My cell phone rang, and I excused myself with a cowardly feeling of having just been saved by the bell. "I'd better get this. Just in case it's . . . um . . . a client or something."

Yeah, right. Fat chance of that.

Rafe nodded politely. I dug in my handbag and pulled the phone out while he turned his back and wandered a few steps. In the opposite direction of the stairs. He obviously wasn't finished with his agenda for the evening. I might yet get that kiss I didn't want.

I put the phone to my ear. "This is Savannah."

Silence, and then a dejected voice said, "It's me."

"Who?"

"Me. You know . . ."

"Alexandra?"

She sniffed. "Yeah."

"What's the matter?"

Sniff. "I need a ride." She sounded pitiful.

"What about your dad?"

Her voice rose. "I can't call him! He'll kill me. He thinks I'm staying over with my friend Lynn. Plus Maybelle's probably there, and she'll treat me like I'm five years old. Please, Savannah!"

I sighed. "Where are you?"

"Maurice's house. On Reinhardt. Loud music. Lots of cars. I don't remember the number."

"I'll find it," I said. "I'll be there in fifteen minutes. Just try to stay safe." I turned the phone off again. Rafe had turned around and was looking at me, hands in his pockets.

"Problem?"

"A girl I know. Alexandra Puckett, Brenda's daughter."

"The one in the black dress at the funeral? Fancy hairdo? Looked about twenty-two?"

"She's actually just sixteen," I said. "Her boyfriend lives on Reinhardt, and apparently something happened. She wants a ride."

"I'll drive you."

"That's not necessary."

"Yeah, it is."

"No, really. I'm just going to go get her and take her home."

"That's what you think." He didn't waste any more time arguing, just headed for the stairs. I didn't have any choice but to follow.

Ten minutes later (traffic being sparse and Rafe being a less-cautious driver than I), we pulled into Reinhardt Street. By now, I was thankful I wasn't alone. Reinhardt is in the same area as Potsdam, but appeared even more alien, especially after dark. It was full of two-story townhouse duplexes and a few small 1950s brick ranchers, all of them with security-bars across the windows and iron security doors. There were no streetlights; or rather, they were there, but unlit. Some of the local kids may have shot out the bulbs, or maybe Metro had given up and stopped turning them on. Most of the houses were dark, too, with an occasional blue flicker of a television here and there, behind tightly closed curtains. There was no sign of Alexandra.

"Over there." I pointed to a townhouse about two-thirds of the way down the street. The lights were on, spilling out onto the dead grass in the tiny front yard, and rap music was thumping. "She said there was loud music and lots of cars."

Rafe drove down to the end of the cul-de-sac and turned around before he slid to a stop at the curb on the other side of the street. I thought about asking why, but then I decided against it. If he thought we might need to make a quick getaway, I'd just as soon not know. Instead I opened the door and swung my legs out. "I'll just be a minute."

He leaned across the gearshift and grabbed my shoulder. "What the hell do you think you're doing?"

I gestured. "I'm going to get Alexandra."

"Like hell you are." He opened his own door and came around the car. "Stay here. I'll get her."

"She's my responsibility."

"No, she ain't. She came here on her own."

"She called me for help."

"That don't make her your responsibility."

"But I promised!"

"I ain't saying we should leave without her, darlin'. Just that I've got a better chance of walking away with her than you do."

"But . . ."

He put both hands on the roof of the car and leaned down until his nose was less than three inches from mine. "Look," he said, "I've got plans for you. And I don't want nobody getting in ahead of me. So stay!" He pushed off from the car.

"I'm not a dog!" I yelled after him. (Plans? Oh, God!)

He tossed me a grin over his shoulder. "Just do it. I'll be back."

He disappeared across the street. I tucked my legs back into the car and closed the door. For good measure, I locked it, too. And at least partially, I put that barrier between myself and Rafe. At the moment, he scared me more than whatever else was out there. I'd have to unlock the doors when he came back, but for the time being, I felt better putting something between us.

All right, so I know this wasn't the first time he had made some off-handed, flirtatious remark about taking me to bed. The implication had been there all along, if not in words, then in his demeanor. But this was the first time he had gone beyond the joke to tell me that he planned to do something about it. And whereas the joke was scary enough, the thought that he might actually act on it at some point was terrifying.

Ever since separating from Bradley, I had kept myself to myself. I had gone out on a date occasionally, like with Todd or for that matter with Rafe himself, but it had never progressed beyond a goodnight kiss outside the door. I had never wanted it to. Mother brought me up to believe that a man isn't going to buy what he can get for free, and that a proposal is the pot of gold at the end of the rainbow. Add to that Bradley's assertion that I was frigid and the fact that I had never enjoyed our sex life, and it won't surprise you that I hadn't felt the need to hop in the sack with anyone since I got divorced. Sex is totally overrated, if you ask me, and I didn't miss it at all. I was certainly not going to ruin my reputation by jumping into bed with Rafael Collier. The thought was, if not actually abhorrent, at least disturbing. Unsettling. Terrifying.

I was so busy with my own scattered thoughts that I neglected to keep an eye on the house and what might be happening there. The music was thumping so loudly there was no way I could have heard voices even if they had been screaming at the top of their lungs, but I believe I would have heard gunshots. I didn't, so I assumed there were none. Whatever had happened to upset Alexandra, it didn't seem as if Maurice was going to put up a fight to keep her.

There was a peremptory rap on the window, and I jumped. Rafe had Alexandra by the arm, and was making motions for me to unlock the doors. I did. "Sorry. I forgot I locked up."

"No problem." He shoved Alexandra into the back seat and closed her door. While he came around the car, I turned around in my seat and contemplated her.

She looked just as shaky in person as she had sounded on the phone. Her makeup had run, giving her the look of a raccoon, and her eyes were red and swollen from crying. She was shaking, and looked pale and scared. "Did he hurt you?" I asked. Rafe, just getting in, glanced over at me. Alexandra shook her head, lips quivering. "Offer you drugs? Force you to do something you didn't want to do? Cheat?"

Alexandra shook her head on everything. I turned to Rafe, who had put the car in gear and was easing out from the curb. "What happened?" He was taking it slow, and it didn't seem like he was worried about anything happening to us. There was certainly no sign of pursuit from the house.

He answered without looking at me. "Not much. She'd locked herself in a bathroom and wouldn't come out till she saw you outside." We slid to a stop at the corner. Alexandra drew a shuddering breath.

"We're going to have to take her home," I said. "She lives on Winding Way."

Alexandra stirred, but didn't object. Maybe she had realized that it was futile, or maybe she wanted the comfort of being home, in her own room, surrounded by her own things, after the ordeal she had been through. Whatever it was, it must have been traumatic to leave her so shaken.

"You're gonna have to give me directions." Rafe looked both ways before turning onto Dresden. We were working amazingly well together, I thought, considering our differences.

"I forgot. You haven't been in town that long, have you? Where was it you used to live again? Memphis, was it?"

He glanced at me. "Who told you that?"

I said it was Sheriff Satterfield in Sweetwater, and he smiled. "I did tell him that, didn't I?"

"You mean it's not true? So where do you live?"

"Right now? A room in south Nashville. Left or right?"

I told him to go left on Potsdam, and turned around in my seat. Alexandra was snuffling softly, with tears pooling in her eyes. I forced myself to be firm. "Are you ready to tell me what happened?"

She shook her head.

"You can't just call and ask me to come bail you out, and then refuse to tell me what's going on, you know. That's not fair."

She sniffed. "I don't want to talk about it."

"You're going to have to talk about it when we get to your house. So if there's anything you don't want me to say in front of your dad, it would be better to tell me now."

Rafe glanced over at me, and I could see amusement in the curve of his mouth. The argument must have been effective, however, for Alexandra sniffed again, and took a deep breath. "I found something."

"What?" My mind started racking up possibilities, from what I'd seen on TV and read in books. "Drugs? Weapons? Lots of cash?" Alexandra shook her head. "Pornography? I hate to be the one to tell you, but that's not unusual. A lot of men seem to enjoy dirty pictures."

Rafe looked at me, but didn't speak.

"A check," Alexandra said miserably.

"A check? What kind of check? For how much? From whom? To whom?"

She sniffed and started digging in the little black bag she kept in her lap. After a few seconds, she pulled out a crumpled piece of paper and handed it over the seat to me. I smoothed it out, and felt my eyes widen. Rafe glanced down, too, and for just a second the car swerved before he righted it. "That's a lot of money," he said evenly.

I nodded. "Where did you find it?"

Alexandra explained that it had been in Maurice's underwear drawer.

"What were you doing in Maurice's underwear drawer?" Alexandra must be a lot more forward than I had been at her age. Or for that matter than I was now. It would never occur to me to go through a guy's underwear. A ghost of a smile tugged at Rafe's mouth, and before he could offer to explain it to me, I added quickly, "Never mind. I don't want to know. So it was in his bureau. Hidden?"

Alexandra nodded. "Underneath everything else."

"So you don't think he intended you to find it?"

She shook her head.

"What do you think it means? Take a right at the light, Rafe."

Rafe turned right as Alexandra answered, "Isn't it obvious? She paid him to stop seeing me. And he took it!" She subsided into another bout of angry and/or distraught tears. Rafe and I exchanged a look, and the same thing was probably going through both of our minds.

The check was for five grand, payable to Maurice Washington. It was drawn on Brenda's personal business account; the one she didn't share with her husband, because the name at the top said only "Brenda Puckett, Realtor." It was signed by her, and dated for last Saturday, the day she died.

"We're here," Rafe said ten minutes later, pulling the car to a halt in front of the massive Tudor house on Winding Way. It was the first time any of us had spoken in what was left of the trip. He looked around and added, "Nice spread."

I smiled in wry appreciation of the understatement. "Thanks for driving. I know I said you didn't have to come along, but I'm glad you did."

He grinned. "Always happy to oblige. You want I should wait?"

I shook my head. "There's no telling how long this will take. I'll get a ride. Or call a cab."

I had thought he might insist, but he didn't. "I'm off, then. Nice to meet you, Alexandra." He turned a melting smile on the girl, who revived enough to give him back a shaky smile.

"Thank you, Rafe. You're my hero." She gave him her hand through the car window. He kissed it before he gave it back to her, lingering over it a second too long. Alexandra blushed. I rolled my eyes.

"Go away, Rafe."

"You got it, darlin'." He put the car into gear and rolled off down the driveway, but not before he had blown me a kiss.

"He is *so* hot!" Alexandra sighed, holding the hand he had kissed against her chest.

"He's a cocky bastard who thinks that all he has to do is smile at a girl and she'll fall into bed with him," I corrected, but without much heat. Alexandra giggled weakly.

"If I were a few years older, *I'd* fall into bed with him."

"If you were a few years older, he'd probably let you. As it is, stay away from him." I turned toward the front steps. Alexandra did the same, as the Town Car's taillights winked off in the distance. She sent me a sideways look.

"Um . . . Savannah?"

I nodded.

"Do I have to tell my dad everything?"

I hesitated. "What do you want to leave out?"

"Well, um . . . I know I'll have to own up to going to a party instead of spending the night with Lynn . . ."

I nodded. There was no hiding that. Her hair and clothes smelled of cigarette smoke, and somewhere along the way, someone—maybe Alexandra herself—had spilled beer on her top. And then there was the sparkly makeup, faded and smudged now, and the dangling rhinestone earrings, and the high heels, and the short skirt, and the tight shirt . . .

". . . but do I have to tell him about Maurice?"

"Don't you think he knows already? Surely your mother told him?" My mother would have been the first to tell my dad something like this.

"He hasn't said anything about it," Alexandra said.

"Well," I answered. "I guess maybe you don't have to, unless he brings it up. Parents can be awfully difficult about boyfriends. Especially boyfriends they don't approve of." Or men they think are boyfriends, but who aren't. If Steven Puckett was anything like Dix, I'd prefer keeping the truth from him, too, if only so I didn't have to sit through the same lecture I'd already listened to regarding Rafe. And we weren't even involved, while Alexandra was going through Maurice's underwear drawer.

"Thanks, Savannah." She managed a smile.

"Don't thank me yet," I warned. "We don't know whether he'll bring it up. And if he does, you'll have to tell him the truth. I won't lie to him."

"Right." She squared her shoulders and turned toward the front door. "Let's go."

We went.

265

It was obvious that Steven had thought Alexandra settled for the night, because when we walked into the foyer, he scrambled out of the sectional in the living room, looking very surprised and somewhat disheveled. Maybelle surfaced a second later, and although she didn't exactly button her blouse, I got the impression that it was a near thing.

To Steven's credit, he rose to the occasion. "Alexandra! Is something wrong, sweetheart?" And then he saw me, and a frown passed over his horsey face. "Savannah?"

"Alexandra has something to tell you," I said, and gave her a nudge. "Go on."

Alexandra took a breath and contrived to look her age: young, ashamed, and vulnerable. The only thing missing was the lisp. "I'm sorry, Daddy. I lied. I told you I was going to spend the night with Lynn, when what I wanted was to go to a party."

Steven looked confused, and Alexandra sent me a pleading glance.

"Alexandra didn't like the party," I explained. "She called and asked me to come pick her up. Which I was happy to do." I smiled. No sense in mentioning Rafe. The fact that he'd been there, too, didn't make any difference to speak of, and although Steven didn't actually know my mother, the fewer people who knew that I'd had dinner with Rafe Collier, the better.

Steven pulled himself together. "Come in. Both of you. Sit down. Savannah, can I get you something to drink?"

I shook my head. "Thanks all the same. I was just on my way home from dinner when Alexandra called."

"And quite lovely you look, too." He looked admiringly at me for a moment before his voice turned severe. "Now you, young lady"—he turned to Alexandra—"from the smell, you've had enough to drink."

Alexandra raised her eyes to his, big and guileless. "It wasn't me, daddy. Someone just spilled some beer on me, that's all." She folded her hands in her lap and endeavored to look demure. It wasn't easy, considering the makeup, and the earrings, and the skirt and top, and all the rest of it. Steven's eyes narrowed.

"Where was this party? Who was there?"

"It was . . . um . . . at a friend's house. In East Nashville. And I don't think you'd know anyone who was there. They were mostly . . . um . . ." She tossed a panicked glance my way. I realized that she had been about to say "*his* friends," which would have been a dead giveaway.

"Alexandra went there with a friend," I explained. "The others were mostly friends of her friend. Nobody she usually associates with." Alexandra nodded, looking grateful. Steven looked suspicious.

"Who is this friend?"

"Oh. Um . . . someone I met a couple of months ago. One night I was having pizza with Lynn and Heather . . ."

"So Lynn and Heather know this person, too?" Alexandra nodded, crossing her fingers unobtrusively. It helped that her hands were already folded. "And what happened tonight?"

"Oh," Alexandra said. "Um . . ." She glanced at me. I lifted a shoulder. She turned back to her dad. "I just didn't like it. They were drinking and smoking, and all of them were older than me, and when I asked if someone could take me home, they said no. I didn't have cab fare, so I called Savannah."

She looked at me. I nodded. Steven looked from one of us to the other for a second before he said, "All right. Alexandra, why don't you go get ready for bed. Take a shower and wash all that paint off your face. I want to talk to Savannah some more, and then I'll be up to say good night."

Alexandra nodded. "Thanks, Savannah." She gave me an awkward hug.

I hugged her back. "You're welcome. Give me a call sometime. We'll talk."

She said she would, and headed for the stairs, her high heels clicking across the hardwood floor. Maybelle got to her feet. "I'll just go up with her and see if she needs any help. Thanks, Miss Martin." She smiled at me. I smiled back, but thought that she was assuming rather a lot if she thought Alexandra was ready for mothering just a week after losing Brenda.

When they were gone, Steven turned to me. "Thank you, Savannah. I appreciate your help. Brenda's death has been difficult for Alexandra."

I nodded. "I guess she probably just wanted to have some fun and forget about it for a while. When my dad died, I went through kind of a weird phase, too." It had manifested itself in gluttonous reading and a refusal to venture outside, but there was no denying that it had been weird. I'd gotten a little bit of perspective since then, although I still missed my dad.

Steven didn't answer, and I added, "I wouldn't worry too much about her. Nothing happened, and I think she probably learned her lesson."

Steven smiled. "If she grows up to be as mature and self-possessed as you, I'll be very happy. She admires you a lot, you know."

"Gee," I said. "Thanks, but . . ." I really didn't feel mature and self-possessed.

Steven continued, "So did Brenda, of course."

"I beg your pardon?" If Brenda had felt anything but contempt for me, I surely hadn't noticed.

His eyes twinkled. "You were everything Brenda wasn't, and everything she wanted Alexandra to be. Beautiful, well-educated, polished . . ."

"My mother sent me to finishing school," I blurted. Steven smiled.

"See? Brenda was born in Bucksnort. All her life she wanted to be a Southern Belle, with everything she thought it entailed. The family mansion, the education, the social standing. All of it was beyond her, so she focused on the one thing she could do, and that was making enough money so that when Alexandra grew up, she would have everything Brenda hadn't had, and become everything Brenda couldn't be. I daresay my wife could have done a better job in some areas than maybe she did, but she meant well."

"I'm sure she did," I said politely. "She—you both—did a good job with Alexandra. She's a nice girl. And now that she's settled at home, I guess maybe I should go. I'm sorry if we interrupted anything."

I got to my feet. Steven stood, too, just as Maybelle came back down the stairs. From the tiny wrinkle between her brows, I guessed that Alexandra had refused the motherly touches Maybelle wanted to administer. Steven didn't seem to notice. "We appreciate you bringing her home, Savannah."

Maybelle went to his side and linked a proprietary hand through his arm. "Are you leaving already, Miss Martin? Where's your car?" She glanced out the French doors to the obviously empty driveway.

"Actually," I said, "my . . . um . . . date dropped us off. I'll have to call a cab."

"Oh, nonsense! I'll drive you." She smiled up at Steven. "That way you can go talk to Alexandra, and Miss Martin and I can become friends." She transferred the smile to me, bright and hard. There wasn't anything I could do but to accept, but I don't mind telling you that the offer made me nervous. Maybelle's single-minded devotion to Steven was more than a little creepy.

I looked around surreptitiously when we got outside, hoping against hope that Rafe had changed his mind and come back to get me, but, of course, he hadn't.

"My car is parked across the street." Maybelle headed for her own, smaller cottage. I trailed behind, keeping an eye on her back and wondering what she'd do if I refused to get into the car with her.

Of all the people I had come across in connection with Brenda's murder, Maybelle was the one who set my sensors to vibrating the fastest. She had the best reason of anyone for wanting Brenda out of the way. She wanted Brenda's husband, Brenda's children, Brenda's house, Brenda's *life*; and she had the kind of personality I could visualize murdering someone who stood in her way. A typical Southern woman: sweet as sugar on the outside, and hiding bubbling cauldrons of malice inside.

"Here we are." She opened the passenger door to a silver Toyota Camry and gestured me in. I hesitated. "It's perfectly clean, I assure you." She smiled.

"Of course. I didn't mean . . ." I got in. There wasn't anything else I could do. She closed the door and trotted around the car.

"Fasten your seatbelt, dear." She put the car into gear and backed out of the driveway. The doors locked automatically as the car started moving. I glanced at the door, then over at Maybelle. She was smiling beatifically.

17.

It was difficult to know what to say, especially since I was afraid of saying the wrong thing. To be safe, I waited for Maybelle to speak. When she didn't, I felt compelled to break the silence myself, with the most innocuous remark I could find. "I really appreciate your driving me home."

"It's the least I can do after you brought Alexandra back home to us." She smiled.

"It was my pleasure," I said, relieved. "She's a nice girl."

"I'm glad you think so." Maybelle said it complacently, as if she had had something to do with it. "No thanks to Brenda, of course. But things will be different from now on."

I didn't doubt it. "I hear congratulations are in order."

She glanced over at me. "I beg your pardon?"

"About you and Steven? The engagement? Congratulations."

She wrinkled her brows. "How did you hear about that?"

"Alexandra told me," I said. Her forehead cleared.

"Of course. I'm sorry if I sounded ungracious. It's just . . . it's very soon, and we've decided to keep it quiet for a while. So as not to give anyone the wrong impression. You understand."

She smiled. I nodded. I understood perfectly. She didn't want anyone to know that the murdered woman's husband had gotten himself engaged to someone else the day after the funeral, and who could blame her? Not only was it in poor taste, but it might set tongues to wagging about the possibility that one or both of them had hastened Brenda's demise.

"Well, I hope you'll be very happy," I said politely. There was no sense trying to question Maybelle about where she and Steven had been the Saturday morning Brenda died, or on Thursday when Clarice supposedly cut her wrists. If they hadn't been together, Maybelle would say they had. She'd probably consider it her sacred duty.

She smiled. "Thank you, dear. I'm sure we will be, once everything goes back to normal. Steven needs a *wife*; someone who puts his needs and the needs of the family first. Not a career-woman like Brenda, who always had other places to go and other people to see."

Her voice was serene. I smiled politely, but once again found I had nothing to say. Although I sensed that Alexandra was in for a lot of cabbage rolls and unwanted mothering as Maybelle attempted to replace Brenda in the Puckett family unit.

It's not a very long drive from Winding Way to my apartment on East Main, and we drove the next few minutes in—mostly—companionable silence. Maybelle didn't appear to have any plans of murdering me, which made me feel silly for my earlier fears, and she didn't veer off course at all. It wasn't until we were on the homestretch, heading down Main Street, that she spoke again. "Savannah, dear . . . you don't mind if I call you Savannah, do you?"

"Of course not," I said.

"It is really so sweet of you to take Alexandra under your wing, and to show her the world, not to mention help her acquire some polish . . ." She pulled up to the curb outside the gate, right where I had hoped—in vain— that Rafe would drop me off just an hour or two ago. "And we're so very grateful that you came to her rescue this evening, believe me . . ." I scooted a little closer to the door as her gentle voice hardened. "But maybe it would be best if you didn't come around again, dear. At least not for a little while. She's still very young, and distraught by her mother's death, and I'm not at all sure she should be subjected to the kind of life you lead. I saw you drive up through the window, and the young man who dropped you both off! Well, I'm sure you understand, dear."

She unlocked the doors. I didn't waste any time getting out of the car, and she didn't waste any in driving away. Nothing more was said by either of us. She'd made her point and I was, frankly, too shocked to respond.

It took a few seconds for the numbness to wear off and anger to kick in. But once there, it kicked with a vengeance. Who the *hell* did she think she was to tell me to stay away from Alexandra? She wasn't the girl's mother, or even her stepmother, yet. And with her horribly ill-timed engagement, surely she didn't imagine she had anything to teach *me* about good manners and proper behavior!

I had worked myself into a fine state of righteous indignation when I sensed—more than heard—a movement behind me. I swung around only to be confronted with a tall, dark figure, menacingly close.

It took just a second for me to recognize him, but it was the longest second of my life. Visions of butcher knives and Brenda Puckett's throat danced before my eyes. And when I did recognize him, it didn't make me feel all that much better. "Dammit, Rafe." My voice sounded weak and breathless. "One of these days you'll scare me into a faint."

He grinned, teeth very white in the semi-darkness. "You didn't think we were done for the night, did you?"

Oh, God. "Um . . ." I said weakly. "I kind of hoped we were."

He chuckled. "It's not that late. I thought maybe you'd wanna have a chat with Maurice Washington."

"Oh." It took a few seconds for my thoughts to switch track from romance—or sexual assault—to murder. "Um . . . sure."

"Let's go, then. Time's a-wasting." He gestured to the Town Car, which I now saw was parked at the curb a few car lengths away. I got in, trying to decide how I felt. I was relieved, of course—for a moment, I had thought he meant that *we* had unfinished business between the two of us, and it was a relief to discover that this wasn't the night when I'd be fighting off his advances—but I was also a little . . . is *insulted* the right word?

We were halfway to Reinhardt Street by the time I'd gotten over my little snit and had managed to convince myself that there were more important things at stake here than my ego. Especially as I didn't even *want* to have anything to do with him. "I've been meaning to ask," I said, "how you got into Brenda's Stor-All unit on Thursday. Did you have a key?"

He shot me a glance out of the corner of his eye. "Where'd I get a key?"

"I thought maybe you'd looked through her purse on Saturday morning. Detective Grimaldi said someone did."

If the suggestion that he might have robbed a dead woman offended him, he didn't show it. "Musta been someone else. I don't need keys."

"You vaporize and slide through the key hole?"

"Not really. I just finesse the lock."

"You're a locksmith?"

He smiled, amused. "Not really. It's one of those useful skills you pick up along the way."

"I haven't picked it up," I said.

"You and me prob'ly haven't travelled in the same circles, darlin'."

No arguing with that. "It's interesting, anyway."

"Glad to hear it. Why?"

"Clarice Webb had a storage locker, too. In the same place as Brenda."

"No kidding."

"The receptionist said she was there just a few days ago. After Brenda's murder, and just before she got dead herself."

"So?"

"So I'm wondering if it had something to do with those papers that Heidi found in her desk. And the manila envelope she came back to pick up the night she died."

"You wanna explain that?" After I had, he thought for a moment. "So you're thinking she went to the storage place to get the papers? And they had something to do with why she killed herself?"

"Or why she was killed."

"She was killed?"

I shrugged. "It's easier for me to believe that someone else killed both of them than to believe that Clarice killed Brenda. I knew her. But either way, I'm hoping that there's something in that unit that can settle it one way or the other."

Rafe didn't say anything for a minute. I assumed he was working on a counter-argument, but as it turned out, he wasn't. "If she took the papers outta the storage unit," he said instead, "they ain't gonna be there no more."

"Not those papers. But as meticulous as Clarice was, she wouldn't have neglected to make extra copies. All of Brenda's paperwork was copied in triplicate: an office copy, a Brenda copy, and a Clarice copy. She would never risk losing her last copy of something. There must be another somewhere, and it's probably in the storage unit. Unless it was at her house, but then the police would have found it."

"I'll take your word for it," Rafe said. "So you're asking if I'll burgle Clarice's locker for you."

I hesitated. "Not burgle it, exactly . . . Just open it so I can have a look around. See, I didn't find a key to Clarice's storage unit anywhere."

He looked at me for a second. "I can't believe you're asking me to break the law."

"Well, if you don't want to . . ."

"I didn't say I didn't want to. Depends on the incentive, don't it?"

"Truth, justice, and liberty for all?" I suggested. He grinned.

"I had something a little different in mind."

"Somehow I knew that." I was trying hard not to blush, but not succeeding very well. Good thing it was dark in the car. Rafe chuckled, and something about it made all the little hairs on my arms stand up. But before he could answer, the turnoff for Reinhardt Street appeared, and we rolled into the cul-de-sac again.

Rafe turned off the engine. "You ready?"

I swallowed. "I guess."

"Still got the check?"

I nodded. It was crumpled up in my handbag, hurriedly stuffed out of sight so Steven wouldn't notice it. "What if he doesn't want to talk to us?"

"I ain't worried about that," Rafe said and opened his door. "Let's go."

Maurice's house still looked much as it had earlier. Light was spilling out of the windows, music was throbbing, and several cars were parked in the driveway. A souped-up green Dodge was among them. "I think this is his," I said, patting the hood on my way past. I don't know why I bothered to lower my voice, because the people inside wouldn't have heard the sounds of a full-scale invasion.

"Likely he's still inside, then," Rafe answered. He walked up on the narrow front porch. I followed.

"Stand here." He pointed to a spot right in front of the door, while he stepped off to the side, where he couldn't be seen. "Don't go in. Just get him to open the door."

"But . . ."

"I need you to get Maurice outside. If he sees me, he won't set foot out here. Not after what happened earlier."

"I thought you said nothing happened earlier."

He grinned and rapped on the door. Hard. "I lied."

He faded into the shadows. I was still gaping when the front door opened and a young black man with a diamond stud in his ear and pants that hung down to his knees appeared in the doorway. The sullen expression on his face looked familiar. Although I had suspected it, it was nice to be able to confirm that he was indeed the same man who had driven his green Dodge past 101 Potsdam Street last Saturday morning, staring insolently at Rafe and myself. What's more, he recognized me, too, although he tried to hide it. I pretended I didn't notice. "Maurice?" I gave him my best smile. "My name is Savannah Martin. Do you have a minute? I'd like to talk to you. In private, if you don't mind."

"C'mon in." He took a step back.

"I'd rather do it out here," I answered, glancing over his shoulder into the smoky living room, where dark shadows were gyrating and rap music was booming loud enough to pierce a person's eardrums. "It's more private. And not so loud."

Maurice hesitated for a second, peering out into the darkness. I did my very best to look innocent and harmless. After a moment he seemed satisfied that I was alone, and he unlocked the screen door and stepped out onto the tiny front porch. The door slammed behind him, and Rafe appeared as if from thin air between Maurice and the door. Maurice jumped, and I could see a flash of fear cross his face before he conquered it. He turned back to me. "You with him?"

I nodded, with an apologetic smile.

"Figures." He pulled his head down between his shoulders like a turtle.

"You carrying?" This was Rafe's contribution. Maurice shook his head, but Rafe patted him down anyway. Maurice didn't object. It looked like it might have happened before. Rafe seemed to be no stranger to the procedure himself.

While Rafe was checking Maurice for hardware, I dug in my handbag and brought out the crumpled check. "We'd like to know about this, please."

Maurice squinted at it, and turned as pale as a man with a complexion like hot chocolate can turn. His eyes flickered from side to side, as if he was thinking about making a break for it. I glanced at Rafe, who grabbed him. "Easy."

Maurice slumped. "You the cops?"

I shook my head. "Just friends of Alexandra's. She found this"—I wiggled the check, but made sure to keep it out of his reach—"in your dresser."

"Stupid bitch." He turned his head and spat. It ended up a few inches from the toe of my shoe. Rafe's eyes narrowed, but he didn't speak.

"She's a sixteen-year-old girl whose mother was murdered last week," I answered coldly. That particular epithet he used is one of my least favorite, even when it isn't applied to me. "And then she finds a check for five grand in her boyfriend's underwear drawer. From her mother. Dated the day her mother died. Oh yes, and her boyfriend wasn't at home that morning, because she stopped by to see him, and he wasn't there."

"I don't have to talk to you," Maurice said. He was probably aiming for tough and truculent, but managed only to sound like a pouty five-year-old. Rafe smiled.

"Why don't you try not talking to us, and see what happens."

Maurice looked up at him. He wasn't much taller than me—five foot ten maybe—and Rafe had him beat by four or five inches, as well as a good thirty pounds. Solid muscle, all of it.

"And watch your language, if you don't mind," I added. Maurice rolled his eyes.

"She called me last week sometime. The old . . . I mean, Alex's ma. Told me to meet her Saturday mornin'."

"Where? And when?"

"Seven thirty, at the house on Potsdam. Said she had a client comin' at eight and wanted me outta there before he showed. Said our business wouldn't take long." His tone when he pronounced the word *business* was sour.

I nodded. That fit well with the notation in Clarice's—Clarissa's—calendar and what Alexandra had said about her mother leaving the house around seven. It isn't a thirty-minute drive from Winding Way to Potsdam Street, but maybe Brenda wanted to go to Starbucks for a muffin and a cup of coffee on the way.

"What happened?"

Maurice shrugged skinny shoulders underneath the oversized T-shirt. "When I got there, the door was standin' open."

"You see anybody else?"

Maurice shook his head.

"What about her car?" I asked.

"Didn't see no car. Just the door standin' open."

"What did you do?"

Maurice had gone in, calling Brenda's name, and found her dead in the library.

"If she was dead, how did you get the check?" I asked.

Maurice folded his arms. "It was in her purse."

"You went through her purse?"

"I wanted to make sure she hadn't got nothin' with my name on it." Maurice's tone indicated that this was something I ought to have figured out for myself. Something anyone sane would have thought to do.

"Why didn't you call an ambulance?" I asked. Maurice turned to Rafe.

"She for real, man? Listen, the old . . . I mean, Mrs. Puckett was *dead*. Wasn't nothin' nobody could do for her. And I got a clean record. Got a scholarship to TSU in a couple weeks. I'm gettin' outta here, goin' places. Why'd I go and fuck that up?"

"Because it was the right thing to do?" I suggested. Maurice looked at me blankly. "Because she was Alexandra's mother and you're dating Alexandra? Because your girlfriend had to hear that her mother was dead from the police?"

Maurice didn't say anything. I glanced at Rafe, who gave a one-shouldered shrug. I turned back to Maurice. "So you took the check and left. What did you do then?"

"Drove around for a while, just to see what happened. Saw *you* get there." He nodded to Rafe. "But you didn't go in. So I drove around some more, and then *she* came." He glanced at me. "Next time I drove by, you were inside, so I figured I could go home. I put the check away and tried to stop thinkin' about it, but it ain't that easy, you know."

I nodded. I knew. It had taken me days to start sleeping through the night again, and I hadn't been in danger of being arrested. Hadn't been dating Brenda's daughter, either.

Maurice added, as much to himself as to us, "Only good thing was Alex ain't been up to gettin' together much. Busy with the funeral and stuff. Tonight was the first time I seen her since it happened."

And then she'd found the check and thought he'd taken money to stop seeing her. And he couldn't tell her the truth, not without admitting that he'd left her mother bleeding to death on the floor. It seemed to me that Maurice was in a bad way however one looked at it.

Rafe said the same thing. "Looks to me like you're screwed, pal."

Maurice shrugged, like it didn't matter, but his eyes said otherwise. Rafe glanced at me. "Anything else you wanna ask, darlin'?" I shook my head. "Looks like we're done here, then. Thanks, man." He released Maurice.

"I guess you can have this back," I added, holding out the check. Maurice eyed it with loathing. "Or I can hang on to it for you, if you'd like."

He nodded. "Yeah. I ain't gonna use it. Only reason I kept it was so I coulda shown it to the cops to prove I didn't have no reason to want the old . . . I mean, Mrs. Puckett dead."

"Works for me," Rafe said. "C'mon, darlin'. The night's young." He winked at Maurice, who dredged up a weak smile from somewhere.

"If you see Alex . . ."

"Yes?"

"Never mind." He turned and disappeared into the house again. We headed for the car.

"So what did you think?" I asked when we were rolling toward the corner once more. Rafe grinned.

"You're a natural, darlin'. Saved me from beating the answers out of him."

"I didn't mean that. Although, do you often . . . um . . . beat answers out of people?"

"It's been known to happen," Rafe said, unrepentantly, and turned the wheel. I watched him in silence for a moment or two while I gathered up my courage.

"Is that what happened with Billy Scruggs?"

He drew his brows together. "Who?"

"Billy Scruggs." Surely he couldn't have forgotten the name of the man who had been responsible for sending him to prison for two years? "You know, the man you had that fight with twelve years ago."

His tone was resigned. "Something else Satterfield's background check dug up?"

I nodded, apologetically. "It sounded like he was hurt pretty badly."

"Not bad enough," Rafe said. He coasted up to the intersection of Dresden and Dickerson and turned right, with no more than a cursory glance to make sure no one else was coming. I wondered where he was taking me—it was in the opposite direction from my apartment, and also in the opposite direction from his, if he had told the truth about living in south Nashville—but I didn't want to interrupt the conversation to ask.

"It doesn't sound like you're very sorry," I said instead.

He glanced at me. "About Billy? I'm sorry I had to spend two years in jail, but I ain't sorry I did it."

"What about your mother? My brother told me that she was so upset she didn't even come to your sentencing."

A sour smile curved his mouth. "That wasn't 'cause she was upset with me, darlin'. It was 'cause Billy'd beat her black and blue, and she didn't want nobody to see her."

For a second or two, my voice deserted me, and I could feel myself turning pale. Then I managed an, "Oh, God."

Rafe didn't answer, just shrugged. After a minute or two, I got over my ladylike vapors enough to continue. "I guess she didn't want to report him, so you decided to go after him yourself."

"Everyone was just waiting for me to fuck up anyway, so I figured I might as well help 'em out."

I nodded. I could understand that. In a way, I was dealing with something similar myself. Everyone thought I was involved with him when I wasn't, so the thought had crossed my mind that I might as well be. At least that way I'd get something out of the situation. Not that I'd actually do it, of course. "But you weren't really trying to kill him, were you?"

He arched a brow, and I blushed. "Never mind. Forget I asked. Um . . ." I looked around, at Apple Annie's motel and the street walkers outside the tinted window. "Where are we going, anyway?"

"Thought you said you wanted me to break into the Stor-All."

"Oh," I said, disconcerted. "I didn't think you'd want to do it tonight."

"Now's the best time. Saturday night. Everybody's out partying. Ain't nobody there."

"True," I admitted, "but . . ."

"What's the matter? You got a Catwoman outfit you were planning to change into for the occasion? I can spare the time for something like that." He grinned.

"Hardly. No, it's just that I don't know which storage unit was Clarice's, and there won't be anyone in the office to tell us."

"We'll figure it out." He changed lanes, and the next second we cruised to a stop outside the Stor-All on Dickerson Pike.

"Looks safe," Rafe commented after a brief overview. I nodded. Perfectly safe. Not a creature was stirring, not even a mouse; let alone anything bigger. He opened his door. I waited while he came around the car and opened mine. "Let's go."

"You're not going to make me wait in the car?"

"You're safer with me than out here by yourself."

He took my elbow. I wasn't sure I believed him, but

I didn't want to be left to cool my heels outside, so I hustled to keep up. The octogenarian receptionist wasn't in evidence tonight; the small cubby where she had been sitting was dark and closed, and no one answered when Rafe knocked on the door.

"It's empty," I said, unnecessarily.

"I can see that. C'mere, darlin'."

"I'm already here," I pointed out, from the safe, arms-length distance to which I had retreated when he dropped my arm.

"Closer." He grabbed my wrist and yanked. Gently, but a yank nonetheless, and hard enough to force me to take a step toward him. He maneuvered me up against the wall next to the door. It would be monotonous, were it not for the fact that every time it happened, a brand-new, stronger wave of panic washed over me.

"Let's see . . ." He tipped my chin up, his dark eyes moving over my face. Simultaneously, his other hand disappeared behind my neck, and I could feel long fingers weaving through my hair. I lost my breath, and I swear my knees buckled. A corner of his mouth turned up.

A second later my prim chignon was history, and the hair I had endeavored to keep from looking tousled and sexy fell over my shoulders.

"Thanks, darlin'," Rafe said and turned away.

18.

It took me a few seconds to put two and two together. Embarrassingly, the conclusion was hard to escape. I had used hairpins to put my hair up. Now my hair was down, so the pins must be gone.

"Like stealing candy from a baby." Rafe grinned at me over his shoulder.

"Huh?" I said. He pushed at the office door, which swung open. "Oh, my God," I added, choking, "you didn't!"

"It's easier than opening every unit. Takes less time, too."

He wasn't kidding. The whole thing had taken less than sixty seconds, from the moment he pulled me to him to the time the door was unlocked.

"Yes," I said, "but . . ." It seemed worse somehow—more like a crime—to break into the office rather than into the storage unit itself.

Rafe didn't seem to have any such qualms. "I'll be right back." He ducked through the door. I waited, looking nervously from side to side, wishing I'd had the chance to put on something different. Not a Catwoman outfit—I wouldn't be caught dead in anything so formfitting—but something less conspicuous than this gleaming white blouse and prim pumps.

But at least I didn't have long to wait. It may have been another minute before he came back out, but no more. "Unit 516, aisle E. I borrowed a master key, too." He brandished it.

"Why did you bother to look for one?" I wanted to know, breathlessly, as I trotted after him. "If you can open the lock just as quickly with hairpins."

"Hairpins are harder to explain away, darlin'. With this, I can just pretend I work here."

"You wouldn't get away with it," I said. "Someone would check."

"I got away with saying I was a cop. Nobody checked that."

"And you should be grateful. There are all sorts of penalties involved in impersonating a police officer."

He shrugged. I added, tentatively, "I know I've asked before, but . . ."

"I ain't."

"Honestly?"

"Would I lie to you, darlin'?"

"Hell, yes," I said. He grinned.

The master key turned as smoothly as butter in the lock of unit E-516, and Rafe pulled up the heavy folding door. Side by side, we peered into Clarice Webb's—Clarissa Webster's—storage space.

It was the same size as Brenda's, and less than half full. What was here was better organized, and wasn't all work related. There were a few pieces of decent furniture—heirlooms, maybe, or pieces that didn't fit with Clarice's current decor. Clothes in plastic bags were hanging on a rack along the wall. Clarice either switched out summer and winter clothes twice a year (difficult in a place like Nashville, where it can be seventy-five degrees in January) or the clothes were like the furniture: out of style, but too financially or sentimentally valuable to throw away.

A couple of cardboard boxes in the corner turned out to hold knick-knacks and assorted junk. Ceramic kittens, vases, framed family photographs. One showed a younger Clarice standing next to an equally young, somewhat weak-chinned man with prematurely thinning hair and eyes that were a smidgen too close together over a pointy nose. "This must be Mr. Webster," I remarked, examining it.

"Looks like the criminal type," Rafe agreed. He was watching over my shoulder, standing close enough to brush against my back. I moved away, fractionally.

"That's pretty funny, coming from you. You didn't get that good at picking locks without considerable practice."

"I'm good at a lot of things." He winked. I fought down a blush, resolving to try harder not to feed him all these straight lines. It was going to be difficult, however, since I had no idea I was doing it until he took my innocent remark and turned it into something I hadn't intended.

"There's a file box over there." He pointed. "I'd guess that'd be where it's at."

"Where what's at?"

"Whatever you're looking for, darlin'. Unless you were planning to ask me to put this on my back and stagger out with it." He patted a heavy dining room table with carved clusters of grapes like goiters on its legs.

"Thanks," I said with a shudder, "but no. I don't mind antiques, but that's really too awful."

"I didn't notice many antiques in your apartment." He was making his way toward the file box, and wasn't looking at me.

"You weren't there very long."

"Long enough."

"And you only saw the hallway."

"I had a look around while you and Todd necked."

"Todd and I didn't neck for more than a second."

Rafe arched a brow, and I sighed. "Our house in Sweetwater had nothing but antiques, but Bradley preferred things more modern. So we furnished our townhouse with leather and chrome and glass." All very cold and angular. An apt metaphor for our marriage, come to think of it; it was no wonder the relationship hadn't lasted. "I left it all behind when I divorced him."

"What happened?" Rafe didn't sound like he cared one way or the other. I folded my arms and watched him navigate the obstacle course to the file box in the corner.

"Other than that we had different tastes in home decor? He cheated." I know I mentioned that that fact was something I didn't want to get around, but I figured it would be safe to tell Rafe. Who could he tell, after all? It wasn't like we moved in the same circles. And, somehow, he was easy to talk to about things like this. I guess maybe because he wasn't in a position to judge me for being less than perfect.

"Figures." He shifted another smaller box out of his way. It clinked, like it was full of porcelain or glass.

I sniffed. "What's that supposed to mean? I'm the kind of woman who gets cheated on? Thanks a lot!"

"I just meant that you pick the wrong guys to get involved with."

"There was nothing wrong with Bradley," I said, stung. I was no fan of Bradley's either, anymore, but I was damned if I would let Rafe Collier lecture me about my love life. Bradley had turned out to be a jerk, yes, but while he courted me, he had seemed like my perfect match. "He was young, wealthy, reasonably good looking, came from a good family, was offered a very good job after graduation . . ."

Rafe murmured something. I couldn't hear what it was, but I heard the tone, and decided not to ask him to repeat it.

"If something wasn't wrong with him," he said instead, "why'd he cheat?"

"Maybe he thought there was something wrong with me."

He straightened up and looked at me. Up and down, for a little longer than strictly necessary. "Ain't nothing wrong with you, darlin'. Any man who has you in his bed and goes somewhere else for his jollies needs his head examined." He turned back to the box.

"Thanks," I said. "I think."

"No sweat. So when you and I get it on . . ."

"I should have known this was just another way for you to try to talk me into bed!"

"Can't fault a man for trying." He grinned at me over his shoulder.

"I can. Plus, I'm frigid." I couldn't imagine why I'd blurted that piece of information out when surely I wasn't *that* comfortable talking to him! But on the upside, maybe it would make him stop asking.

"Just 'cause Bradley couldn't get the job done, don't mean I can't."

Or maybe not. I shrugged. "Are you finding anything?"

"Papers. Old bills. College transcripts. Looks like she studied accounting half a century ago. Title to her house. She lived in Sylvan Park. Any reason we have to go there?"

"None I can think of." Breaking into Clarice's storage unit was one thing; breaking into her house was something totally different.

"Glad to hear it," Rafe said. "Houses are close together out there. Someone'd probably see us. Here's a will—everything she owns to someone named Laura Curtis of Des Moines."

"I doubt she had much to leave," I said. "The house is probably worth something, if it isn't mortgaged to the rafters, but her husband went bankrupt and left her destitute, and for the past fifteen years, she's been a glorified file clerk for Brenda Puckett. Who wasn't the world's most generous employer, by all accounts. Alexandra told me she was always complaining about the money she had to pay Clarice. Which is *so* unfair, because if I know—knew—Brenda, she probably had Clarice earning eight fifty an hour!"

Rafe didn't answer, and I turned to look at him. He was staring at something he had just pulled from the box.

"What's that?" I picked my way closer to him.

He held it out. "IRA statement. Says she had just under four million dollars in her account."

"What?" I grabbed the statement. "But if she had that kind of money, why did she continue to work for Brenda?"

"Maybe she liked her," Rafe said. I snorted, handing the statement back to him.

"I don't think there was a single person in the whole world who liked Brenda Puckett. Except maybe her family, and I'm not sure about them. Plus, Alexandra told me they weren't friends."

"So maybe Brenda had some kind of hold on her."

"Blackmail, you mean? I suppose it's possible. I wouldn't put it past her. If Clarice was involved in her husband's embezzling scheme, for instance, and Brenda knew about it . . . Clarice was an accountant. Maybe she helped Graham cook the books. And maybe Brenda hired Clarice in order to squeeze as much work out of her as she could, knowing that Clarice couldn't quit. Although that doesn't explain how Clarice ended up with four million dollars . . ."

"This does."

He handed me another piece of paper. I looked at it and gulped. "What on earth? But this isn't . . . Oh, my God!"

Rafe arched a brow. I waved him off as I cast my mind back a couple of days to the morning I'd heard that Clarice was dead. Heidi had told me she'd seen Clarice's contract with Brenda, and that it was the same as her own. Heidi paid Brenda 40 percent of her income, and kept 60 percent after Walker took out the company's share.

"But this doesn't say that, does it?" I asked Rafe after I had detailed what I remembered. "This says that Brenda has to pay Clarice 40 percent of everything she makes. Everything *Brenda* makes. Right?"

Rafe nodded.

"But that's . . . that's *criminal*! No wonder Brenda complained!"

"Explains a lot, don't it?"

"It sure does! Brenda sells a couple of million dollars worth of real estate every month, and sometimes a lot more. Three percent of two million is . . . um . . ."

"Sixty grand," Rafe said. "Sounds like I'm in the wrong business."

"We're not all that successful. Walker gets 15 percent off the top. That's . . . um . . ."

"Nine grand."

"Which leaves . . . um . . . fifty-one grand?"

He nodded.

"Brenda keeps 60 percent, and Clarice gets 40 percent. That's . . . um . . ."

"That's $20,400 for Clarice, $30,600 for Brenda."

"Thank you. Over a year, that would be . . ."

It didn't take him more than five seconds. "Just less than 245 grand for Clarice, and just over 367 for Brenda."

"You're good at this. Are you in banking? A CPA? How about a bookmaker?"

"Shame on you," Rafe said lightly, "don't you know that gambling is illegal in Tennessee?"

"Like that would stop you? Two hundred and forty-five grand. That's not bad for typing and filing and keeping track of Brenda's appointments."

Rafe agreed. "For that kind of money, I'd go to work for her myself."

"I wouldn't. There's not enough money in the world to pay me to work for Brenda Puckett. Plus, she didn't like me." I hesitated for a second before I added, "She wouldn't have liked you either."

"Most women like me just fine." He grinned.

"Brenda wasn't most women," I said. "All she cared about was money, and you don't have any. All the sex appeal in the world wouldn't make up for that. Plus, she liked people she could bully, and you're just not pliable enough."

"Depends on who's doing the plying, darlin'."

I rolled my eyes. "Give it a rest, would you? It's getting almost as old as my family throwing every eligible bachelor they can find at me."

He smiled, but didn't answer. Instead he looked around. "We done here?"

I did the same. "I guess we are. Unless you think there's something else we might find if we keep looking?"

"I think we've found enough, don't you?"

I nodded. I guess we had.

So we locked up again, and hoofed it back to the office, where Rafe went back inside and put the master key wherever he found it and just generally made sure no one could tell he'd been there. If they came through with a fingerprinting kit, they'd find his prints, of course, but as long as everything looked normal, there was no reason why anyone would suspect we'd ever been here.

"All right," I said when we were driving down Dickerson Pike again. "Let's see if we can figure this out."

Rafe nodded encouragingly.

"Fifteen years ago, Clarice's husband got involved in a business deal with Brenda. When it fell apart, he killed himself."

Rafe nodded.

"Clarice filed a suit with the Real Estate Commission. But nothing ever came of it, because Brenda paid Clarice to withdraw the charges."

Rafe nodded.

"So Clarissa Webster became Clarice Webb, and went to work for Brenda. As the years went by, Brenda—

thanks in no small part to Clarice—became more and more successful, and Clarice became richer and richer. She had every reason in the world to help Brenda make money, because the more money Brenda made, the more Clarice made."

Rafe nodded.

"And she had absolutely no reason to want Brenda dead. Brenda was much more valuable to her alive. So Clarice didn't kill her."

"Unless there's something you don't know," Rafe said. "Like, Brenda got tired of sharing and fired her, or something."

I nodded, grudgingly. "True. What did you think of Maurice Washington, by the way?"

"Nasty tick," Rafe said, but without excitement. "I don't think he killed Miz Puckett, if that's what you're asking. Not man enough. That prob'ly happened as soon as she got to the house. Whoever did it would wanna get it over with, just in case Maurice was early. It don't take long to cut someone's throat."

I swallowed. "Not to be rude or anything, but how do you know that?"

"Not 'cause I ever had occasion to do it to anyone. Old Jim used'ta take me out hunting. Ain't much difference when it comes to it."

"Ugh!" I said. He shrugged. "All right. So the murderer cut Brenda's throat and then got in the Lincoln Navigator and drove it down to the Milton House, where he or she exchanged Brenda's car for his or her own car. Then he or she drove home, and waited. Meanwhile, Maurice showed up and found Brenda dead. He rifled her handbag, just to be sure she hadn't written his name anywhere, and made off with the check she was presumably planning to use to make him stay away from Alexandra. You realize that he had every reason in the world to do away with her? She wouldn't have stood for Alexandra continuing to see him. The poor girl would have been on her way to finishing school in Charleston before you could have said 'boo.'"

Rafe looked at me askance, but didn't ask. "He don't have the guts," he said instead, dismissively.

"I'll take your word for it. By the way, do you think whoever killed Brenda missed the check, or did they leave it on purpose, to implicate Maurice?"

"Depends on whether they knew about Maurice or not. If they didn't, maybe they were hoping to pin it on me." He didn't sound too bothered by the possibility.

"Clarice knew," I said. "She was the one who saw Maurice and Alexandra together, and told Brenda. Although she might not have known that Brenda had set up an appointment with him that morning."

Rafe shrugged.

"Anyway, Maurice doesn't call the cops, but he hangs around to make sure someone else does. You know, I agree with you. He lacks spine. Anyway, then you show up. But you don't go in, and when you get tired of waiting, you call me, and between us, we find Brenda. And Maurice goes home to hide the check in his underwear drawer."

Rafe nodded.

"The next thing that happened was that Clarice died. No, wait. That's not true. The next thing that happened was that the *Nashville Voice* ran a derogatory article about Brenda, and dredged up the whole Kress-building fiasco. It could be unrelated, but then again, maybe not. Maybe someone tipped them off. Maybe the murderer did it."

"Why?"

"Who knows? Out of plain maliciousness, or to throw suspicion on Clarice. Or to give her another reason for supposedly committing suicide, if the murderer had already decided to do away with her."

Rafe nodded. I added, "But Clarice wouldn't have done it, would she? She wouldn't want to implicate herself, or dredge up the old business."

"Don't seem that way." Rafe turned the car onto East Main Street. I was almost home. I began to talk faster. I wanted it all said by the time we got to my apartment, because there was no way I was inviting him in to continue the exposition. This time, come hell or high water, I would say goodnight in the car, outside the gate.

"So someone else did it. And then that same someone made an appointment with Clarice on Thursday night, and killed her too. With the same knife he or she used on Brenda. To make it look like Clarice had killed Brenda and then herself."

"Works for me." Was it my imagination, or was he driving more slowly? The roof of my apartment building was visible just over the next crest, so he might also want me to finish what I had to say before we got there. Maybe he thought the evening had been long enough. Maybe he couldn't wait to get rid of me . . .

"The only thing left to do is figure out who it was. Someone with a reason for wanting Brenda dead. That's practically all of Nashville. Her husband, his mistress, her daughter, her daughter's boyfriend, every real estate agent who's ever worked with her, and at least half her clients, current and former, including you and your grandmother. Not to mention the wacko who peppered her billboard with buckshot last month. Who'd want to kill Clarice, though? And why?"

"As a guess," Rafe said, slowing down a little more; I was sure by now I wasn't imagining it, "she prob'ly knew who Brenda took with her on Saturday morning, and decided to try another spot of blackmail. It worked out real good last time, after all."

I nodded. That made sense. "Someone they both knew, then. Tim, maybe. He has plenty of income, and I don't see him letting himself be blackmailed. The receptionist at the Stor-All did say she saw him on Monday morning, when he had no business being there. He said she'd made a mistake, but that's what he'd say anyway, isn't it? On the other hand, I can't really see him cut someone's throat. Too squeamish, don't you think? Maybelle Driscoll would take it in stride, but I'm not too sure about Steven. Surely he'd find it hard to cold-bloodedly cut the throat of the woman he had lived with and slept with for twenty years, and who had given him two children? Austin is too young, and I just can't believe it of Alexandra. But then there's . . . um . . . your grandmother."

He sent me a black look. "Keep my grandmother out of this."

"I wish I could," I said sincerely, "but she had every reason in the world for wanting to kill Brenda, either because she thought Brenda had broken into her house or because she understood that Brenda had cheated her out of it. And it's not like she would go to jail even if she did do it. She's clearly *non compos mentis.*"

I trailed off as I watched Rafe's hands tighten on the steering wheel until the knuckles showed white. It looked like he was imagining squeezing something soft, like my throat.

"You're right," I said, "let's keep your grandmother out of it."

"Thank you."

"No problem. By the way, while I'm still thinking about it, Walker asked me if I thought you'd be interested in getting the house back, without having to pay the hundred grand, if he could arrange it. The only stipulation is that you keep it quiet."

He sent me a suspicious glance. "Why?"

"He's hoping to be elected for a spot on the Real Estate Commission next spring. He's been working toward it for a long time, and all of these tragedies haven't improved his chances, poor man. I promised I'd ask you."

"Sure." He shrugged. "I ain't proud."

"I'll let him know." I leaned back in my seat and watched my apartment building come closer. This time I wasn't going to be caught off-guard.

When he slid up to the curb, I had the door open before we'd even come to a complete stop. "Thanks again. For everything."

"You sure you don't want me to walk you up?"

I shook my head, a little too emphatically. His eyes crinkled. "You afraid of a repeat of last time, darlin'?"

I shrugged. No sense in denying the obvious.

He smiled. "I ain't gonna hurt you, you know."

"I know. It's just . . . my mother would kill me."

He cocked his head. "You planning on telling her?"

I shook my head. "Oh, no." I would never breathe a word of this evening to my mother. Not for all the money in Clarice's IRA account. But I wasn't about to compound the offenses I had already committed by allowing myself to be kissed by him, either. There are limits.

I had been prepared for a prolonged argument, but to my surprise and—dare I say it?—merest hint of disappointment, he didn't quibble. "Guess that's it, then. Good night, darlin'. And thanks for a good time."

He extended a hand through the car window. It seemed churlish and ungrateful not to take it, considering everything I'd put him through, so I placed my hand in his and prepared to shake. I daresay I should have known better. He lifted it to his mouth and brushed his lips over my knuckles before turning my hand over and kissing my palm. Scrubbing it against my thigh to get rid of the feeling of his lips on my skin would only make me look like I cared, so the kiss stayed there the whole way across the courtyard and up the stairs to my door, like the niggling of a mosquito bite.

19.

So that was that, I reflected the next morning. I had made it through the previous night without being arrested for burglary and, more importantly, without being kissed by Rafe. And considering the terms on which we had parted, it seemed as if he had realized—finally!—that any hopes he harbored in my direction, if he harbored any, and he didn't just attempt to talk me into bed on principle, were bound to be unfulfilled. What a relief. That he realized it, I mean. Of course, the rest of it was a relief, too; I didn't mean to imply otherwise. But in this case, I mostly meant that it was a relief that he realized it and so, presumably, would stop bugging me. Not that I actually minded the bugging all that much, so long as he was just joking. It was the idea that he might not be that was scary. And that was why it was a relief that he seemed to have accepted that I wouldn't ever have anything of a sexual or romantic nature to do with him. It removed quite a load from my mind.

That settled, I moved on to more important things. After a leisurely breakfast of black coffee and the cheesecake from yesterday—yes, I'll eat dessert as long as nobody masculine is around to see me do it—I spent a couple of hours freshening my manicure and pedicure, and doing my hair and makeup. Once noon rolled around and it was acceptable to call people—it was a Sunday, after all, and we Southerners take our religion seriously—I got on the horn.

My first call was to Dix, who was having brunch at The Wayside Inn and Restaurant in Sweetwater, as he explained when I asked about the noise I could hear in the background.

"Who's with you?" I inquired, since his voice had that unnaturally cheerful quality that voices tend to have when someone is listening. I could hear his children—three-year-old Hannah and five-year-old Abby—squabbling just far enough away that I couldn't make out what the argument was about.

"Sheila and the kids, of course. And Todd Satterfield and his dad, and um . . . Mom."

In that case, I had probably better not tell him—and by extension the rest of them—who I'd had dinner with last night. Or, as had been my intention, ask advice about Rafe's dilemma with regards to Mrs. Jenkins.

"Say hello to them all for me, would you?" I said instead, brightly. "I had something of a professional nature I wanted to ask you, but it sounds like you're busy just now. Why don't you give me a call later, when you have a few minutes to talk?"

"Sure. Bye, sis." He hung up without waiting for my answer. I leaned back, gnawing the newly applied lipstick from my lower lip. Had he been so abrupt because he—bless him—didn't want the rest of the family (and Todd and Sheriff Satterfield) to insist on interrogating me, or was there something going on that he didn't want me to know about? Were they, perhaps, having a council of war, discussing my supposed involvement with Rafe, and what they could do about it?

But no, I told myself, that was surely paranoia rearing its ugly head. They were probably just having brunch together, like family and friends were wont to do after church on a Sunday, and it had nothing whatsoever to do with me.

My next call was to Walker, whom I caught at home. "Yes, Savannah," he said promptly when I introduced myself, "what can I do for you this morning?"

I explained that I had spoken to Rafe the night before, "about what we discussed in the ladies' room last night. Remember?"

"Of course," Walker said smoothly. "How did Mr. Collier feel about the idea?"

"He seemed to feel just fine about it. I'm sure he'd appreciate anything you could do."

"And you made sure he understands that this depends on us being able to keep the transaction quiet?"

I assured him I had done everything I could to impart that understanding. "I don't think he'll say anything to anyone. Although I suppose you could always get it in writing."

"I'd prefer to keep that part of the agreement verbal," Walker said blandly. "However, does he strike you as someone who'd come back later with demands?"

"For money, you mean? Like Cla—I mean, like he'd try to blackmail you?"

Walker might not—probably didn't—know that Clarice had been blackmailing Brenda all these years, and it wasn't my place to tell him. That agreement had been between Clarice and Brenda, and hadn't affected Walker in any way, and what he didn't know really couldn't hurt him, so I didn't even feel a twinge of guilty conscience over keeping mum. When he didn't say anything, either, I added, "No, I don't think so. He might steal your money, but he'll steal it honestly. He's not someone who'll sneak around behind your back."

"In that case," Walker said, "I'll see if I can't take care of this right away. Thank you for letting me know so promptly, Savannah."

"My pleasure," I said. "Is there anything I can do to help out?"

It sounded like he hesitated for a moment. "Actually, there is. I had scheduled an open house over at Potsdam Street today, from two to four. It is still our listing, and until we hear otherwise, it is our responsibility to do our best for our client."

"Of course," I said.

"But now, with this problem to work out, it would be more convenient if I didn't have to be there. I don't suppose you're available to do it instead?"

"I'd love to," I said (although, between you and me, I didn't love the idea as much as I said I did).

"There's nothing to it," Walker said bracingly. "Just talk to people and be your usual charming self, and all will be well."

"Charming I can do. I spent a year in Charleston learning how to be charming."

"There you go, then. I know you'll do wonderfully. And if I can work this little problem out in time, I might see you there myself."

"That would be great," I said. Walker excused himself to get to work, and I did the same.

In my naiveté, I thought that not many people would come to an open house at 101 Potsdam Street. It wasn't a property that would appeal to the masses, after all. Too expensive, needing too much work, and in the wrong part of town. Just to have something to do in case nobody showed up, I stuffed my most recent romance novel purchase in my handbag before I headed out. It was the latest release by Barbara Botticelli, my favorite writer. All Barbara's heroines were blonde, beautiful, and well-bred—I could relate, at least to the blonde and well-bred part—and all her heroes, from highwaymen and pirates to Indian braves and Bedouins, were dark and dangerous and not at all well-bred. The cover showed an impressively muscled native dressed in nothing but war paint and a skimpy loincloth crushing the swooning heroine to his manly chest. Her double-D-cup breasts were threatening to explode out of her half-undone bodice, and she was clearly both weak-kneed and dizzy. At the last minute, I added a sedate real estate magazine to the bag, to have something to hide the book behind in case someone should sneak up on me while I was reading. I wouldn't look very professional sitting there devouring *Apache Amour*.

After a stop at the store and another few stops to put arrow signs with balloons pointing the way on the corners near the house, I arrived at 101 Potsdam Street at ten minutes to two, to find a half dozen people already waiting in the driveway, panting to get inside, and not only because of the heat. I wish I could say I thought they were potential buyers, but as far as I could tell, they were all more interested in the murder than in the house itself. Several had cameras they kept using, and one woman even went so far as to ask me in which room the "tragedy" had taken place. Would I mind pointing to the exact spot on the floor where Brenda had breathed her last? When I did, she sat down cross-legged on the hardwood, rolled her eyes back into her head, and emitted mooing sounds while she attempted to contact Brenda's lingering spirit. It was enough to put me off my feed for another week. The rest of the looky-loos gave her a wide berth while they stared avidly at the remains of bloodstains on the floor and munched on cookies, scattering crumbs everywhere.

One young couple had some potential, though. As clients, I mean. They came through the door about thirty minutes into the ordeal, bright-eyed and bushy-tailed as squirrels, looking around curiously. I greeted them with a smile. "Good afternoon. I'm Savannah Martin with Walker Lamont Realty."

"Gary Lee Hodges." The young man grinned at the girl next to him. "This is my wife, Charlene." Charlene giggled and clung to his arm. They acted like newlyweds, and looked to be in their early twenties. I hoped for their sake that they'd fare better than Bradley and I had. Then again, I'd never giggled and clung to Bradley the way Charlene did to Gary Lee, so maybe they'd do all right.

"Nice to meet you both," I said. "And welcome to 101 Potsdam Street. The kitchen is through there, down the hallway. There are some cookies and lemonade out there if you want a snack, and also a sign-in sheet, if you wouldn't mind. We like to keep track of how many visitors we have. Would you like a brochure?" I offered them one, and Charlene took it. They bent their heads over it; one dark and disheveled—Gary Lee looked like he might be a musician, or belong to some other profession where they keep their hair long—and one fair and sleek. Charlene's hoop earrings were big enough to fit around my upper arm.

"Where are the bedrooms?" Gary Lee asked.

"All the bedrooms are on the second floor. There's a third floor, too, but that's just one big ballroom. And down here there is a dining room, a parlor, a library, and a kitchen, plus a laundry room and a pantry."

"Thanks. Come on, Charlene." He tugged on her hand. She followed, giggling.

"Let me know if you have any questions," I called after them as they ascended the stairs.

I got busy after that, and didn't see them for twenty or thirty minutes. Other people arrived, some people left, and almost everyone wanted to know about the murder. I said as little as I could and did my best not to give anyone the impression that I knew more about it than the average person. Above all, I wanted to avoid letting anyone know that I'd actually found Brenda and had seen the whole messy, awful scene. If I did, I'd have to talk about it, and I still felt a little queasy whenever I thought too hard about what it had been like. (The memory of fainting dead away in Rafe's arms wasn't one I particularly wanted to relive, either. Not that I'd have to talk about that, but I didn't even want to have to think about it.) The lady— and I use the word loosely—who was trying to contact Brenda's wandering soul went into a trance right there on the library floor, and started moaning and groaning in a way that bore very little resemblance to the shrill tones of the late Brenda Puckett. The rest of the group looked on with a blend of amusement, pity, and exasperation. A few rolled their eyes. I wondered if I ought to interfere, but I was afraid of what might happen to me if I did.

And then Charlene and Gary Lee came back downstairs, still giggling and holding hands, and saved me from having to get involved in the séance. I ignored the rest of the assembly to escort them into the kitchen, just to be sure I could get their contact information on the sign-in sheet. I suspected they were first-time buyers, newlyweds looking for their first home, and semi-serious about buying something. If I could get my hooks into them and hold on, I might get a commission at some point. Maybe not in what was left of this year, but eventually.

"So how long have you been married?" I asked while Gary Lee was writing their information on the sheet. His handwriting looked like the rest of him: spiky, uneven, and dramatic. Charlene giggled and looked adoringly at him. "Two months."

"Congratulations. And now you're looking for your first house?"

She nodded.

"What do you think of this one?"

"Too big," Gary Lee said without looking up. "Too expensive. Needs too much work."

"But it was a good house, didn't you think, honey?" Charlene squeezed his arm. He nodded.

"Yeah. It was good. But too big."

"What sort of size were you looking for?" I asked. They agreed that something with at least two, maybe three bedrooms would be good. I crossed my fingers. "I'd be happy to help you find something. Unless you're already working with another Realtor . . ."

They looked at each other. "No."

"If you'll give me your e-mail address, I can send you a list of all the houses for sale in your price range. Then we can narrow it down to the ones you're interested in and go look at them."

They exchanged another look. "Yeah. That'd be good."

"Great." *Yes!* "Here's my card. I'll send you a list of properties this evening, and then you can let me know which ones you'd like to see."

"Sure." They nodded eagerly. I watched them walk out the door, still hand in hand and giggling, and although I managed to restrain myself from jumping up and down in undignified excitement, it was difficult.

Dix called at three thirty, just as things were starting to slow down. The lady in the library had come out of her trance and departed. I was glad to see her go; if there was one thing I didn't need, it was for Brenda's spirit to be summoned back to haunt the house. Not that I'd be likely to see her if she came back, but if Mrs. Jenkins returned, or Rafe moved in, or someone else bought the place and renovated it, I doubted they'd be any happier about her presence than I.

When the medium left, most of the others did too, as it seemed the entertainment was over. A single guy was roaming around on the second floor, so I took the phone out on the porch to talk to Dix.

"Sorry," Dix said. "I've been busy."

"No problem," I answered. "I've been busy, too. So what was going on earlier?"

"What do you mean?"

"It sounded like you were having a family conference. Is something wrong?"

"Why would you think that?" Dix asked.

"No reason. Well, call it paranoia, but both you and Todd have been lecturing me about getting involved with Rafe Collier, and I thought maybe . . ."

"We'd all get together for Sunday brunch and talk about you and the guy you claim you're not involved with? Sorry, sis. I believed you when you said there wasn't anything going on between you. Now I'm starting to wonder, though. It sounds like a guilty conscience to me."

"You're wasted in family law," I muttered. Dix snorted. I added, reluctantly, "All right, so I've got a guilty conscience. I had dinner with him yesterday. But only so I could make sure he understands that I'm not going to get involved with him. It wasn't a date or anything. Please don't tell Mom!"

"Is he giving you a hard time?" Dix wanted to know, without promising that he wouldn't tell our mother.

"No, he's not. Not at all. I promise. He's actually quite nice." He'd certainly given me plenty of help the night before. Fetching Alexandra, interrogating Maurice, and picking the lock on Clarice's storage unit. "Not my type, of course."

"Yes, you've said that before."

"Well, he isn't. Could you imagine mom's face if I brought Rafe Collier home to meet her?"

"She'd be polite," Dix said fairly. "Mom's always polite."

"Of course she is. She taught us, didn't she? But she'd never let me hear the end of it if I started dating a man with a criminal record. So I would consider it a personal favor if you wouldn't mention anything about it."

Dix hesitated for a second. "I suppose what mom doesn't know can't hurt her," he agreed, finally. "As long as you're telling the truth. He's not bothering you, right?"

"He's not. I swear." It wasn't even really a lie. In fact, it was amazing how un-bothered I was. "Thanks, Dix. You always were my favorite brother."

"I'm your only brother," Dix pointed out.

"That, too. And that's why I'm sure you won't mind giving me some free advice."

"Does this have to do with Collier?" He sounded suspicious.

"Only indirectly." I explained the situation with Mrs. Jenkins—in hypothetical terms, without mentioning any names—and asked Dix's advice for what to do. He waxed poetic for minute after minute while I made mental notes. The lone browser came out of the house while Dix was talking, and I lowered the phone to tell him goodbye and thanks for coming. Dix didn't even notice; when I put the phone back to my ear, he was still going strong.

"Thanks," I interrupted eventually. "That's great. Lots of information. Once I figure out what it means, I'm sure I'll know exactly what to do."

"Give me a break, sis. You took pre-law. You understood every word."

True, I had. "I appreciate it. You're a brick, Dix. If you weren't my brother, I'd kiss you."

"That's all right," Dix said. "Just don't go kissing anyone else. And tell Collier that next time he wants information, he can call me himself, instead of making my sister do his dirty work for him."

"It was my idea. I wasn't sure you'd be willing to help if he called."

"I'm always willing to help," Dix said. "For a fee."

He hung up. I stuck my tongue out at the phone, for all the good it did me.

It was almost a quarter to four by now, and it appeared as if the rush of visitors was over. I stayed on the porch, rocking gently in the creaky, peeling swing, admiring my newly manicured toes, and enjoying the fact that the temperature had finally dropped below ninety degrees. That, and avoiding being alone inside the house.

After a couple of minutes, I was rewarded by the sight of a small figure trotting up the driveway. (If *rewarded* is the right word.) It was old Mrs. Jenkins, still wearing the same dirty housecoat and the same slippers, with her hair sticking out in every direction. If Rafe didn't do something about her living situation soon, I'd damned well do it myself. I wasn't family, so my options were much more limited than his, if he could ever prove he was her grandson, but surely I could do *something*. It wasn't right that the poor old dear should have to live in that sorry excuse for a home, where no one even bothered to comb her hair or make sure she changed her clothes once a week. For a hundred grand, Brenda ought to have been able to do better, and if she hadn't been such a greedy witch, and had paid Mrs. Jenkins even half of what the property was worth, Mrs. Jenkins could have been sitting pretty for the rest of her life.

"Good afternoon, Mrs. Jenkins," I said politely when she came within range. I wondered what sort of state she was in today and what kind of behavior I could expect to see. Would she remember me? And if she did, would she know who I was, or think I was LaDonna Collier?

Her first words gave me no clue at all. "Hi, baby. What you doin' here?"

"I'm having an open house," I said. She nodded vaguely and looked around.

"Where's that handsome boy of yours?"

"Um . . ." Rafe? Or Tyrell? "Not here, I'm afraid. It's just me today."

"You're being careful, ain't you? He'd be just sick if summat happened to you or the baby."

Tyrell, then. Rafe couldn't care less what happened to me. And I wasn't—thank God!—expecting his child. "Yes, I'm being careful. I don't want anything to happen to me, either."

"That's good." She patted my hand; her own was tiny and spotted and wrinkled and brown. I smiled back, and although I suspected it wouldn't make any difference, I tried anyway.

"You know, Mrs. Jenkins, I'm not LaDonna. LaDonna was Tyrell's girlfriend and Rafe's mother. Rafe's your grandson, not your son. And I'm Rafe's . . . um . . . well, Rafe and I are just friends. But I'm not LaDonna. I'm Savannah."

Mrs. Jenkins nodded, but vaguely, her eyes on a car that was slowing down out on the road. It turned into the driveway and then started crunching its way up to the house. Mrs. Jenkins jumped. "He's comin' to get me!"

"That's not the police . . ." I began, remembering what had happened the first time I'd met her, when Spicer and Truman appeared to take her back to the Milton House.

She snorted. "I know it ain't the police, baby. That's the bad man!"

I shook my head. "You must have him confused with somebody else. That's just my boss. He's coming to talk to me about something."

Mrs. Jenkins shook her head right back at me. "He's gonna hurt me. He said so. He showed me his gun, and then he said if I told anyone I'd seen him, he'd kill me, too. Just like my baby. I gotta get inside!"

"Oh!" I said, as light dawned. "You mean . . ."

But she was already gone, into the house as quickly as her ancient legs and fuzzy slippers could carry her. The door slammed behind her.

While we'd been talking, Walker had pulled his Mercedes up to the bottom of the stairs and stepped out. Because it was Sunday, he was more casually dressed than at the office, but the khakis had a knife-edged pleat down the front, and the pale canary yellow Oxford shirt was starched to within an inch of its life. I could have seen my reflection in his loafers, and not a hair on his dignified, salt-and-pepper head was out of place. He was quite amazingly good looking, and if he hadn't been my boss, and gay, and about fifteen years too old, I would have made a dead set for him. As it was, I smiled in a friendly, but distinctly non-sexy manner. "Hi, Walker."

"Savannah." He nodded cordially at me, although his eyes were on the door. He must have seen Mrs. Jenkins scurry away from him, and now he was wondering why.

"That was Tondalia Jenkins," I said apologetically. "I think I told you she's old and somewhat confused."

Walker nodded warily.

"Well, today she's living thirty years in the past. She thinks I'm LaDonna Collier, pregnant with her grandchild, and that you're my disapproving father. See, Mrs. Jenkins's son Tyrell was shot by LaDonna's daddy because old Jim Collier didn't want his daughter involved with a black boy. Or at least I think that's what happened."

"I see," Walker said. I nodded.

"I guess old Jim must have been hanging out, waiting for Tyrell, because Mrs. Jenkins said she'd seen him. You, that is. And that he'd shown her his gun and told her he'd kill her, too, if she told anyone about him. Except, of course, you don't have a gun and you had nothing to do with killing Tyrell." I smiled. Walker didn't. I guess he didn't think it was funny. I added, "She's got a little bit of paranoia anyway, because the nursing home always sends the police after her when she wanders off."

"Really?" Walker threw a glance over his shoulder. There was no police car coming up Potsdam Street. I shrugged.

"I guess they haven't gotten the message yet. Or maybe they've got more important things to do than chase down a harmless old lady."

Walker moved his gaze back to the door. "Shouldn't we make sure she's all right? If she was upset when she went in . . ."

"Maybe that would be a good idea." I walked to the door and tried the knob. It was locked. "Uh oh."

"What?" Walker said.

"I left the key inside, so I wouldn't forget it when it was time to leave. She must have locked herself in. Maybe she'll answer." I started knocking on the door. "Mrs. Jenkins? Can you hear me? Come open the door, Mrs. Jenkins. It's just me. Savannah. Nobody's going to hurt you. Please, Mrs. Jenkins, can you hear me?"

"Here." Walker pushed me aside and bent over the lock. I heard a click, and then he turned the knob and pushed the door open. I stared.

"Where did you . . . ?"

"There was a spare key at the office." He waved me in, and then followed me through the door and locked it behind us. I opened my mouth.

"Mrs. Jenkins?"

Nothing. Walker took a breath and added his voice to mine. "Mrs. Jenkins? This is Walker Lamont, Savannah's boss. Please show yourself. We're worried about you."

There was no answer this time either, but we heard a soft shuffling noise. Walker's gray eyes met mine. "Sounds like she's in back," I said softly. "Kitchen or . . . um . . . library."

He nodded.

I headed down the hallway with him right behind, and believe me, I tried not to draw a parallel between this and going into the library with Rafe a week ago. But at least I wouldn't encounter a butchered body today. Mrs. Jenkins had been alive and well just five minutes ago, and although she was old and demented and paranoid, I wasn't worried that she was suicidal, or homicidal.

That is, until I walked through the kitchen door and found her in the middle of the cracked vinyl floor, holding a serrated carving knife the size of a saber with both hands.

20.

"Whoa!"

I stopped, so abruptly that Walker walked into me and knocked me forward a step. We all froze for a moment, suspended in time, and then I pulled myself together. My voice was calmer than I felt on the inside. "You'll want to be careful with that, Mrs. Jenkins. You could hurt yourself, or someone else."

Her eyes flicked to me for a second, and then she went back to staring unblinkingly past me at Walker. I made another effort to defuse the situation. "This is my boss, Mrs. Jenkins. He's not here to hurt you. He just came to talk to me about something."

"I seen him before," Mrs. Jenkins said.

"Excuse me?"

"I seen him. Here."

"Well, he was Brenda's boss, too. You know, the woman who listed your house for sale."

"The one who's dead," Mrs. Jenkins said, flatly.

I nodded, even as I felt a shiver of fear down my back. Was it possible that Mrs. Jenkins had murdered Brenda after all? I hadn't thought she had the strength, but maybe I'd been wrong. She was feeling threatened now, and it had caused her to brandish a carving knife as long as her arm. Maybe Brenda had underestimated Mrs. Jenkins's strength, too, and that was what had allowed Mrs. Jenkins to kill her.

While all of these thoughts were scurrying through my head, I was talking calmly, trying to reason with her. "If Walker was here, it was probably just to see the place. He was responsible for Brenda, just as he is for me. All the listings are his. They belong to the brokerage, not the individual agent. He probably just wanted to make sure that everything was okay."

Although if he'd been here before the murder, he must have known about the listing, and that it was a net listing, then. I didn't have time to follow this particular train of thought to its final destination at the moment, however.

It didn't seem as if Mrs. Jenkins had heard me. "They was busy talkin', in there." She nodded in the direction of the library. I felt another *frisson*, stronger this time, and for a different reason.

"Who were?"

"Him," Mrs. Jenkins used the knife to point at Walker, "and the lady who died."

I glanced at Walker. He was shaking his head mutely, but without conviction. His usually kind, gray eyes were darting from side to side, like a trapped animal, and suddenly a lot of little bits and pieces of the puzzle were falling into place in my head. The thought-train came out of the tunnel into blinding light, and I had the dizzying feeling that someone had shaken a kaleidoscope and changed the picture inside. The new pattern was one I hadn't considered before.

Of course, Brenda would ask a man to accompany her to Potsdam Street on Saturday morning. A woman would be no help if Maurice decided to fight for Alexandra. Tim would have been about as useless as Clarice or Heidi, and if Brenda wanted to keep Alexandra's involvement with Maurice from Steven, Walker was the obvious choice. I guess she didn't realize just how upset he was over her illegal wrangling of Mrs. Jenkins, or how far he'd go to protect his reputation and snag that coveted spot on the Real Estate Commission.

It had taken just a few seconds for all the facts to rearrange themselves in my mind, in nice, neat, damning rows, but it was too long. Walker had seen my expression change, and knew I had figured it out. His handsome face hardened and his eyes turned the color and consistency of bullets: steel gray and hard. He reached behind him and whipped out a little handgun. It looked dainty and harmless, like a toy, but the hand that held it was steady as a rock. I took a step back, next to Mrs. Jenkins.

My mother trained me to be, among other things, a good hostess and an amusing conversationalist. I can talk to practically anyone about practically anything, and it isn't often I find myself lost for words. This time I didn't know what to say. What does one say to a man one has admired and looked up to, when one has realized that he's a cold-blooded murderer who's likely to kill one in the next few minutes?

As often happens to me, my mouth took charge independently of my brain. "I can understand about Brenda—Lord knows I've wanted to murder her myself, more than once—but why Clarice? What did she do?"

"The old bitch tried to blackmail me," Walker said disgustedly. I chalked a mental point up to Rafe, who had suggested it. And I hoped devoutly that I would get the chance to tell him he'd been right. In the meantime, I talked.

"She tried to get you to give her a percentage of everything the company took in?"

The same thing she had done with Brenda fifteen years ago, but on a much larger scale. Walker Lamont Realty sells tens of millions of dollars worth of real estate, and brings in hundreds of thousands in commissions every month. Booty like that would be well worth a little blackmail.

Walker nodded. "Like I'd roll over and give her whatever she wanted just because she figured out I'd got rid of that fat cow Brenda Puckett. Who deserved everything she got, let me tell ya! Even Clarice said so."

Walker's cultivated accent was degenerating rapidly. Any minute now he'd probably turn and spit on the floor.

"I didn't like Brenda, either," I said soothingly, while my thoughts ticked over as fast as they could, like a hamster on a wheel. Maybe if I could keep him talking, the police would show up looking for Mrs. Jenkins, and save us all. Walker smiled, but it didn't reach his eyes.

"You're a nice girl, Savannah. I'm sorry I have to kill you."

"I'm sorry, too," I said, doing my best to keep my voice level. And although he probably expected me to beg for mercy, I wasn't going to give him the satisfaction. Not on my own behalf, anyway. "You can leave Mrs. Jenkins be, though, can't you? She's old and senile. Nobody's going to believe anything she says."

Walker glanced at her. She still had the knife in her hands, although those hands were trembling with effort now, and her eyes were vague and unfocused. I've rarely seen a knife-wielding lunatic look less threatening. Nevertheless, Walker shook his head. "Sorry, Savannah. I can't do that. She saw me. She has to go, too. But I'll make it quick. I have no need to make either of you suffer."

"Gee, thanks," I said, wondering if he'd dragged out the inevitable for Brenda or Clarice. No, surely not Brenda; there hadn't been enough time. Clarice, maybe . . .

The thought was unpleasant, and I forced my mind back to more immediate concerns. Namely, dragging the inevitable out for myself as long as I possibly could. "You must have been pretty upset with Clarice. You probably thought you'd gotten away with Brenda's murder until she tried to extort money from you."

"I could have killed her on the spot," Walker agreed, with a faint smile at his own pun. "But, of course, I couldn't do that. Not right there at Brenda's memorial service. So I arranged to meet her later instead. The next day, as it was."

"So that article in the *Voice*—the one about Clarice's husband and the whole Kress-building fiasco . . ."

Walker nodded, and a shadow of vexation crossed his no-longer-quite-so-handsome features. Funny how I had never noticed before how deep the lines at the corners of his eyes were, or how tight the lips when they weren't smiling.

"Did you leak it, to frame her?

"Hardly," Walker said grimly. "Tim did it."

It didn't come as much of a surprise. I had suspected as much yesterday evening, when Tim talked about wanting to get rid of Clarice. I also remembered the phone call I had heard the beginning of last Sunday, when Tim had told someone named Larry he had a story for him. And the *Voice* reporter's name had been Lawrence Derryberry.

"What did Tim have to do with any of it?"

"Nothing," Walker said. "Not a thing. He knew about the—as you say—Kress-building fiasco, and that Brenda gave Clarice a job after Clarice's husband died, but that was all he knew. But Clarice never liked him, so with Brenda out of the picture, he wanted to get rid of her as well. I've had a talk with him about it." He closed his teeth with a snap. I didn't envy Tim's conversation with Walker, although it was much to be preferred over the one I was having at the moment.

"But what was he doing at the Stor-All last Monday morning?" I asked. "The receptionist said she'd seen him."

And then it dawned on me that Tim wasn't the only good-looking gay guy that Brenda worked with. I had just suspected Tim because it hadn't crossed my mind to suspect Walker.

"He wasn't there," Walker said, confirming my conclusion. "I was."

"To do what?"

"Change the date on the Potsdam Street listing agreement, of course. If the police saw that I'd signed the paperwork on the second instead of the twelfth, they'd know I knew about the net listing before the murder. But if I didn't sign it until the twelfth, *after* the murder, I would have had no reason to kill Brenda." He smiled tightly.

"And I guess you let Clarice believe that she was going to get what she wanted, and then you killed her?"

Walker nodded. "I wined and dined her at her favorite restaurant, and put a little harmless powder in her drink, and then I drove her home and helped her upstairs. She was already passed out when I made the first cut."

My stomach turned at the picture he painted, and the offhanded way he talked about slicing into flesh, but I forced myself to stay focused. "Brenda wasn't, though.

Although I've been told that for someone who knows what they're doing, it's both quick and easy to cut a throat. Funny, I wouldn't have pegged you for the hunting type."

Walker showed his perfect teeth in another smile that didn't reach his eyes. "I guess I never told you my life story, Savannah. You will appreciate this, I'm sure. I grew up in a small town in Kentucky. My daddy was a redneck. He drove a pick-up truck with a gun rack and a mongrel dog in the back, and went hunting on the weekends. I used to have to come along, because he hoped it'd make a man out of me. So I cut my first throat before I was ten. It's like riding a bicycle: once you know how, you never forget."

"I see," I said, weakly. "Your dad?"

"Sadly, he's passed on. A hunting accident. Very unfortunate." Walker's voice was cold, and I felt his words settle in the pit of my stomach like a block of ice. But before I had time to blurt out an unguarded question as to whether he'd shot his father—ill-advised under the circumstances—there came the sound of car tires from outside.

Time went into slow motion. I could see the thoughts chasing each other across Walker's face—shock, fear, uncertainty, anger—and the gun wavered for a crucial tenth of a second. I grabbed the opportunity and gave Mrs. Jenkins a shove in one direction while I hurled myself in the other. The bullet sliced through the air where we had stood just a second ago. Mrs. Jenkins landed hard, face first on the cracked vinyl, and stayed there. I ran, stumbling and skittering on high heels, out the kitchen door into the hallway. Behind me, I could hear Walker following. Simultaneously, someone began hammering on the front door.

"Heeelp!" I shrieked. "Somebody help me!"

The hammering intensified, and I heard masculine bellows outside the door, much too far away for me to recognize. My plan, if I had one and wasn't just mindlessly trying to get away, was to run to the front hall and open the door, but Walker cut me off before I got there. I changed course and backed into the library instead. Walker followed. He had the gun in a steady grip again, and a light of homicidal mania in his eyes.

I was just about to start praying when we heard a scrabbling noise in the hallway. Walker whirled around and went for the door. I followed, since there was nowhere else for me to go, and because I had an idea of what was going on. It didn't come as a surprise to see old Mrs. Jenkins determinedly crawling down the hallway toward the door. She had just a few yards to go, and Walker did the only thing he could think of. He aimed the gun at her. I threw myself forward, pushing him with everything I had. The bullet went wild, and the gun went flying. So did Walker. The gun crashed through the hall window and landed in the rose bushes outside amidst the tinkling of glass. Walker landed on top of Mrs. Jenkins, and I could hear all the air being squeezed out of her body in a *whooosh*. The front door was vibrating under the onslaught of blows.

I recognize a heaven-sent opportunity when it hits me over the head, and I didn't waste any time in taking advantage of this one. For me to land on top of Walker would only mash poor Mrs. Jenkins's face and body deeper into the floor, so I stayed where I was, digging in my handbag. No, I'm not one of those realtors who carries a gun (although after this experience, I thought I might start), but after a moment, I found a lipstick. One of my customers at the makeup counter had told me about this trick. I had giggled at the time, but under the circumstances, it was worth a shot. It would possibly distract Walker for long enough to allow the police to get through the door and take over, with *real* guns. I shoved the cylinder against Walker's back. "Stay where you are. I have a gun."

Walker froze, like a dead weight on top of poor, frail Mrs. Jenkins. She groaned.

A voice outside the door muttered something, and the hammering stopped. There was a breathless moment of silence, as if the house was bracing itself, and then the heavy oak door exploded inward with an almighty bang and a splintering noise. Officer Truman stumbled through the doorway, blinking.

"You took your time about it," I commented.

Officer Spicer followed more slowly, and I could see his lips quirk when he saw me with my Mauve Heather #56 pressed against Walker's back.

"You can lower your weapon now, Miz Martin," he said blandly. "Truman's got him covered."

I dropped the lipstick back in my purse while Truman prudently handcuffed Walker before lifting him off Mrs. Jenkins.

"Um, boss?" he ventured. "What're we charging him with?"

"Yes," Walker drawled, in his well-bred, snooty voice, "I'd like to know that, myself." Had his hands not been cuffed behind him, he'd probably be brushing invisible lint off his sleeve as he spoke.

Spicer looked from me—I grimaced—to Mrs. Jenkins, still prone on the dusty floor. "Assault with the intent to harm will do, for the moment. Put him in the back of the car."

Truman moved to obey. Walker allowed himself to be walked outside and loaded into the police car, without protest and without so much as a glance at me. Truman closed the door behind them while I turned my attention to Mrs. Jenkins, who was just starting to stir and moan. Spicer joined me in helping her to sit up. "What *are* we charging him with?" he asked, *sotto voce*.

"You mean you don't know? He killed Brenda Puckett. Then he killed Clarice Webb. Then he threatened to kill Mrs. Jenkins and myself. Then he attacked Mrs. Jenkins."

"What was she tryin' to do?" Spicer asked, curiosity mixed with awe in his voice, as he assiduously brushed the new dust off Mrs. Jenkins's already filthy housecoat. She was sitting upright, but still had a vacant look on her face, like she wasn't quite sure what was happening.

"He had me cornered in the library," I explained. "I guess he thought she was passed out in the kitchen, but then we heard her crawling down the corridor. Walker left me and threw himself on her."

"So he killed Miz Puckett, did he? And the other one, too? Miz Webster?"

I nodded.

"And said he'd kill you? You're gonna have to come downtown with us and make a statement. Detective Grimaldi's gonna wanna talk to you."

"My pleasure," I said. "Just let me lock up here first. Um . . . how about if I follow you in my car? I don't really want to share the squad car with Walker. And that way I can drive Mrs. Jenkins home first. Unless you're going to need to talk to her, too?"

Officer Spicer glanced at her, sitting there on the floor muttering to herself, with tiny trickles of blood running down her legs and face from the slide along the hardwood floors. "I don't think we need bother with that. Ain't nothing she can tell us that we can't get from you. And she oughta have some medical attention, anyway. Them scratches ain't too bad, but the old bird got the wind knocked out of her pretty bad. You want I should radio for an ambulance?"

I shook my head. "I think it'll be faster just to drive her down to the nursing home. It's just down the street—you know that—and I'm sure they're equipped to take care of minor cuts and bruises. Would you mind getting her situated in my car—it's the blue Volvo—while I lock the door? I'll come back for my things later."

"Sure thing." Spicer grabbed old Mrs. Jenkins under her arms and heaved her to her feet. She was too shook up even to attempt to bite him. While he loaded her into the passenger seat, I locked the door and hurried around the car and into the driver's seat. With Mrs. Jenkins dozing beside me, I steered with one hand and dialed my cell phone with the other. (Bad, I know, but I figured Spicer and Truman had better things to do just now than bust me for illegal cell phone use.)

"Pawn shop," a gruff voice muttered. I hesitated.

"Didn't you say 'car lot' last time?"

"Beg pardon?"

"Never mind. I'm looking for Rafe Collier."

"Nobody here by that name," the voice said.

"Don't give me that," I retorted. Mother would have quailed. "It's Wendell, isn't it? We met yesterday, when you drove me to Fidelio's Restaurant. I have a message for Rafe. Get hold of him, please, and tell him that his grandmother has had an accident and needs his help. I'm on my way to the police station, or I'd stay with her myself. And while he's at it, tell him to get her out of that god-awful place and into someplace nicer, or I'll do it myself. Can you do that for me?"

Wendell agreed, somewhat reluctantly, that he could, and I reverted to good manners before I hung up, just long enough to thank him.

Rafe wasn't there yet when Mrs. Jenkins and I got to the Milton House, but I didn't really have time to wait around for him. There was no telling where he was or how long it would take Wendell to track him down; he could be in Sweetwater for all I knew!—so I washed Mrs. Jenkins's scratches and put her to bed. I extracted a promise from her that she wouldn't leave before he came, although I wasn't positive she knew who I was talking about. The ordeal with Walker and the gun seemed to have scattered what little wits she had.

That done, I headed downtown, back to police headquarters. Things were very different this time around. I found a parking space on the street nearby and went in through the visitors' entrance. I didn't wait for more than two minutes before Detective Grimaldi herself appeared to escort me upstairs. She ushered me into another interview room; friendlier than the one I'd seen last week, and with no two-way mirror. I guess I had graduated from suspect to witness. "Would you like something to drink? Diet Coke, right?"

I accepted her offer, and she went and got it herself, along with a can of Dr. Pepper. Another sign of approbation, I thought, if she'd unbent far enough to have a soda with me.

She sat down on the other side of the table and popped the top on the Dr. Pepper. "Officer Spicer tells me I have you to thank for the apprehension of Mr. Lamont."

I shrugged modestly.

"So tell me about it. From the beginning."

I took a sip of Diet Coke and began. "Walker Lamont is my boss. He owns Walker Lamont Realty, and has for about twenty years."

Detective Grimaldi opened her mouth to say something—probably that she didn't expect me to begin quite that far back—and I continued, before she could protest, "He grew up in some hick town somewhere in Kentucky, with a redneck daddy who used to take him hunting. He told me about it earlier. And you may want to look into what happened to his father, because I wouldn't be surprised if Walker shot him. He said it was a hunting accident. Very tragic."

Grimaldi shut her mouth and started taking notes. I continued. "At some point he came to Nashville, probably because as a gay man, he wasn't happy or accepted where he was. Then he discovered that there was money and a reputation to be made in real estate. He started his own company after a while, and became both very successful, and very well-respected. He was being considered for a spot on the Real Estate Commission next year, did you know that?"

"He didn't mention it," Detective Grimaldi said, jotting it down on her legal pad.

"No reason why he would. Especially since it was the reason he killed Brenda."

"Is it financially beneficial?"

I shook my head. "Oh, no. Walker isn't concerned with money. Not that he doesn't have plenty, but I think he cares more about his reputation and his standing in the real estate community. Being invited to join the Real Estate Commission is an honor. The rest of the world couldn't care less, but to those of us in the business, it's a very big deal."

"And Mrs. Puckett was a threat to his realizing that?"

I nodded. "Walker's responsible for all the rest of us. His job is to keep the agents under him in line. That only goes as far as we allow, of course, and I can't imagine that Brenda allowed much interference, but the buck still stops—stopped—with him. When Brenda took 101 Potsdam as a net listing, she broke the law, and even if he didn't have anything to do with it on the front end, the responsibility was ultimately his, as her boss."

"What's a net listing?" Grimaldi wanted to know. I explained how a net listing works and why it's illegal to take one, while she took notes. "So once word got out that Mrs. Puckett had taken this net listing, Mr. Lamont would be held responsible right along with her, and that would put his appointment to the Real Estate Commission in jeopardy?"

I nodded. "If it had been a one time occurrence, maybe not, but I think that sort of thing may have been going on a lot. Brenda had already been investigated by the commission once. And Alexandra Puckett told me that she had a habit of handling certain paperwork and listings outside the office, to keep the details from Walker."

"Why didn't he just fire her?"

I shrugged. "Who knows? Maybe he didn't dare to. If her files are full of illegal deals, she could still cause trouble. And he probably liked the money she brought in. She was insanely successful, you know. Plus, Mrs. Jenkins really isn't capable of taking care of the house, so in a way, Brenda was doing her a favor. Or would have been, if she'd treated Mrs. Jenkins fairly and paid her what the house was worth."

"What changed his mind?" Detective Grimaldi was scribbling busily now. I hesitated. It wasn't really my place to reveal any of this, but on the other hand, it was just a matter of time before it became public knowledge anyway. Grimaldi arched her brows at me, and I sighed.

"It's just a guess, but I think that when Rafael Collier called Brenda the Thursday before she died, he may have asked questions about the owner of 101 Potsdam. You see, it turns out that Tondalia Jenkins is his grandmother." I explained the convoluted story behind Rafe's birth, trying not to feel like I was gossiping. It didn't work, and I was squirming guiltily by the time I finished.

Detective Grimaldi fixed me with a steely stare. "How long have you known this? Is it definite?"

"As definite as it can be, when all the people involved are dead. He showed me a picture of Tyrell Jenkins, the way Tyrell looked at the time he died, and the resemblance is scary. Mrs. Jenkins probably has a photo she'll show you, and you can see for yourself."

"So Mr. Collier was asking Mrs. Puckett questions about the Jenkins family when he called her last Thursday?"

"I think he probably was. He would have been cautious, I think, but he may have dug deep enough to put Brenda on alert. Maybe she told Walker, or maybe she just told Clarice, and he overheard. There wasn't much going on in the office that he didn't know about. Either way, I think he probably realized that Rafe was someone who might cause trouble, and he decided to take care of the problem."

"Why not just remove Mr. Collier?"

It was my turn to shrug. "It was probably simpler and easier to get rid of Brenda. Being a real estate agent isn't always a safe profession. Rafe was an unknown entity who wouldn't have stood still to have his throat slit, plus Brenda might have done it again. Or something else that would ruin Walker's reputation. He'd be much safer with her out of the way. And I wouldn't be surprised if he hoped Rafe would be suspected of it. Two birds with one stone, and all that."

"Makes sense," Grimaldi said, writing. I nodded. It did. Unfortunately.

"Walker may have offered to come with her on Saturday morning, or maybe she asked him to come, for protection." I explained my reasoning with regards to Clarice, Heidi, and Tim. Grimaldi nodded understanding. While she was busy writing, I waited, hesitating over Maurice Washington and the check. In the end, I decided that nothing would be gained by mentioning either. If

Rafe and I hadn't shown up, Maurice would probably have gotten around to reporting the death himself eventually. Anonymously, of course.

"And Mrs. Webster?"

"Clarice knew Walker had gone out that morning with Brenda. She tried to blackmail him. See, she blackmailed Brenda fifteen years ago. That was how she came to be working for Brenda in the first place, and she was still doing it when Brenda died. I guess with Brenda gone, Clarice wanted to find another source of income."

"What did she have on Mrs. Puckett?"

I explained about the Kress building and Mr. Webster's suicide, and Detective Grimaldi nodded. "We know about that. I guess I just didn't realize that what was happening was blackmail. It seemed like a straightforward business contract."

"It *was* a straight-forward business contract. That's the beauty of it. But Clarice should have been working for five hundred bucks a week, not taking home almost half of what Brenda made. Brenda must have been desperate to agree to something like that!"

"Not as desperate as Mr. Lamont," Detective Grimaldi said dryly. "I take it he agreed to meet Mrs. Webster's demands, and then accompanied her home and killed her, using the same knife he had used to kill Brenda Puckett, to make it seem as if Mrs. Webster had killed Mrs. Puckett."

"That's what he said. And then he probably went over to her house on Friday morning to 'discover' her, just in case you came across his DNA there."

Grimaldi nodded. "It all makes sense so far. Now tell me what happened today."

I explained about the open house. "Then Mrs. Jenkins showed up. She's in the habit of wandering off from the nursing home and going back to the house. And then Walker dropped by."

"Why?"

I hesitated. "He didn't have time to say. Although he had a gun with him, so maybe I said something earlier in the day that made him think I knew more than I did."

The thought was unsettling. The image of Walker putting bullets into his gun, each and every one of them with my name on it, gave me goose bumps up and down my arms. I hugged myself.

"Take your time," Grimaldi said, without a hint of condescension in her voice.

I explained how Mrs. Jenkins had told me that Walker was a "bad man," and my mistaken belief that she was confused and had mistaken him for Jim Collier. "I think Old Jim shot Tyrell, although I don't know how you'd be able to prove that at this point. I doubt the Colliers were big picture-takers, although Rafe may have found a picture of his grandfather somewhere among LaDonna's stuff. You could ask him. Or maybe the Sweetwater jail has a mug shot. Old Jim was certainly arrested enough. Mrs. Jenkins may be able to identify Old Jim from a photograph. Then again, I don't know how reliable her identification would be. And anyway, he's dead, so it wouldn't really matter one way or the other. But at least you'd know."

I was babbling, and realized it, so I reined myself in. "Anyway, Mrs. Jenkins told me he'd hurt her, that he'd shown her his gun and told her that if she told anyone she'd seen him, he'd kill her, too. I thought she had confused him with Jim Collier, but when I told Walker, of course, *he* realized that she had recognized him."

Detective Grimaldi nodded. "We checked with the nursing home, and she *was* missing for a while on Saturday morning. But they didn't actually realize that she was gone until she came back, so they never called it in. The nurse who spoke to her said she was muttering about blood and the bad man, but apparently she frequently talks about what happened to her son, so they didn't realize that this was anything different."

"Totally useless people," I muttered. Tamara Grimaldi shrugged. "Anyway, she locked herself in the house, and when she wouldn't open the door, Walker brought out a key. He said he'd had a spare at the office. I thought it was strange, because I'd already gotten the spare from Brenda's desk, but I was worried about Mrs. Jenkins, so I didn't think too much about it. I should have realized that it was the original key, the one he'd taken with him after he killed Brenda last week."

"There wasn't any way that you could have known," Tamara Grimaldi said comfortingly. "There was no reason to suspect him. We didn't. No more than anyone else whose DNA was found in the Lincoln Navigator. He did a very good job of covering his tracks. If you hadn't caught him for us, I'm not sure we would have been able to."

"Thank you very much, but sooner or later you would have gotten around to suspecting him. Or he would have made a mistake. Just out of curiosity, who did you suspect?"

Her lips quirked. "Not you. There was nothing at all about you that led me to believe you'd be capable of cutting someone's throat."

"That's nice to know. But . . ."

"I've been focusing a lot of attention on Mr. Collier," Detective Grimaldi said blandly. "Like you, I found it suspicious that he had arranged to meet Mrs. Puckett to see the house when he didn't have the financial resources to buy it. And, of course, he already has a record for violence." She paused. I nodded.

"Billy Scruggs had beaten LaDonna. Rafe's mother. She was too ashamed, or maybe too afraid, to report it."

"None of that is in the arrest report," Grimaldi said. I shook my head.

"Rafe wouldn't have said anything about it. Not if his mother didn't want it to come out. But I asked and he told me."

"And you believed him?"

I shrugged. "He didn't have any reason to lie. Anyway, when we got inside, Walker pulled out a gun and threatened to kill us both. I kept him talking for as long as I could because I was hoping that the nursing home had called the police again. When the car pulled up outside and distracted Walker, I pushed Mrs. Jenkins out of the way and ran. He followed me. Just when I thought he was going to kill me, we heard Mrs. Jenkins crawl down the hallway, and he turned around and went after her instead."

"I've heard Officer Spicer's report," Grimaldi nodded, with an expression that might almost have been a smile in someone less severe. "Good job with the lipstick."

"It was nothing."

This time it was a real smile, no doubt about it. It transformed her angular face, and made her almost attractive. "Well, Ms. Martin, unless you have something to add, I think that's it for now. I'll have a statement typed up for you to sign. How about I contact you tomorrow?"

I said that that would be just fine, and left. On the way home from picking up my open-house paraphernalia from 101 Potsdam Street, I drove by the Milton House Nursing Home, and when I didn't see Rafe's motorcycle in the parking lot, I stopped and went in, just to make sure that everything was all right. But when I inquired in the lobby, I was informed that Tondalia Jenkins had moved out suddenly, leaving no forwarding address. The nurse on duty this weekend was different from the one who'd been here afternoons during the week. She had no idea who I was, and when I asked if Mrs. Jenkins had left with her grandson, she said she was sure she had no idea, and popped a pink bubblegum bubble in my face. I smiled sweetly and gave her my business card, "in case you have need of a realtor," and went home.

21.

The weekly sales meeting on Monday morning was interesting. Most people had no idea that Walker had been arrested, and for the first few minutes after I imparted the news, everyone was buzzing. Several people refused to believe it, and I guess I couldn't blame them. I hadn't believed it myself, until I had no other choice. Then Detective Grimaldi appeared and addressed the assembly, explaining that Walker had in fact confessed to murdering Brenda and Clarice. She refused to go into detail, although Tim said, with a malicious gleam in his baby blue eyes, that he, for one, wasn't surprised. Detective Grimaldi didn't dignify his statement with an answer, other than to advise him that if he had something of importance to say, if he would please contact her privately. Tim smirked.

To my, and I'm sure several of the others', surprise, Walker had, at some point, arranged for Tim to take over the management of the office if something were to happen to Walker himself. Heidi Hoppenfeldt and I shared an uncomfortable moment of unity as we both contemplated the fact that we would have to work for Tim from now on. I wasn't sure I had it in me, and from the expression on Heidi's round face, she felt the same way.

Detective Grimaldi came to visit me in my cubby after the meeting broke up, to get me to sign my statement from yesterday and, surprisingly, to ask me to have lunch with her. "Don't worry," she added, with something that wasn't even a smile, but a grin, "I won't interrogate you. It's just that we got off on the wrong foot last week, and I wanted to make amends. I have a feeling we could get along quite well if we tried." Now that I had proven I wasn't as wimpy and helpless as she had previously thought, I assumed.

"And you won't ask intrusive questions about my love life and whether I'm involved with . . . um . . . certain individuals?"

"Certain individuals being Mr. Collier, I suppose? I guess I can avoid talking about him. If you can."

"I definitely can," I said firmly. "In that case, I'll be happy to have lunch with you. As long as we don't go to Fidelio's. That would totally ruin my reputation."

"I was thinking more of McDonald's or Burger King. Somewhere fast. I have a case to close."

"That's fine." With the way things were going, I was going to have to get used to eating like normal people, anyway.

I led the way through the lobby with the detective trailing behind. Tim was standing over a pouting Brittany, giving her orders, and he smirked when he saw us.

"Have a good time, Savannah. Detective. Have her home by midnight."

"Very funny," I answered coldly, while Detective Grimaldi merely showed Tim her teeth and said, "I'll be in touch, Mr. Briggs. A few questions; nothing to worry about." Her voice was a little overly reassuring, and so failed to be reassuring at all. It was a pleasure to see Tim's expression fade from gloating enjoyment to uncertainty.

Lunch was actually quite enjoyable, apart from the cuisine, and the detective kept her promise not to interrogate me. She didn't keep the one about Rafe, but rather than trying to get me to admit that there was something going on between us, she seemed more interested in getting me to assure her that there wasn't. So maybe she was hankering for him herself. Just because a woman eschews makeup and feminine clothes, doesn't mean she's gay. They'd make an interesting couple, anyhow, although I admit I had a hard time seeing the amorous Rafe being attracted to the business-like Grimaldi. But if we became better acquainted, maybe I would have the opportunity to give her some friendly advice about her hair and clothes. It was the least I could do.

When word got around of what had happened, my phone started ringing. Reporters called to interview me, friends and family called to congratulate me and/or to make sure I was okay, Lila called to invite me to lunch to dish the dirt, and Alexandra Puckett called to talk to me about Maurice. As soon as he'd heard that someone else had been arrested for the murders, he'd gotten in touch with Alexandra to tell her everything, and she wanted my opinion on what she ought to do.

"Why haven't you called me?" she demanded. "I thought you'd call to tell me that Walker killed my mom. Not that I'd hear it from the police. I thought we were *friends*!"

"We are," I assured her. "I'm sorry. You're right, I should have called and told you myself. It's just . . ."

"What? Tell me!"

"Well, on Saturday night, when she drove me home, Maybelle told me it would be better if I stayed away from you."

Alexandra breathed a word she had probably learned from Maurice. I won't repeat it. "Well, she can just lump it, because daddy likes you, and he won't mind if you call." She sounded triumphant.

"If Maybelle is going to marry your dad, though . . ."

"They're not married yet!" The implication was that if Alexandra had anything to say about it, they wouldn't be, either. "So tell me what to do, Savannah. About Maurice, I mean. *You* know men!"

"Not as well as you think," I said dryly. "I guess it depends on how you feel about him, after everything that's happened. He came clean and told you the truth, and you know that he didn't actually accept money from your mother to stop seeing you, but he left her on the floor without calling an ambulance, and that argues a degree of cowardice, don't you think?"

"He was afraid he'd be arrested," Alexandra said, but halfheartedly. I nodded, and then realized she couldn't see me.

"He probably had good reason to be. I'm just not sure I could date a man who found my mother bleeding on the floor and didn't do anything. No, let me change that. I'm sure I couldn't."

Alexandra sighed. "I'm sure you're right, Savannah. He just sounded so pitiful, you know."

I was certain he had. "You'll be going back to school in a couple of weeks, and he'll start college soon. Why don't you give it some time?"

Who knew, maybe they'd both get busy with their separate lives and the relationship would just die a natural death, without anyone having to say or do anything to end it.

"That's a good idea," Alexandra said gratefully. "Thanks, Savannah."

"No problem. I didn't really do much. Let me know how it goes."

She promised she would, and I hung up, pretending I didn't hear her parting shot. "And give Rafe a big kiss for me!"

My mother called, of course, to make sure I was all right, and Dix, and even Catherine. Lila and I squeezed in a power lunch, during which I dumped everything that had happened in her lap and she told me how clever I had been in figuring it out, and on Tuesday, Todd called and asked if I'd go to dinner with him. I accepted, and we ended up at Fidelio's again. Todd appeared to have deemed it "our" place, and since it didn't seem to have occurred to him that I might prefer to go somewhere else, I didn't say anything, just grinned and bore it. The gray-haired maitre d' beamed paternally at me when I showed up with Todd; I guess he hadn't approved of Rafe any more than anyone else did.

We sat at the other end of the restaurant, near where Walker and Tim had dined on Saturday, and talked mostly of inconsequential things. Todd's work, my work, how I had caught a two-time murderer and nearly gotten killed in the process . . . Until Todd told me that his father had retired LaDonna Collier's case file for lack of evidence. "I thought you'd like to know," he said stiffly, "since you seemed so concerned about Collier taking the fall for it."

"I wasn't concerned," I said. And amended it to, "Or only because I don't think he did it."

"He's gotten away with it, anyway," Todd said, "whether he had something to do with it or not."

"He didn't. So you don't have to worry."

Todd didn't answer. "So what's happening now?" he asked instead. "With you and with the house?"

"With me, not much. Walker had a back-up broker assigned, in case of emergency, and he's taken over running the company. I expect the name will change at some point, since being associated with Walker is no longer a benefit to us. As for the house on Potsdam Street, Mrs. Jenkins is getting it back. She didn't actually sell it, you know, even if Brenda did pay the Milton House a hundred grand for her room and board there. Maybe she'll put it back on the market and get to keep all the proceeds this time."

If so, I hoped she'd consider using me to list it. Of course, Tim was hoping the same thing, and he hadn't been pleased when I had explained the situation to him on Monday morning. There wasn't anything he could do about it, though; Walker had taken the house out of our inventory and off the Multiple Listing Service, and that was just as well, as far as Tim was concerned.

"So I guess you won't be seeing Collier again," Todd said. I shook my head.

"Now that the house business is settled, and the murders solved, there's no reason why I would. He hasn't even called." And as I had mentioned to Lila, it rankled. After I had single-handedly (with the aid of a lipstick) stopped a cold-blooded murderer from shooting his grandmother, the least he could do was call to thank me, I thought. But no, not a word.

"I guess blood will tell," Todd said, with—I couldn't help but notice—a certain amount of satisfaction. "He's just not a gentleman."

"That he's not," I agreed.

"So what are your plans for the rest of the week? Would you like to have dinner with me again one night? Friday? Or Saturday?"

"Either would be fine." Life is really too short to play hard to get, no matter what mother says. I could be dead tomorrow. "And I don't have many plans. Other than that I have to go out to Riverbend Prison tomorrow. Detective Grimaldi called and said Walker had asked to see me."

Todd looked concerned. "Are you sure you want to, Savannah? It could be unpleasant."

"I'm sure it will be," I agreed. "But yes, I do have to. He asked, and we've always had a good relationship." Up until the moment he apologized for having to kill me, at least.

"Would you like me to go with you?" Todd offered.

"Thank you," I said, "but that won't be necessary. Tamara Grimaldi is coming. She'll make sure he doesn't do anything to me." Not that he'd try. Walker wasn't crazy. He got rid of Brenda and Clarice because they stood in the way of his getting what he wanted, and he would have killed Mrs. Jenkins and me for the same reason, but now, with nothing left to protect, he had no reason to hurt me. "He'll probably just apologize again, and try to make amends."

Todd looked as if he wasn't quite convinced, but as it turned out, I was right. Walker seemed much like his old self again, suave and polite, and looking very out of place in the orange jumpsuit. I hoped he wouldn't have too hard a time of it in prison, but at the same time, I realized that he was a lot tougher than he looked. A man who can slit throats and cut wrists and not bat an eye is not a sissy.

"Thank you for coming, Savannah," he said softly. We were seated on opposite sides of a long table, with an impassive guard standing a few feet away at the door and Detective Grimaldi hovering anxiously in the hallway outside. Walker had asked to see me alone, and I had agreed to it, and although she didn't approve, there wasn't a whole lot she could do.

"No problem," I answered cautiously.

"I wanted to apologize again. I don't know what came over me."

"It's all right," I said. "I understand." Of course I didn't, but politesse commanded that I say I did. "I'm sure you would only have done what you thought was necessary."

He smiled faintly. "That's kind of you. I have something for you."

I must have looked nervous, because he added, "Not here. Go see my lawyer, Barry Vinson. He'll give you an envelope with all the paperwork for 101 Potsdam Street. I took it out of inventory and off the MLS."

"I noticed," I said. "Thank you."

Walker nodded. "The envelope will take care of the rest. Steven Puckett and I worked it all out to where Mrs. Jenkins can get the house back and the nursing home gets to keep the money they were given, while Brenda's reputation won't get any more damaged than it is. Steven is going to claim it as a charitable contribution. Let me give you the number." He recited the lawyer's phone number, and I plugged it into my cell phone. "Call him and tell him who you are and that you want to come get the envelope. He'll give it to you."

"I appreciate it," I said. "Um . . . I'm sorry, too."

He smiled. "I'm sure you only did what you had to do."

Touché. I shrugged.

He added, "It appears I underestimated you, Savannah. I didn't realize you carry a gun."

"I don't," I said sweetly. "It was lipstick."

And I admit it, I enjoyed seeing the incredulous look on Walker's face as I got up and walked—no, make that *sashayed*—to the door.

I picked up the envelope from the lawyer's office the next morning. And so it was noon on Thursday before I made it back to 101 Potsdam Street.

I had tried calling Rafe a couple of times, at Wendell's number, but I had never gotten an answer. The car lot/pawn shop must have gone out of business. Either that or they had caller ID and didn't want to hear from me. LaDonna's shack in the Bog was about to be razed by bulldozers, and I had no idea where Rafe's room on the south side of town was, so the house on Potsdam Street was the only place I could look for the two of them. I figured if they were anywhere, they'd be there. All the same, as I crunched up the circular drive on Thursday afternoon, I wasn't feeling confident. The yard was still sadly overgrown and unkempt, and the house looked just as neglected and empty as the last time I'd seen it. Nevertheless, I stopped the car and got out, and made my way onto the peeling porch.

The lockbox was gone from the door handle, and I knocked and waited. Nothing happened. I was just about to give up and go home when the door opened. My friendly, professional smile froze into an uncertain grimace.

"What *you* doin' here?" Marquita asked, her stance confrontational and her elbows out and blocking the doorway. She was dressed in pale pink nurse's scrubs—size 18, if I had to venture a guess—and her yellow hair was braided into a complicated style that did nothing for her globular face.

I could have asked her the same thing, but I decided not to. "I'm here to see Mrs. Jenkins," I said instead, calmly.

"She ain't seein' nobody." She tried to close the door. I put my foot in the gap, the way I've seen people do on TV. Marquita pushed harder. It hurt, and didn't do my Italian leather slingback any good, but the door remained open.

"She'll see me," I squeezed out between gritted teeth.

Marquita scowled, but under the circumstances she couldn't do anything but let me in. I swept past her with my head held high, trying not to limp conspicuously. Mother would have been proud.

Inside, everything looked pretty much the same, except that it was cleaner. There was the fresh smell of paint in the air, and the sound of a TV from the kitchen. I headed down the hallway and found Mrs. Jenkins sitting on a folding chair at a rickety card table, watching a talk show and spreading peanut butter on Ritz crackers. She lit up when she saw me. "Hi, baby! I ain't seen you in forever!"

She looked about 110 percent better, and even seemed to be acting more lucid. The scratches on her face and legs were healing, her hair was washed and combed, and she was wearing a brand-new housecoat and new fuzzy slippers. Whatever else was wrong with Marquita—and I could see plenty—she seemed to be good at her job.

"I've been busy the past few days," I explained. "With Walker in prison and Tim in charge, there's a lot to do. You look good. How have you been?"

Mrs. Jenkins beamed toothlessly. "That handsome boy o' mine came to the nursing home, just like you said. He walked me right outta there, and nobody said nothin'. And then he brought me back here, and got me new clothes, and a TV, and a new bed, and got the water turned on again, and brought Marquita to stay with me."

"It sounds like he's taking good care of you."

She nodded. "He's a good boy. You lookin' for him, baby?"

Marquita scowled. I hesitated. I probably should talk to Rafe. Mrs. Jenkins wasn't in any kind of condition to understand about the paperwork I had brought, and it was none of Marquita's business. Unless Rafe planned to marry her, but then she could damn well wait until after the ceremony to hear the details. "I suppose I'd better. Is he at work? When will he be back?" *And by the way, what sort of work does he do?*

"Oh, he ain't gone. He's just upstairs. You go on up, baby. He won't mind." She glanced over at the TV. Marquita's face went stony, and I was too entertained by the whole thing to even try to resist temptation.

"I don't expect he will. I'll see you later, Mrs. Jenkins. Nurse." I smiled sweetly at the scowling Marquita. She watched me as I went up the stairs. I wriggled my fingers in a friendly wave, and she huffed and turned on her heel, waddling back to the kitchen table.

It was anybody's guess in which of the upstairs rooms Rafe was, so rather than walking from room to room in what was now a private residence, I stopped in the upstairs hallway and raised my voice. "Rafe?"

"In here." It came from a bedroom on the left, overlooking the overgrown side yard. I walked there and stuck my head in. My jaw dropped.

Two weeks ago, there had been a moldy mattress full of rodents in here. Chunks of the ceiling had fallen onto the floor, and there had been debris in all of the corners. Now, it was a different room. The mattress and the mice were gone, and in their place was a good quality four-poster bed and matching dresser. The bed and the top of the dresser were covered with newspaper, but I could see lilac-printed sheets through the gaps. The ceiling was freshly dry-walled—so fresh that the gaps between the pieces hadn't been mudded yet—and the walls were in the process of being painted a soft lavender.

"Speechless?" Rafe's voice was amused, and I pulled myself together and looked for him. He was standing in one corner, paintbrush in hand. Both his jeans and t-shirt were liberally sprinkled with paint stains, not all of them lavender. When I didn't say anything, he added, gesturing with the paintbrush, "Whaddaya think?"

"It's beautiful," I said honestly. "You've done a great job. It looks like you might have had some experience doing this sort of thing." I paused, hoping that maybe he'd let slip some information about having done this before.

"I've got experience doing all sorts of things." He grinned when he saw my expression, and added, "It's my grandma's room."

"I thought it must be. It doesn't suit you, somehow."

"Good to know. Mine's down the hall. Wanna see?" He winked.

"I don't think I'd better," I said, fighting back a blush. I wanted to, sure—not because it was his, but because I was curious to see what he was doing to it—but the idea of willingly stepping into Rafe's bedroom with him didn't seem smart. The old story about Goosy Loosy and Foxy Loxy came to mind. His eyes brightened with amusement.

"You afraid I'm gonna throw you down on the bed and have my way with you? Don't worry, darlin'. I ain't so hard up that I have to force myself on anyone."

"I imagine you're not," I said sweetly. "I saw Marquita downstairs."

He turned away, balancing the paintbrush on the edge of the bucket. "She needed a job, we needed a nurse.

That's all. I told you before, ain't nothing going on with Marquita and me."

"Yes, I remember hearing you say that. I actually just came by to give you this." I handed him the envelope I'd gotten from the lawyer. "It's the listing agreement for the house, cancelled by Walker, and all the other papers that your grandmother signed. The Milton House will get to keep the hundred grand, but at least the house is yours again, or your grandmother's. Steven Puckett came through in a big way, bless his heart."

Rafe took the envelope, but didn't open it. Instead he looked at me. "Looks like I owe you one."

I shook my head. "No, you don't. You helped me burglarize Clarice's locker, and fetch Alexandra, and intimidate Maurice, and you caught me when I fainted and bought me cheesecake and made sure I got home safe."

"That's true. Maybe you owe me one instead." He grinned.

"One what?" Try as I might, I couldn't help the nervous glance at the newspaper-covered four-poster. He wouldn't really try to seduce me in his grandmother's bed, would he?

He laughed. "Not that."

"What, then?" My heart began to thud uncomfortably fast and hard as he dropped the envelope on the dresser and took a step toward me.

"Nothing too painful. Though I've earned a kiss, don't you think?"

"I . . . suppose." After enumerating all the things he had done for me lately, I could hardly say anything else. Although I admit I was worried about Marquita coming upstairs and finding us *in flagrante*, as it were, and what she'd do to me.

"Glad you agree. That mean you'll stand still and enjoy it?"

My eyes wavered. "I'll . . . um . . . try."

"Good. Now just relax, darlin'. This ain't gonna hurt a bit." He tipped my chin up and leaned down. My knees buckled and my eyes rolled back in my head. From very far away, I heard a chuckle and felt a pair of arms settle around my body. A voice murmured in my ear. "Not *that* relaxed. Try to stay awake, darlin'. You don't wanna miss nothing."

And I tried, I really did. The idea of being unconscious and completely at his mercy—and with a bed within easy reach, too!—was too dreadful to contemplate. But then his lips moved from my ear, across my cheek, and over to close over mine, and the next second, everything went black. My last coherent thought was that if I got out of this room with my virtue and my sanity intact, I'd never let him get within touching distance ever again.

ACKNOWLEDGEMENTS

This particular book—the first I wrote—wouldn't have made it into print without the help, support, and encouragement of a lot of people. Chief among them:

My wonderful agent, Stephany Evans. You're one of a kind, and I'll always be grateful for the way you took me, Savannah and Rafe under your wing, and didn't give up on us over the two years it took to find us a home.

Everyone at PublishingWorks, for your excitement and enthusiasm for me and my characters. You're a fine bunch of folks, and I'm proud to be associated with you.

My family and friends, here and abroad, especially my husband and my two boys, who share daily life with me and love me anyway. It isn't easy to live with someone who spends half her time in another world, but the three of you manage to thrive in spite of me. You're a constant source of inspiration, amazement, and awe, and I feel so fortunate to have ended up with you.

Last, but certainly not least, Tasha Alexander. Sometimes, through no particular act or ability of our own, Fate blesses us with the gift of someone who changes who we are and makes us believe that anything's possible. You've been my friend and my mentor, my cheering section and my sounding board. A girl wanting to write a book couldn't have a better role model than you. This one is all yours.

ABOUT THE AUTHOR

Bente Gallagher is a former Realtor® and home renovator. She is also the nationally bestselling author of the acclaimed *Do-It-Yourself Home Renovation* mysteries from Berkley Prime Crime, written as Jennie Bentley. She lives in Nashville with a husband and two boys, a hyperactive dog, a killer parakeet, two frogs, and a couple of goldfish. A native of Norway, she's been hanging out in the U.S. for the past twenty years and still hasn't been able to kick her native accent. You can learn more about Bente and her various doings and undoings on her website, www.BenteGallagher.com.